REFINING THE DEBUTANTE

OTHER COVENANT BOOKS AND AUDIOBOOKS

BY ANNEKA R. WALKER

Love in Disguise

The Masked Baron

"Lord Blakely's Gift" in *A Hopeful Christmas*

REFINING THE DEBUTANTE

a regency romance

ANNEKA R. WALKER

Covenant Communications, Inc.

Cover image © Ysbrand Cosijn / Trevillion Images

Cover design copyright © 2021 by Covenant Communications, Inc.

Published by Covenant Communications, Inc.
American Fork, Utah

Printed in the United States of America
First Printing: March 2021

27 26 25 24 23 22 21   10 9 8 7 6 5 4 3 2 1

ISBN 978-1-52441-694-2

PRAISE FOR
ANNEKA R. WALKER

THE MASKED BARON

"Romance, suspense, and the supernatural effectively intertwine in this captivating Regency from Walker (*Love in Disguise*) . . . The engrossing central mystery and electric chemistry between the spirited characters keep the pages turning. This rousing romance is sure to win Walker new readers."

—*Publishers Weekly*

"The sinister forest backdrop is atmospheric, and the mystery surrounding the baron and his lost family creates a diverting, gothic read with supernatural elements. The romance arcs towards a natural conclusion, but the author's techniques add tension, which makes the inevitable very beguiling. The manor house staff members are all integral to the story. Themes of self-forgiveness and trust are dealt with compassionately, integrated into a very well-thought-out tale. Recommended for readers who love a clean romance with a difference."

—*Historical Novels Review*

"A superbly crafted and fully entertaining novel that combines elements of romance and suspense, The Masked Baron by Anneka R. Walker will prove to be an enduringly popular and appreciated addition to community library general fiction collections."

—Midwest Book Review

"*The Masked Baron* [is] a unique take on a retelling of *Beauty and the Beast* during the Regency era, with a mystery weaved throughout."

—Timeless Novels Review

"Anneka R. Walker has written a charming and sweet *Beauty and the Beast* meets masked highwayman story that readers will delight in. It's filled with a fun twist on the *Beauty and the Beast* fairy tale woven through the story, along [with] a bit of mystery and danger, making the story engaging and enticing. Throughout the story, readers will enjoy watching the ebb and flow as the relationship between Ellis and Andalin blooms . . . a cute and memorable read. Readers will be watching for more from this enjoyable author."

—Singing Librarian Books

TO THE SOCIETY OF
OBSTINATE, HEADSTRONG GIRLS

ACKNOWLEDGMENTS

MY LIST OF PEOPLE TO thank seems to get longer with each story I write. My first thanks is to God for inspiring me to use the themes of love and redemption. I clearly remember the day I opened my scriptures and read the story of the prodigal son and the idea for this book came to my mind. This is very much a different story, but it was meant to be told.

Once it was written, this book passed through a dozen hands. Emily Bradshaw and Heather Okeson read this book in its rawest form—bless you both! Mindy Strunk and Esther Hatch had the privilege of hearing me read the first chapters *out loud*. Lucky women! Esther put aside time during her own deadline to help give me feedback. My brother Taylor Riddoch helped me analyze every inch of my story to make sure all the dots were connected. Julianne Donaldson stayed up all night reading my book just so she could give me last-minute advice on how to make it shine. The result was a lot of cutting and rewriting, but it was worth it! Jill Warner fell in love with my characters and rooted for them through all their changes. Jennie Goutet was my angel with a red pen. She helped me fine-tune my manuscript and cheered me on right up to my deadline. She saved my story and my sanity with her professional-level edits.

The submissions editor and evaluators at Covenant don't get enough credit. Their feedback is always so helpful, and I make many adjustments because of them. As always, my editor, Kami, is the one I trust most to polish my manuscript and get it ready for readers. She is such a joy to work with! I feel bad for every writer who doesn't have a Kami in their life. The rest of the Covenant team deserves a shout-out too. The graphic artists always give me beautiful covers to reflect my stories. Amy Parker, our marketing manager, does so much to get my books out into the world. She sacrifices so much time and energy on behalf of her authors. Thank you!

Last, but definitely not least, is my family. My husband listens to me squeal about cute story ideas and then holds me when I cry over plot problems. He is, hands down, my biggest support on this writing journey. There is no way I could do this without him, nor would I want to. Many thanks to our parents for cheering me on with each and every book. And I am ever grateful for my children for being generous with their time and patience while I work. I love you all so much!

CHAPTER 1

London, January 1816

WHAT EXACTLY WAS A MAN supposed to do in a dressmaker's shop? His mother's headache, brought on by his sister Jane's sour temper, necessitated an early return home. This left Ethan to retrieve Jane from her appointment. He suddenly felt envious of his youngest sister, who remained home at their country estate, and even his younger brother, who was at school. Ethan would rather be anywhere else.

With a fortifying breath, he entered the narrow building of the most popular modiste in London and removed his beaver hat. He grimaced at the rainbow of colors before him. His sister had better hurry. To say he was out of his element, with the crowded bolts of fabric and the framed sketches of women's attire, was an understatement.

Jane was in the adjoining room, standing on a raised platform. Her back was to him, but through the doorway, he could see her staring at the reflection of her new gown in the long gilded mirror in front of her. He stepped closer to gain her attention but paused when he saw her expression. She looked as if she might cry. Was this dress the reason for his mother's headache? Eyeing the gown, he wondered what part offended his sister. It seemed nice enough to him.

The shop's front door opened to let in a woman. He shuffled to the side of the small vestibule and dipped his head in a polite greeting. The woman curtsied and smiled up at him. Ethan did not easily get his head turned by a pretty face, but when she boldly met his gaze, he could not look away. She wore a jonquil-yellow redingote with a brown velvet collar. She did not remove her heavily trimmed bonnet, but it did little to hide the golden-brown curls framing her large eyes, small nose, and full lips. While he had no intention of speaking to her, his mouth opened of its own accord. No sound emitted, and he floundered for a moment to close it again.

She looked away before he did, breaking the strange spell her presence had cast over him. He was still thinking about his reaction to this perfect stranger when she spoke in a near whisper.

"You really ought to tell your wife how wonderful she looks in her new gown."

"Pardon?" Ethan stole a glance at the stranger. Had he imagined her soft words?

"It would do her a world of good," she whispered again.

He looked at her. "Are you speaking to me?"

Her eyes snapped to meet his. "Who else would I be speaking to?" She motioned to Jane. "Look at your darling little wife. She is terribly insecure. She needs you to buoy her spirits with a compliment or two."

He raised his brows in disbelief. Sisters did not care what brothers thought of their dresses, and he was nobody's husband. "You are mistaken."

"There is no mistake. Don't be hurt that you cannot see what I can. A woman senses this sort of thing." She gave him a look of pity. "It isn't your fault. You were born a man; it is harder for you. But I do not mind helping. Go ahead. Look at her. See the way she stares in the looking glass? See the worry line between her eyes?" She leaned near him as if doing so would allow him to see what she did.

He had never met a more impertinent woman. "Why would she be worried? That dress cost a fortune."

A sigh emitted from her mouth. "She needs to *feel* beautiful. Only you can do that for her. Tell her."

"I don't think—"

"Do it. Go on."

Why had he agreed to come here in the first place? He cleared his throat, anxious for the woman to let him be, and stepped across the threshold of the adjoining room. "You look well," he said to Jane.

"What are you doing in here?" Jane swiveled on the platform to face him. She batted at a dark ringlet by her face, then dropped her hands to her hips. "Wait outside. I am embarrassed you would speak to me in such a place."

He shuffled backward.

The strange woman tsked her tongue. "You did a very poor job of it. A husband must learn the best way to compliment his wife. Let me demonstrate."

The woman stepped past him. She looked back at him once, shaking her head as if he'd disappointed her, then waltzed into the room as if she were the proprietor. "Excuse me, but I mustn't stay silent for another moment."

"What is it?" Jane asked.

"It's your dress. It's exquisite. I must have an exact replica."

"You? But why? Your dress is far superior."

"Nonsense. You can barely see it beneath my redingote. You are far too kind." The woman put her hand out as if she were stroking the fabric of Jane's dress but was not actually close enough to touch it. "This muslin is some of the finest I've seen so far this Season. You are a natural beauty, but do not underestimate the power of a beautiful gown."

"You think so? It is rather pretty, I guess. I am not sure about the fit."

The woman looked her over as if she were the mantua-maker. "You're right. Madame Gillespie? A half inch at each shoulder." The dressmaker pinned the material in the place where the stranger told her to. "Your shoulders are slender indeed. What do you think now?" She turned to Madame Gillespie before Jane could answer. "Fetch that gold shawl on the table." The woman accepted it and draped it over Jane's shoulders. "Stunning. Wear it a little lower. Just there."

Then she crossed to a table and selected a green feather. She placed it in Jane's hair. "Sometimes the little accents give a dress greater personality."

Ethan stared. A little charm made the personality of a woman shine too. He turned his gaze from the vexing but delightful woman to see Jane's reaction. His sister's cheeks flushed with pleasure.

"It's far lovelier with your adaptions. I never would have been able to put this combination together." Jane turned and preened in front of the mirror. "Thank you."

Madame Gillespie clasped her hands together in front of her chest. "Miss Bartley has excellent taste. She sometimes sketches designs inspired by her travels."

"I am most impressed," Jane said.

Ethan was too. *Miss Bartley.* He would remember her name.

"I am happy to share one with you, although my skills pale compared to Madame Gillespie's," Miss Bartley said. She pulled out a sketch from her reticule. "I happen to have one I did just this morning. What do you think of this? Oh, forgive me; I don't even know your name."

"This is Miss Roderick," Madame Gillespie supplied.

"May I?" Jane took the picture and gasped. "It's like a Grecian princess."

"I think an English lady like yourself could do it justice too. It's yours. I believe a soft blue would do well with your coloring."

"Thank you, Miss Bartley," Jane cooed.

Miss Bartley smiled at her and stepped back into the vestibule. Jane returned to studying her reflection in the mirror, her eyes sparkling.

Ethan chuckled. "You've made my sister feel very beautiful."

"She seems most deserving."

"You were right about her insecurity and the worry lines on her face. You have done something in minutes that my family hasn't managed in two years."

"Well, I—" Her eyes widened. "Your sister? She is not your wife?"

"Jane is my sister. But don't worry. When I marry, I will be sure to compliment my wife just as you've instructed. I will insist on having an exact replica of her dress made to fit me. I will select her shawls and feathers. And I will sketch all the designs for her gowns."

"Oh . . ." She sputtered. "That would be most extraordinary of you." She took a step backward. "Perhaps I should return for my appointment when your sister is through."

"I'm disappointed. You cannot be finished instructing me on my behavior already," he teased.

"Instructing?" She looked perfectly bewildered—as innocent as a dove. "Why would I do that? We have not even been properly introduced. I wouldn't dare speak with a stranger."

He bit back a grin. "Heaven forbid."

"My thoughts exactly."

Madame Gillespie stepped out of the room at that moment and gasped. "Don't move!" She returned with a piece of parchment and a pencil and started sketching something. "Just one more minute."

"What is she doing?" Ethan asked Miss Bartley.

"Don't interrupt an artist at work."

He couldn't help the movement of his lips. He grinned. This woman was a great deal more outspoken than most. "An artist?"

"She draws fashion plates for *La Belle Assemblée*, the lady's magazine."

"Oh." Ethan frowned. "I hardly think—"

"You will be famous."

"Me? In a lady's magazine?" He cringed.

Madame Gillespie lifted her pencil from the paper and studied her work. "What do you think?" She handed it to Miss Bartley, but Ethan could easily see it. Miss Bartley was the focus of the sketch, which did not surprise him.

"Add a scalloped edge to the hem of my dress and give Mr. Roderick a pale-green scarf."

"Oh, I like that."

Ethan groaned.

Miss Bartley put her gloved hand up to hide a smile.

"You won't speak to a stranger, but you'll laugh at one?" he asked.

"You must have imagined it," she said, looking up at him. "I have a refined sense of humor."

"Which is probably why you have guilted me into complimenting my sister and then memorialized me in a lady's magazine. Your sense of humor is most unique."

The door opened, and in stepped a woman and her daughter, crowding him closer to Miss Bartley. He turned and was nearly touching her. She blushed and maneuvered back against the wall.

"You're still here!" Jane said to Miss Bartley, walking out with her cloak clasped around her throat. "Please, come to the teahouse with us."

"My appointment is next. My apologies."

Ethan didn't know what possessed him to step forward and ask, "Another time, then?"

She turned her head to meet his gaze. Did she think him insincere after his teasing? He had no reason to pursue this woman, except that he couldn't let this be the last time he saw her. She wasn't part of his plan, but with her in front of him, he couldn't remember why his plan was so important.

She smiled. "I should like that."

❋

May 1816 (Four months later)

Ethan usually enjoyed Mrs. Grantham's card parties since they were an opportunity to see his favorite friends, but tonight he could not keep his eyes off the door. If he had learned anything from courting Miss Miranda Bartley, it was that she was unpredictable. She was also charming, maddening, and utterly captivating. She made him question his ability to reason. Even when she was not with him, his thoughts never strayed far from her.

When the door opened and Mr. Bartley and his daughter entered, the tone in the subdued room quickly changed. Miranda arrived overdressed and laughing at something her father had said. Her golden-brown curls were pulled high on her head with a large bow above one ear. Ethan's heart stuttered in anticipation to be near her.

Her sparkling eyes found his, and she grinned, unabashed. She left her father greeting the host and hostess and made her way directly to Ethan. "Mr. Roderick, I have you to thank for extending this invitation to us."

Ethan bowed in greeting. No one made him feel the way Miranda did. He stepped closer to her. "I wanted you to meet some of my friends outside of my parents' circle."

"I daresay you are friends with everyone." Miranda took in the room of people. "I should dearly love to meet any and all of them."

Ethan's lips quirked, and he leaned closer. "I know you better than to think you wanted to come. However, I will introduce you quickly so you might see my friends improve with further acquaintance." He put out his arm to her, and she readily accepted.

He brought her over to three men—some of the greatest philanthropists he knew.

"The working class will not be silenced," his friend Mr. Thomas said to the others. "Things are escalating. We need to help if we can."

Ethan stepped forward. "We need to raise more funds first."

His friends turned their eyes on him, and their smiles showed their appreciation of his input.

General Stoker motioned to Miranda. "So this is the woman who has claimed all of your attention as of late."

"Gentlemen, may I present Miss Bartley?"

Miranda curtsied. "Please don't tell me you are discussing the state of the poor at a party. It isn't in good taste." She playfully put her hand on Mr. Thomas's arm and lightly tapped it. "You must all cease this serious talk at once. I don't see many games started yet, but we can be the ones to remedy this. Who is up for a game of charades?" She turned to Ethan, her eyes bright with enthusiasm.

Ethan cleared his throat to break the awkwardness of the moment. These men were much too dignified to play silly games. And their *poor taste* translated to saving lives. This was his fault. He should have prepared Miranda. He covered her hand on his arm with his own. "Shall we finish the introductions first?"

"Of course. We must invite the others to play as well."

Ethan smiled apologetically to his friends and pulled Miranda away. Nearest to them were two young ladies at a table. They were chatting, their cards neglected in front of them. This was a safe introduction.

"Miss Withers, Miss Karlson, might I introduce Miss Bartley?"

"Please, join us," Miss Withers said, pointing to the open chairs. "We aren't playing a game, but we wouldn't mind more company."

Ethan pulled out a chair for Miranda, and they both sat. "Miss Withers and her family have recently settled near Stonebrook Hall, my family estate." Miss Withers's beauty nearly rivaled Miranda's, but her russet curls were dressed more conservatively, as was her gown.

"Oh?" Miranda's eyes darted from him to Miss Withers. "Have you known each other long?"

"No," Miss Withers answered, "but as a new neighbor, I hope to deepen my acquaintance with the family." She turned her gracious smile on him.

Miranda lifted her brows. "I see." She tucked her arm possessively under Ethan's. "Perhaps you hope to know Mr. Roderick's *sister* Jane better. I must warn you, living in the same part of the country does not mean you are equal in Society. Jane is a very fine lady—my dearest friend."

Miss Withers wrinkled her nose. "I see."

Miranda turned her gaze to Miss Karlson. "And do you also want to endear yourself to Mr. Roderick's family?"

Miss Karlson paled. "I . . . ah . . ."

Ethan didn't understand what was happening. Miranda's words seemed to hold a barely veiled threat. It was time to withdraw from this conversation too. "I see Mrs. Jones has arrived. She is a widow and an old friend. I should greet her. Will you join me, Miss Bartley?"

"I would love to meet Mrs. Jones." Miranda gave him a smile to make his knees quake.

He couldn't stay frustrated with her for long. He took her hand and assisted her from her seat. Before he stepped away, he tipped his head to Miss Karlson and then Miss Withers. "I will look forward to seeing more of you at Stonebrook. You are most welcome."

Miss Withers's smile blossomed, and Ethan hoped he had repaired any offense. He directed Miranda over to where Mrs. Jones sat, her eyes glossed over as the party happened around her.

"Mrs. Jones, I am pleased to see you tonight."

Mrs. Jones blinked as if surprised to be addressed. "Ah, Mr. Roderick. I thank you for sending your carriage for me."

"You need to leave your house more often." Ethan directed Miranda to a sofa across from the older woman. "How is your health?"

Her shoddy dress glared in his eyes compared to Miranda's finery, and he hoped Miranda would not comment on it—she could be unpredictable in her naivety.

"My health is very poor indeed. I suffer greatly," Mrs. Jones replied. "My back aches, my feet tingle, my heart hiccups, and my head throbs. The doctors don't know what to make of it. They have tried all the regular medicines, and you know, I think they have given up on me. You will speak to them, won't you? If my husband were still alive, he would not let them disregard my pains."

"Of course. I am always glad to help when I can."

"You are the only one. Why, just the other day, I had such a festering sore on my side, and my doctor couldn't even see it. Three times I called him back, and at the last, he threw up his hands and told me to find some-one else. I daresay the physicians in London are the most uneducated in all the world." Mrs. Jones glanced at Miranda. "I'm sorry, who is this?"

"Forgive me. This is Miss Bartley."

"No, you must both forgive me," Miranda said with a lighthearted air. "I see my father motioning for me to join him. Please, carry on without me." She brushed Ethan with her hand as she stood.

Disappointment sank deep into his gut.

"Oh, Mrs. Jones," Miranda said, turning to face his friend. He held his breath until she spoke. "Have you tried pink?"

"Pink?"

"Yes, I believe it is your color. You have beautiful rosy tones to your cheeks. A pink dress will not cure your ailments, but it might do just the trick in lifting your spirits."

Mrs. Jones put her hand to her chest. "How thoughtful! I will try it."

Ethan groaned inwardly. He could not predict Miranda at all tonight. He wanted to focus on the smile she had brought to Mrs. Jones's lips, but her earlier comments had ruffled him. His gaze followed her as she approached her father, who lovingly put his arm around her small shoulders and introduced her to an older gentleman at his side. She was special, to be sure, but her naivety worried him. Could such a strong-willed woman fit into his world? Ethan caught sight of Miss Withers—calm, soft-spoken, an advocate for underprivileged women. It was forward-thinking, perhaps, but part of him wanted the woman he married to support him in his dreams. What if he had grown attached to the wrong woman? His heart told him one thing, but his head said differently.

CHAPTER 2

A PROPOSAL OF MARRIAGE WAS the single most desirable goal for a young lady of good social standing. *This* was Miranda's moment.

Sitting very near the Honorable Ethan Roderick on the bench of his curricle, she could feel his steady breathing during the smooth stretches of road. The clouds weaved a heavy gray carpet across the sky, and a cool London breeze encircled her neck. Not even a little rain could dampen her spirits. Everything was going as planned. All the right people at Gunter's tearoom had seen them together, though her grape molded ice had chilled her more than she cared to admit, and now they were alone. The anticipation of a declaration of love made her heart flutter.

"I told you Gunter's was a splendid idea," Miranda said, twirling her parasol as Berkeley Square faded behind them. "Except, not a soul complimented me on my new bonnet. I assure you, it was the finest seen today." She wanted him to feel proud to have her by his side and had been extra particular about her wardrobe that morning. Miranda fingered the wide red ribbon tied under her chin and tilted her head in a flirtatious manner. "You do like it, don't you? I bought it especially for this ride."

Mr. Roderick—Ethan, as she liked to call him in her mind, which was infinitely more personal—took a cursory glance but did not smile. "It becomes you."

There was an emptiness in his voice Miranda did not like. Surely it was from nerves and not because of *the incident* the night before.

"Why, thank you." She waited for Ethan to say something more, but he did not. Sometimes he grew too grave when a matter weighed on his mind. Marriage was certainly a serious subject. Miranda attempted to speak of other pleasantries to help him relax. "What did you think of Mrs.

Grantham's card party?" She immediately regretted the question. The party had been an absolute disaster. Perhaps they needed to talk it out and be done with it. "I did my best to lighten the tone, but your friends are altogether too solemn. I don't think anyone appreciated my efforts. I daresay Mrs. Grantham shouldn't have invited Miss Withers and Miss Karlson. I've never met a more desperate pair. Truly, they were dreadful."

Ethan cleared his throat, and his gaze remained on the road. "I thought the hostess and company exceptional."

"I did not object to all of them, mind you." There was no use arguing further on the subject, even if she did not like the way Miss Withers had looked at Ethan or the familiar way Ethan had spoken to the woman. It was no surprise when he refrained from responding. He didn't like to be disagreeable. His character was impeccable. He said all the right things, wore the right clothes, and possessed the right position in Society. The only thing that was not perfect was his cravat, and likely because he could not see under his chin well enough to know when it was crooked. It brought out an adorable boyish side to him, so she did not mind.

It wasn't just that he was tall and handsome that made her care for him, but because she trusted him. He was a good man—a noble man—exceeding all her expectations in a suitor. Her admiration for him increased with every passing day. Only—he had yet to speak with her father about an engagement. What was taking him so long?

Ethan pulled up to Miranda's family town house. He turned to her instead of hastening to help her down, his chocolate-brown eyes capturing hers. How she loved chocolate. "Miss Bartley, I hope this is not too untoward."

Miranda smiled boldly. She had always made it a point to be very open with Ethan. "No topic you address could offend me." Here it was. The moment he would profess his love. Ethan's mouth drew downward in an adorable little frown, and Miranda almost laughed at the gravity in his expression. He must be nervous indeed.

"I tell you this to spare your feelings as much as possible. Despite the expectation everyone has—that you may have—I cannot continue my attentions toward you. I intend to leave London in the morning."

She shook her head in confusion, her golden-brown curls bouncing in front of her face. "Surely you cannot be in earnest."

Ethan stared at her in solemn silence.

Merciful heavens. He was serious.

"Miss Bartley, we are not a good match."

"Don't be silly. We complement each other perfectly." *Didn't they?* She could make him smile when no one else could, and he . . . well, he was everything to her. Wasn't she enough for him? She had a desirable figure, a pleasing complexion; she even had straight upper teeth!

"No," he said. "It seemed that way in the beginning, but it can never be."

His words were like flies buzzing in her head. They made no sense at all. "But your sister and even your mother have expressed how greatly they desire for us to wed. You said a woman like myself must've inspired the great poets."

Closing his eyes, he breathed through his nose with evident frustration. "It's a matter of principle." Mr. Roderick seemed to regret his words—even seemed torn. With a sigh, he removed his hat and ran his hand through his thick dark hair before replacing it. "Forgive me. I thought I could . . . but I can't. I hope in time you will understand why."

Her lungs squeezed tight in her chest, strangling her. Think. She must think. Perhaps he didn't love her after all. The thought stole away her breath. She'd never really cared what people said about her, but this . . . this was bigger than whispers about her outspoken manner or laughing louder than was proper. Calling things off now, when they were as good as engaged, would ruin her reputation. She had one opportunity to rectify this mess before her failings as a debutante were printed in the Society papers come morning. "I'll never understand unless you tell me plainly."

"As you wish." Ethan's chiseled jaw tightened, and his words created a coldness far more uncomfortable than the flavored ice or chilly spring weather. "I cannot marry someone so vain. Your contempt for others is shameful. You think more of your silly dresses and bonnets than you do the state of the country."

A wave of dizziness washed over her. Miranda put her gloved hand to her head. "Perhaps a little less plainly would have been sufficient." A gulp of air steadied her. Her dignity demanded she leave the carriage and his presence. "Very well. If you will be so good as to help me down."

Ethan escorted her to her front door and bowed ceremoniously over her hand. His eyes lingered on hers for just a fraction of a moment. "Good day, Miss Bartley."

Miranda wanted to show him an indifferent face, but tears blurred her vision. Good day indeed. She stuck her chin defiantly in the air and refused to answer or even look at him. She let herself inside, eager to be alone. She made it to her bedchamber before the first sob escaped. Why must she be attracted to someone so self-righteous? Of course he wanted to marry someone equal to his nature. He was kindhearted, and she was clearly shallow in comparison. She should have known better than to fall in love with such a man.

⚹

After saying goodbye to his parents and closest friends, Ethan saw no reason to delay his departure another moment. He couldn't stay in the same place as Miranda if he had any hope of conquering his attachment to her. He would ride his horse ahead to Stonebrook Hall, his family's country seat, and have his valet follow with his things. Ethan handed his valet a detailed list of everything he wanted packed for his trip home to Sussex.

"I wager that list is numbered in order of priority," his sister Jane said from the doorway to his bedchamber. Her tone and expression revealed her barely restrained anger.

His town house in London was supposed to offer him privacy from his family, but his sister was forever coming to visit so she could nag and criticize him.

"What is the point of a list if not succinct?" Ethan said, refusing to be baited and drawn into another discussion about Miranda—er, Miss Bartley. He must only think of her as Miss Bartley.

Jane began unbuttoning her spencer jacket, as if she intended to stay a while. "I only worry about your propensity for order. Your life revolves around your carefully constructed plans. Finding a wife this Season was on the top of your list. I do not think it healthy for you to leave before you have accomplished such an important task."

It irked him to no end how Jane had helped herself to his private papers and had seen such revealing details. "Plans change." Ethan pulled on his cloak. She might be staying, but he was leaving.

"You despise change," Jane said. "Besides, why alter a course set for success?"

Ethan pulled at the cravat his valet always tied insufferably tight, no matter how many times he insisted otherwise. How could he explain to his sister? There had been a million little reasons for his decision. He knew women in Miranda's station often refrained from participating in discussions of worldly topics such as political or economic struggles, but the final straw had been her complete ignorance and lack of human sympathy for those affected by the rioting around England. News of the Ely and Littleport riots, and the subsequent deaths, had reached their ears the morning of their last carriage ride. It was the talk of the *ton* in every drawing room, and Ethan knew Miranda had at least overheard the gossipmongers at Gunter's tearoom discussing the report. Yet all she could speak about was her silly bonnet.

Jane would never understand. He folded his arms across his chest. "Perhaps I am wise enough to acknowledge when a course correction is needed."

"Oh, get off your high horse and see reason." Jane slumped into a chair by his bed in a very unladylike fashion. "I need Miranda to help me find a husband. What if she abandons me now that you are no longer interested in her?"

"Jane," Ethan huffed. "She cares for your friendship. That won't happen."

Jane's mouth turned down into a pout, an expression saved for when she spoke to her family. "It is so unfair. Why can you not find peace with her? She adores you, and you recently adored her. I know you consider yourself too principled a man to prize your bachelorhood over a woman's good name. What happened?"

"I *did* care for her." More than he could even admit. He stopped in the doorway and rested his hand heavily on the post. "But it was not a good fit. Surely you cannot argue away a man's conscience."

"What man today has a conscience?" Jane put her hand over her eyes. "If you insist on being a gentleman, don't misapply it."

Ethan's scowl deepened; he knew her surliness was her way of coping with the situation, but he found he had little patience for her under the circumstances. It wasn't just Miranda's heart breaking. "Maybe that is a failing in your sight, but not for me. When you are ready, please see yourself out." He spun on his heel and marched down the single flight of stairs, right by his sister's maid, and through the front door. To his relief, he found his horse saddled and waiting for him. He wasn't walking away from his problems. Fleeing, more like. But a man of conscience had a level of pride. There was no way he would face anyone after jilting Miranda. Besides, he had more important matters on his mind—like saving lives.

CHAPTER 3

July 1816

Dancing normally cheered Miranda, but none of her partners pleased her—too boisterous, too short, or too desperate. She moved to a corner of the room where she would have a moment of respite. It was a miracle she had secured an invitation to the duke's ball at Grosvenor Square, and this was her last opportunity to salvage her reputation. What was wrong with her tonight? Had she eaten something that disagreed with her? As she looked over the glittering ballroom, she knew the answer. It was Ethan. His hurtful departure over a month before still felt fresh in her mind.

Jane, who had become her dearest friend, saw her escape and came to her side. She lifted her fan to hide her words. "First, Lord Byron and Beau Brummell flee England, and soon you will be gone too."

Miranda sighed. "It is already July. With Parliament at an end, you and most of Society will be leaving London anyway."

"I suppose," Jane said, "but a tour of Europe will keep you away from London for two whole years! There will be no one to talk about or talk to when my family returns from Stonebrook. It's cast a pall over the party tonight, and I know I am not the only one to feel it." Jane's dark hair gleamed in the low light, reminding Miranda of Ethan with his similar coloring.

"Others missing my society is precisely the point," Miranda explained. "It will make my return all the sweeter." Besides, she needed to get away . . . to forget. She had never been one for making plans, but this seemed like the best course under the circumstances. Thankfully, it had not taken much begging to get her father to agree.

"If only my brother were here." Jane's lips turned down into a pout. "I have written to him twice a day since he left. You are going to be snatched up, and we will never be sisters. If he loves me at all, he will come back and marry you. How you must despise me! I swear—"

"Jane, stop!" Every reference to Ethan felt like salt to her wound. "Someone might hear you, and then what? Your brother was . . ." She paused, pushing back the deep hurt creeping into her voice. "Not who I thought he was, but our friendship will not suffer because of it. I will secure someone else's affection, and just like I promised, I will help you win over whomever you choose. Your husband will be a rich Adonis."

Jane seemed to hang on her every word, and Miranda couldn't understand how such a beautiful woman could be so lacking in confidence. Jane could find a husband without Miranda's help, but she would never believe it. Her presence felt smothering now and again, but moments like this made Miranda grateful for a true friend.

"We can't let anything hold us back, Jane." Miranda realized now why women schemed and plotted for suitors. She had failed abysmally that dark evening of the card party, but she had learned her lesson. She would not fail twice. She put up her fan like Jane, but it gave her pause. She had taught Ethan the secret language of the fan, and they had shared many laughs through the subtle gestures. A sudden onslaught of tears threatened to break her composure. She would be strong tomorrow. Tonight, however, she was not quite ready for matrimonial games.

With a subtle hint or two to the right gentleman, Miranda sent Jane off to dance and made her escape. She found her father in a back room playing cards and reaching for a drink.

"Papa, I feel a headache coming on." She looked at him pointedly.

"Oh, ah . . ." Her father wiped his brow with a handkerchief. "Give your father a few minutes, and I will see you home."

With her emotions shredding to pieces, she wanted to demand they leave immediately, but something was off. She felt the awkward stares before she saw them. "Of course, Papa." She retreated outside the game room and heaved a sigh.

Several minutes passed, and her father came out pale and wiping his forehead again.

"Are you well?" Miranda laid her hand on his arm.

"Well enough." Her father shrugged off her touch. "It's that blasted volcanic eruption in the Dutch East Indies last year that ruined all my crops. Nothing has been right in the world since then. Not the weather, not the circumstance, not my luck. Never mind, dear, let's return home."

She welcomed her father's comforting arm. She wished she could blame her mood on a volcano, but it was a broken heart that had blown her world off its axis. Neither one of them would be happy until they left Town. The sooner they were on their tour of Europe, the better.

❊

Ethan sat in his father's study, content to be back at Stonebrook Hall with its clear country air. Theirs was a small but comfortable community, and his efforts to manage the family estate would keep his mind busy, if only he could sleep. Mr. Buehler, their butler of more than thirty-five years, brought in a tray of letters for him.

"Very good. Bring them here." Ethan accepted the letters, riffling through the small stack, and stopped at one addressed to him from his family. He reached for a letter opener and slit open the sealed missive, perusing it quickly. Something, something, duke's ball. Ah, there. His parents were bringing Jane here to Sussex to be with him and his youngest sister, Hannah, who had not yet been introduced to Society, and then leaving to Bath as Ethan had suggested. They would be taking his brother, Richard, who was on holiday from school, with them. Pleased with the arrangement, Ethan sank back in the armchair.

His father also required a holiday after a session in Parliament and owing to a recent attack of gout, as there would be no relaxation for him here—not with the east wing of Stonebrook Hall under renovation. The amount of powders his father needed with each flare of pain in his foot and leg worried Ethan. Although the medicine helped considerably with the pain, Ethan had noticed his father's increasing reliance on it and had encouraged something new, like partaking of the waters. He was pleased to see his advice being followed.

Ethan reached for another letter, this one from Jane. With a small groan, he set it aside to read later. No doubt she meant to harangue him again about marrying Miranda. He shook his head. Why could he still not think of her as Miss Bartley? Putting his elbows on the table, he clasped his hands together and rested his head atop them. The view of Grandfather's portrait on the wall opposite him did little to distract his tired mind from the lovely image of Miranda he'd conjured. Guilt had been robbing him of sleep. What kind of gentleman walked away from a woman after leading her to believe there would be an engagement? And his words haunted him too. He should not have been so harsh.

Miranda likely did not even notice her behavior, as it came naturally. She attracted men like a dog would fleas. Her coquettish giggle and her coy smiles in response to every compliment bestowed by other men might have been unconsciously done, but they drove him to the brink of insanity. With effort, the harmless tendencies he could ignore, but her selfish nature he could not. Flipping open his father's record book, Ethan found the ribbon marking the current numbers to date. He would forget her. He sat back and ran his fingers down a column, attempting to do the figures in his head. As if in response to his deep-set frown, a thought teased him from his concentration.

"You have a very handsome smile, though I do not know why you hide it."

Good heavens. Was he hearing her voice in his head now?

He wouldn't smile. He refused.

"Not everyone can be as carefree as you," he whispered out loud to the taunting memory. Her own wide smile always unnerved him. No doubt a womanly trick to entrap him. Perhaps he was more tired than he thought, because his mind easily fell into the memory of that day in Hyde Park when she'd tricked him into climbing a tree.

"You must not care what anyone else thinks about you." She threw her head back so the sunshine could make it past her bonnet to her face. *"You deserve to be happy and to show it."*

"And you do not care? I find that impossible in the world we live in."

Miranda shrugged her dainty shoulders. "To an extent, perhaps. We all care about something, but caring too much robs you of the chance to enjoy life. Trust me; people respect me for being the only debutante who is not demure and mundane."

She definitely drew a crowd wherever she went, with her beauty and confidence. And somehow, she acted as if he were the one she wanted to be with.

He slapped his face. "Focus, man!"

Caring too much was what he was good at. He'd always wanted to do what his father expected of him, and that meant taking life seriously. While he and his father did not see eye to eye on everything, they both appreciated order—and Miranda seemed to turn everything on its head.

She was unpredictable and outspoken. Someday, Ethan would inherit the title of Gibson and the barony, and upholding tradition was important.

He knew what Miranda would have said.

"It's not about sacrificing your pride; it is about shedding your inhibitions." She'd said that very thing to him before she'd tricked him into climbing that infernal tree and he'd embarrassed himself. He blinked away the memory. He shouldn't have listened to her then, and he wouldn't listen now.

Ethan stood from behind his desk and stretched his back. He needed to do something active to keep his mind off this woman—and the reckless way she made him think. Perhaps this was a good time to go through his clothes and put together some castoffs for the school.

He found a maid dusting a vase in the corridor outside his father's study. "Have a footman bring a crate to my bedchamber about this size." He put his arms out, parallel with his body, to suggest the dimension he would need.

The maid bobbed a curtsy and hurried to do his bidding. Instead of walking the rest of the way to his room, he took the staircase two steps at a time and jogged past the other bedchambers. He'd been pushing himself physically with every opportunity he had as a way of keeping his mind clear. He'd even taken up running just after sunrise. He opened his closet and pulled out a few pairs of trousers he rarely wore. They could easily be sized down for a younger boy—

"Miss Bartley, I am not a young boy. However, if it should please you, I will climb this measly tree to prove a point. It will not change me in any way." He removed his tailcoat but refused to look to see who might be watching. Of course he cared about whether or not he was making a fool of himself, but Miranda's playful behavior brought out a side of him that he had buried after his days at Eton.

He rubbed his hands together and reached for a branch near his shoulders. He swung his feet up onto a lower branch. Miranda's giggles inspired him to climb higher. He reached his leg up a second time, but his pants snagged on a branch. He yanked at it, but it would not free itself. With his weight dangling by his arms, his balance grew precarious. Another sharp yank disrupted his hold, and he found himself pitching face-forward to the ground. He hit with a hard thud. He had not climbed very high, but pain did not know height.

Shrieking, Miranda whisked herself to his side. "Are you alive?"

Ethan moaned and pulled himself into a sitting position. He spit out the dirt, wondering how he had managed to get a mouthful. "Dead people do not hurt as I do." Ethan tested his arm to see if it was broken. "I am very much alive."

Miranda's sympathetic expression made him laugh despite the discomfort he felt in every part of his body. She put her hand over her mouth, but it was too late; her giggles joined his.

"I'm sorry," she said over and over again. "Truly, I should not have suggested this."

"No, I should not have tried so hard to impress you." It was beyond ridiculous what he would do for this woman.

When their laughter diminished, Miranda pulled out a handkerchief. She bent over and tenderly wiped the dirt from his face. Her eyes met his—blue as a perfect summer sky—and drew him in. He reached for her wrist to keep her from pulling away. How warm she'd felt beneath his touch.

They sat there, staring at each other, mesmerized in a world all their own. His other hand cupped her face, and he caressed the curve of her cheek, stopping at her full lips.

Ethan coughed, jarred by that tender moment. Why did he torture himself with memories? There had been no kiss, thank the stars. A few ladies and a gentleman had seen his fall and hurried over to see if he was all right. Somehow, he had pulled his bruised body off the ground and dusted himself off. The story had never even reached the ears of the gossipers. Miranda had taken complete blame for his behavior, making up a silly story about him rescuing her handkerchief from the tree.

It was no wonder he could not forget her. At the end of their drive, she had taken the same handkerchief she had trailed along his cheek and, with mischievous eyes, kissed the cloth and handed it to him.

"A favor for a favor."

That alluring woman needed a husband to tie her down—just not him. The attraction drawing them together was not enough to excuse certain behaviors Ethan later learned he could not overlook. Her beauty and charms had intoxicated him until he was almost too blind to see her true character. He shoved a few spare shirts on top of the pile of trousers with greater force than necessary. He desired a wife he could trust as the future mother to his children.

That gave him pause. She would likely be a good mother. He did believe her capable of that.

But did she have the ability to run his social calendar without jeopardizing important relations with her pettiness? He might regret the way he'd gone about it, but not the ending of their courtship.

"Excuse me, sir." A footman interrupted his thoughts with the delivery of the requested wooden crate.

"Thank you. Set it here beside me." Ethan scooped up the articles of clothing in his arms and systematically placed them inside the crate. He craved order, and Miranda Bartley was a wildflower that could quickly overrun his neatly arranged life.

Returning to his closet, he added several old books he'd taken from Stonebrook Hall's library. Then he pulled out a pair of barely worn boots his brother, Richard, had left behind, claiming they rubbed the outside of his feet when he walked, and added them atop his growing pile. Anytime weakness tested his fortitude, he needed to remember why he had made this decision in the first place. He picked up the crate and grunted at the weight. The footman could take care of it, but Ethan wanted to feel the pain in his fingers and the pull of muscles. He would forget this woman if it killed him.

Each step toward the front door of his home added to his determination as did a growing mental list—one Jane would never find. Stop wearing the color blue—Miranda favored it on him. Stop drinking chocolate—the woman adored the stuff. Burn the handkerchief with her kiss upon it that she had brazenly pressed into his hand. Take his neighbor Miss Withers for a ride in his barouche. The last on his list gleamed like a beacon of hope as he set the crate by the door. She was the perfect combination of beauty and sweetness. There lay the ideal solution to his problems. And this time, he wouldn't get so emotionally involved.

CHAPTER 4

MIRANDA'S ABIGAIL, SARAH, WRAPPED A scarf around the outside of Miranda's large bun in a half-turban look, the end of the scarf dangling over her shoulder, with a feather and gaudy pin poking out a few inches above her ear. Sarah fingered the silky fabric, and Miranda noticed the way her eyes lingered, admiring the fine colors.

"What do you think? Too bold?" Miranda tweaked the curls around her face. "It seems only the most eccentric older ladies can pull off a full turban, but I find it a fashion oversight to dismiss them altogether—never mind it is just for a dinner at home with Father."

Sarah dropped her hands from Miranda's hair and cleared her throat. "It suits you, miss."

Miranda ignored her maid's opinion and observed herself in the mirror. Ethan's condemning words about her vanity caused her eye to twitch. Beauty and vanity went hand in hand. All women desired beauty. Didn't they? "You can go now. I am off to find my father to ascertain our travel details. I imagine you will be packing my things soon enough."

Leaving Sarah behind her, Miranda skipped down the stairs, feeling lighter than she had in a long time. It was wonderful to have a change of scenery to look forward to. She heard a clatter coming from her father's study and turned at the end of the staircase in that direction. She pulled open the door to find his desk in disarray, with him hastily shoving things into a travel bag.

"Papa, what on earth are you about?"

"Oh good, you're here," he said, glancing at her. "Hurry and pack your things. I've called a carriage for you. We're leaving."

"Whatever are you talking about?" A sinking sensation started in her chest.

"We are ruined. They will be coming for me soon enough, and I can't be here when they do." He frantically moved about the room as if searching for something important. "I refuse to rot in some blasted clink."

The hair on the back of Miranda's exposed neck stood on end as every sensation in her body responded in alarm. "You speak nonsense. We cannot be *ruined*!"

Her father stopped shoving papers in his bag long enough to meet her gaze fully. She saw panic in his eyes. "I am sorry, dearest. Bad luck is all."

Miranda rushed behind his desk and grabbed at her father's greatcoat. "Stop! For all that is good in the world, I demand an explanation!"

"And you should have one." His voice trembled, and his pallor resembled the ash in the cold fireplace behind him. He thumbed through a few papers scattered on his desk.

"Well?" she prompted. He seemed childlike with his sheepish expression, as if a little scold from her could set everything to right. She put her hand to her chest to still the beating inside. "Just tell me and be done with it."

"The money is all gone." His words were numbing. "My investments in the Dutch Indies came to ruin with that dratted volcano. I tried to recover what I could at the tables, but my creditors are calling in my debts. If only I had more time."

Miranda sputtered while she searched for a solution. "What about our friends?"

"Why do you think I must escape to the Continent? I have borrowed from everyone, and there is no one else to turn to." He grabbed his writing box and shoved it into his bag.

Miranda shook her head. "No! It cannot be." Times like this made her wish her mother had not died in childbirth. She longed for motherly comfort—someone who could help her father make sense of this impossible situation. "You should have told me," she cried, a storm of panic and anger building inside her.

Her father held out his hands, then dropped them in defeat.

Miranda hugged her arms to her chest. "Well, what of the town house? My dowry? Surely there are assets we can use to rectify this."

"Gone to my creditors. We will not see a farthing of it."

"And we must flee into the night like criminals?" Miranda swallowed back her angry tears. "Where will we go? How will we live?"

Mr. Bartley's whole posture drooped. "I will make my way to France and then to Spain. It matters not where. I will lie low until I can earn enough to send for you. But I can never return to London. Our life here is over."

Putting her hand over her mouth, Miranda squeezed her eyes shut. She had known of her father's strong pull to the gaming hells and the horse races; it had always seemed like harmless entertainment. Now the last of their resources were lost over an unexpected volcano and a few bad bets. Or years of bad investments—she was not privy to her father's business. It didn't matter. Thousands of miles away, an unforgivable explosion had ruined her entire life.

"And where shall I go?" Miranda dreaded his answer, but she had to know.

Her father dropped his head. "I have arranged for a carriage to take you and your lady's maid to my brother's house in Folkestone. He is a cantankerous old fool, but he will not turn you away."

"Your estranged brother? He swore he would kill you if he ever saw your face."

"Which is why you are going, not I."

The shock dissipated enough for her to imagine following her father's plan. She'd be living in an obscure seaside town with a stranger. "Can you be sure he will have me?"

"No, I cannot. Nor can I depend on his aid for my debts. As far as I know, he has no heir, and he would never sign over a farthing to me. But who else is there to protect you? His title can help you retain a presence in Society." Her father came forward and wrapped his arms awkwardly around her. "There, there, sweet. I would do anything for you, you know that. It is just that if I stay even a minute longer, I could spend the rest of my days in debtors' prison. That is no life for either of us."

Miranda knew every second was crucial, but she leaned her head against his shoulder anyway, blinking back tears. "This is a perfect disaster."

"Yes, dear, it is."

One tear leaked free and then another. With the same rapid fall of the moisture on her cheeks, life as she knew it dripped away. "Will you at least write to me?"

Her father pulled away and dropped his arms to his sides. He stared at her long and hard. "I promise to send for you as soon as I can afford to. I will write, but it could be some time before I am settled."

Miranda could not imagine life without her father. They had never been parted for long. Even as a child, she and her governess had traveled everywhere with him. But she found herself wiping her eyes dry and nodding. "I shall miss you." She meant it, even though right now, she felt mostly anger and hurt.

"And I you. Now, go. The carriage I sent for you is on its way."

⚜

Miranda pointed to her trunk. "If you hurry, you might have time to gather a few things of your own."

"Me?" Sarah glanced up at her, her petite frame suddenly tense.

"Well, yes, you must come with me." Miranda felt a shiver of fear pass down her spine. What if Sarah said no? Miranda couldn't travel alone—not to see her uncle, of all people. "I haven't the time to write you a recommendation, and we both know you would never find another job as a lady's maid without one."

Sarah continued packing Miranda's truck without a word, her cheeks as pale as the white-blonde lock of hair that had escaped her mobcap.

Miranda drummed her fingers on the side of her dress. This was taking much too long with just one of them working. She hurried to her dressing table and gathered her toiletries.

"Perhaps—" Sarah's hesitant words broke the harried silence. "Perhaps I could join you with your trunk tomorrow. There is a great deal to pack, and—"

"No," Miranda said sharply, remembering her father's dire words. The last thing she wanted was to face the humiliation of creditors banging on their doors. "We must leave straightaway."

Sarah's jaw went tight, and she began shoving the dresses into the trunk without her usual care.

"This is not convenient for either of us, Sarah." Miranda hoped to convey the desperate situation they both faced. "I have not forgotten the small fact about there being more laborers than jobs. I am doing you a favor." Miranda tucked her toiletries into a smaller trunk while Sarah rushed to place silver paper between the gowns in the larger trunk. "Honestly, Mr. Roderick was always whispering about the state of unemployment with his friends. They think the ladies don't hear anything because we are too busy simpering behind our fans."

Miranda could see Sarah turning the situation over in her mind before her features turned stoic and accepting of her fate. Her maid might not be the most competent with the latest fashions, but she did know how to be compliant. Still, Miranda could not breathe until the hired post chaise arrived and her hastily packed trunk was loaded, along with Sarah's meager belongings. Her father gave her a tight hug at the door, but she pulled back. She didn't want to remember his face lined with worry or the brandy on his breath. When she walked away, she felt like an orphan.

The door to their town house shut with a resounding thud, the dark street empty beside the chaise. Before she and Sarah stepped inside, Miranda paid the driver a handsome tip. "I require a quick stop." She relayed to the driver the address of Jane's family town house. She was not going all the way to Kent if Jane would take her in. Perhaps Lord Gibson, Jane's titled father, could help smooth her situation. Money and reputation went a long way with the *haut ton*, and the Rodericks had both.

Only a few minutes later, the carriage lurched to a stop, and Miranda eyed the lit windows of Lord Gibson's place. After a few slams of the knocker, the door opened to her. She was led into the vestibule right as Jane stepped down the stairs. Thank heavens it was her and not her parents. Miranda needed another minute to prepare herself to speak with them—she'd not spoken with either Lord or Lady Gibson since before Ethan had left Town. Would the rumors of her father's ruination have reached them already?

Jane frowned. "You are much too late for calling hours. Did Mother invite you to dine with us? Never mind that, I have a delicious story to tell you about our friends, the Fosters. Come sit down, and I shall tell you every scandalous detail!"

"Jane," Miranda whispered, pulling her close. "I have much to tell of my own, and I really must make haste."

Jane leaned toward her. "Of course, dear friend, you must tell me!" She looped her arm with Miranda's and pulled her into her family's opulent sitting room. Gold-colored curtains were pulled closed for the evening, and candlelight illuminated the many paintings of Venice and Rome.

"This is for your ears only. Promise me." Miranda and Jane took a seat close to one another.

Jane crossed her heart with her hand. "I am the soul of discretion. You know that."

While Jane gossiped with her about other families, Miranda knew she could be trusted with her secret. "It is my father. He has fled London. We have lost everything."

Jane gasped. "You are ruined?"

"Through and through."

"No, it is not fair!" Jane cried, sitting up straight in her seat.

"Trust me, I feel it keenly."

"But where shall you go?"

Miranda stared hard at her. "Here, I hope. You must take me in."

Jane's face paled. She said nothing for a good, long minute. Then she stood and backed away from Miranda. "You know I cannot. My parents are leaving for Bath. I am to travel to our Sussex estate to be with Ethan and my sister, Hannah."

Miranda dropped her gaze. The last thing she could do was ask Ethan to rescue her. "Perhaps if you and I were to go to Bath. Couldn't you ask your parents?"

"You ask too much. You cannot expect me to speak with you after this. We cannot even be friends."

Miranda's eyes darted upward again. "Cannot be friends? What nonsense."

The anguish in Jane's face disappeared and was replaced with a hardened expression. "I can't let anything hold me back."

Jane's words slapped Miranda in the face and took away her breath. She had flippantly said the same thing to Jane at the ball. "Jane, you are misapplying my words." She searched for a trace of compassion but saw only insecurity and fear in Jane's eyes. Or perhaps it was a reflection of Miranda's own desperate feelings.

"Surely you would do the same," Jane said quickly. "Please do not come back."

Would Miranda abandon Jane if the situation were reversed? Shame erupted like an ugly pox on her soul, and deep down she knew the answer. Being poor was worse than having a disease. Miranda's blood pulsed in her veins, and she stood abruptly. Her only hope lay with her uncle at Gray House. Time would not allow her to tarry another moment.

Jane turned her back on Miranda, cutting off any need for a goodbye. Miranda swallowed back the pain of another rejection and hurried from the room. She hid under the hood of her cloak, knowing anonymity was safest, and departed the house. Sarah was waiting for her in the carriage, looking curious and worried. Once shut inside, Miranda turned away from her maid and laid her head on the velvet upholstery. Silent tears coursed down her cheeks. She had not a single person to turn to.

No real friends.

CHAPTER 5

Gray House, Kent

A HOUSE HAD NEVER LOOKED more unwelcoming. The cool gray stone of the building matched the glimpses of the billowing ocean she'd seen from her carriage window. Alone the house might have been passably pretty, but it was cast in a shadow from the storm clouds threatening to unleash a torrent of rain. Everything in Miranda's sight seemed to quiver in the wind. Even the overgrown juniper shrubs seemed to reach out as if to snatch her. When the door opened, she stepped into the unfamiliar place with great trepidation.

"Miss Bartley to see Lord Aldington," she said in a shaky voice she hardly recognized as her own. "I'm his niece."

The butler's look was cold and curious, but he motioned her inside. He directed her to the drawing room, and Sarah followed her inside. The furniture was dated, the room absent of accents of color, and the hearth cold. This was where she was to live?

She sat on the edge of a sofa, and Sarah took a seat near her. Something about this room struck her as odd. Whether it was a feeling or an observation, she could not be sure, but it seemed as if no one had used this room in ages. Miranda pulled at her elegant sleeves trimmed with lace. At least she had been able to pack a few decent dresses in her haste to leave London. Her uncle would see a real lady as his guest and would not dare turn her away. Miranda lifted her chin. Money was not the only making of a lady.

Miranda turned when the door opened to present her uncle.

The man before her looked to be the same age as her father, with the same salt-and-pepper hair. In contrast, her uncle was taller and had long whiskers that stretched to his mouth. From his rumpled clothes to his facial features, everything about him drooped.

"Why have you come?" he asked without so much as a greeting.

Miranda leapt to her feet and curtsied, squeezing her hands together. She mustn't let a display of nerves ruin his impression of her. If only her father had written a letter of introduction so she might avoid this awkwardness. "My father finds himself in a difficult situation and has been called out of the country. He sent me to live with you for the time being."

Lord Aldington's drooping features hardened. "Impertinent girl. You lie to my face about my indulgent and useless brother and then demand to live here. Don't those governesses teach their charges any manners?" Lord Aldington waved his hand toward the door for her to take her leave. "I do not require a houseguest at this time."

She stared at him, hoping his sense of decency would get the better of him. How could he turn out his own flesh and blood? She stood rooted in place. Feelings of defiance and utter fear fought for control inside her.

Lord Aldington glared at her. "Speak, girl. Do you have something to say before you depart?"

Miranda debated her choices. She could leave, but where would she go? She needed money to do anything. Anyone she'd once claimed as a close acquaintance surely shared the same opinion as Jane. This was her only family connection. Her only option.

"My father lost our fortune." The degrading truth ripped free from her lips. "If you do not take mercy on me, I will be forced onto the streets." She was no beggar, but humility was the only way. Anguish pressed against her chest, making it hard to breathe.

Lord Aldington grunted. "That was not so hard, was it? I see a generation is not a sufficient gap to water down the haughty nature of one's parentage. At least you resemble your mother, not that her appearance did her any favors in life."

It was Miranda's turn to glare, but her words now would come at a price, so she held her tongue.

"You can stay," her uncle finally said, walking to the cold fireplace. He stared into it as if sheer frustration could cause a spark. Then he turned and gave her a shrewd look. "But I will not spoil you. You will earn your keep like the rest of this household. If you can agree to the terms, I will have a room at the far end of the house aired for you. You will take your meals alone. I cannot abide chatter at my table."

Appalled, Miranda gaped. She sputtered for a moment but then pressed her lips together, refusing to invite more censure. She had let him see that he had affected her this time. But never again. She would take his charity because she had no other choice. She stuck up her nose again. "Very well."

Lord Aldington raised an incredulous eyebrow but said nothing. He turned sharply on his heels and strode from the room.

What had she gotten herself into? She had fallen from a pit of despair into the fire of hell.

※

"Come in, Mr. Buehler. I'm terribly busy reading the same page over and over again, but I think I can hear whatever it is you have to tell me." Ethan didn't so much as sit up from his relaxed position as his butler entered. He occupied one of four sofas in the extensive library—two were perpendicular to the hearth, and the other two backed the central ones. The bookshelves of his childhood lined either side of the stone-encased fireplace, and the treasure trove of literature comforted him. Opposite the shelves was a line of windows, making the room one of the brightest in the house, and the perfect place to think. He looked at Mr. Buehler, half-expecting him to say Ethan's sisters needed him for some useless task—it wasn't easy being a substitute parent.

Mr. Buehler pushed back the few hairs left on his head and cleared his throat. "Mrs. Withers and her daughter just arrived and are in the drawing room with your sisters."

Ethan snapped his book shut and pulled himself upward. "How is my cravat, man?"

"Crooked."

Ethan peered down at it, nearly crossing his eyes. He yanked on it a few times but couldn't see the damage underneath his chin. "Good enough?"

Mr. Buehler's vague nod was sufficient for him.

"Excellent. If I'm going to marry Miss Withers, I had better get a little acquainted first." Ethan had moped over Miranda for two miserable months. It was time to be aggressive about putting her from his mind.

"Very good, sir." Mr. Buehler held the door out for him as Ethan passed through it.

The ladies stood as he entered the drawing room. He bowed, and the Witherses curtsied.

"Please be seated." Ethan couldn't help the sudden spring to his step as he made his way to an elbow chair beside his two sisters and across from his guests. Step one was happening without him even interfering. "A fine day, is it not?"

Varied murmurs of agreement sounded around the room.

Miss Withers was the picture of perfection. She sat primly in her seat, hands in her lap, and bore a contented quiet in her expression. She reflected her mother's fair coloring, but that was all. Everything about Miss Withers's features was petite—small eyes, small nose, and dainty lips—but with a figure as tempting as Miranda's.

Ethan laughed under his breath in a sort of giddy anticipation. "Good-bye, Miranda."

"What is that you said, sir?" Miss Withers asked.

"Just a little congestion." Ethan cleared his throat and pointed to his neck. "There. All better. Tell me, Miss Withers, are you in good health?"

"Yes, sir. All of us Witherses have excellent constitutions."

"Wonderful." He didn't want to marry a sickly woman. Heaven forbid. Was he smiling too wide? "And how have you spent your time since arriving in the country?"

"I am sewing infant quilts for the newborns in the village. There is a mother of twins who has a particular need for linens."

Mrs. Withers leaned over and set her hand affectionately on her daughter's arm. "My Georgina is the most charitable girl, is she not, Mr. Roderick?"

The size of Ethan's eyes should have already answered the question for him. "Indeed. I am duly impressed."

"I think it remarkable." Jane put her hand to her chest. "Do you know my brother regularly sends funds and necessities to a boys' school? You two are quite matched in nature."

"Do you think so?" Miss Withers asked. "I would never presume to compare myself to Mr. Roderick. My sewing is nothing to the efforts he surely makes."

A maid brought in tea, and Jane served their company first. When she handed a cup to Ethan, she whispered, "Don't ruin this."

Ethan said much louder, "You're a great comfort to me, Jane."

She glared at him and then served their younger sister, who usually never said a word in company. Why could Jane not be more like Hannah and even Richard, who could both sit beside him in silence? His sisters looked alike with their matching dark-brown hair and eyes and rosy cheeks—though Hannah was a smaller build—but their temperament could not be more different.

"What other pursuits do you enjoy, Miss Withers?" Ethan asked, drawing his attention back to his guests.

"I am fond of music and art, but please, I do hate to direct conversation to myself. What of your interests?"

Ah, a modest woman. Another box seemed to check itself in his mind. "I enjoy physical exercise, hunting, and a good afternoon nap."

Miss Withers smiled. "I should think a nap is needed if you are as active as you lead me to believe."

"He has spent the entire day lying around in the library," Hannah said.

Ethan sputtered on his tea. Why had Hannah decided this was a good moment to talk? This was clearly Jane's influence. Hannah was the sweet one. "I have been trying to study some laws," he said by way of explanation. "It's a long, dreadful story and certainly too boring for such delicate ears."

"I agree," Jane said.

"You have piqued *my* curiosity, Mr. Roderick," Miss Withers said. She tilted her head to one side, and he could tell she was attempting to read his character as well.

He might as well do his best to impress her. "I am making a study of the rights of the poor, but I am afraid I do not possess the mind of a barrister; each statute is convoluted, and I need an interpreter to discover the buried meaning."

"When you find an interpreter, I would be interested to know what you have learned."

Ethan caught an approving smile from Mrs. Withers. She was following the conversation with rapt attention. He met Miss Withers's gaze and grinned. "I would be glad to share such knowledge with you." Her enthusiasm for a passion he shared impressed him.

"Are you long at Stonebrook, sir?" Mrs. Withers asked. Were her fingers crossed in her lap? It seemed her excitement about her daughter's conversation with Ethan rivalled his own.

"I have a business trip in a month and then will return to Stonebrook until the new year."

"Well then, you must come to our picnic." Mrs. Withers said. He was beginning to wonder if she had created the picnic just for the opportunity to push his daughter toward him.

"A picnic?" If he said yes, would he come across as overeager? "I wouldn't want to ruin any fun by intruding."

"Nothing of the sort," Mrs. Withers said. "I was going to copy a few invitations tomorrow. Nothing formal—just an intimate gathering under my shade trees. We are going to have *ice cream*."

"Ice cream?" Ethan leaned forward as if coconspiring. "I would not want to miss something so delightful."

"No, you mustn't," Miss Withers said, picking up where her mother had left off. How could he say no to such a sweetly delivered plea? "And your sisters must come too."

"Thank you," Jane said. "That is most kind." After a moment, she elbowed Hannah.

Hannah squeaked a quiet thank-you.

Ethan eyed Miss Withers. "And you will be there, of course?"

"Undoubtedly." She smiled at him.

Miranda would have teased him for asking such an obvious question. He might have laughed with her. But Miss Withers was not the laughing type. She was sedate in both behavior and expression. Such an opposite nature to Miranda's made her a prudent choice for him. He only wanted his intentions toward Miss Withers to be clear before she left his house.

CHAPTER 6

"I AM NOT A SERVANT." Miranda folded her arms across her chest, defiance burning behind her eyes. She had not slept well in her new bed, but had she anticipated such a rude reception from Mrs. Guttridge, the housekeeper of Gray House, she would have stayed put.

Mrs. Guttridge had the physique of a burly man. Her wiry gray hair was pinned tightly beneath her mobcap, and her neck and cheeks bulged, whereas her eyes were tiny slits. She stood to her full height and drew her face very near to Miranda's. "If ye want to eat or have a roof over yer head, ye'd better mind me. Yer to contribute to the upkeep of the house to earn yer meals. Lord Aldington said there's to be no special favors for ye."

Her voice boomed, and a fleck of spit landed on Miranda's cheek, causing her to cower and step backward into the passage and away from the kitchen. This woman was not someone Miranda wanted for an enemy; that much was clear.

"Is this some sort of test?" Miranda reached up and wiped the spit from her face. "I do what you ask, and then my uncle lets bygones be bygones?"

A sharp bellow of a laugh burst from Mrs. Guttridge's mouth, revealing several missing teeth. "There ain't no end for the rest of us."

A sinking sensation started in Miranda's chest and moved to her stomach. "I am not suited for such tasks."

Mrs. Guttridge smirked. "It ain't proper-like, but ye'll be appreciating the hands that serve ye by the time yer done."

The pit inside Miranda began to swirl, and she clutched her stomach. She barely managed to move her hand before Mrs. Guttridge shoved a mop bucket into her gut. Miranda clasped the handle of the rusted, dented bucket and cringed at the very feel of such filth. It smelled of feet and lye.

This was the furthest thing from what she had dreamed for herself. How could her uncle subject her to this?

Mrs. Guttridge rattled off a list of chores, each one a nail in Miranda's social coffin. She looked around for a savior, but the deserted corridor reflected the past twenty-four hours of her new life. With reluctant steps, she began to mop the passage, only to spill the dirty water all over the floor as soon as she finished. Later, she broke a vase while dusting, and Mrs. Guttridge shrieked for several long minutes about it being Lord Aldington's favorite. When she stood over several dark-green rows in the garden, Miranda had no idea where to begin. She examined each plant and pulled the ones that seemed offending in shape and size. How was she supposed to know she had pulled up all the vegetables and left the weeds behind?

"Ye ain't got a lick of sense in ye," Mrs. Guttridge said, analyzing the pitiful basket of fruit Miranda had collected on her way back from the garden. The woman placed her hands on her wide hips. "Let's see if ye can handle the kitchen."

The cook, a tall and wiry woman, glared when they entered the warm room. Several kitchen maids were scattered about the place, and they all rushed to look busier than they likely were. Sarah was there too, but she hesitated in her sweeping, and her soft eyes met Miranda's.

"Ye there!" Mrs. Guttridge said to Sarah. "Teach this sad creature to boil a kettle." The housekeeper was apparently so used to being obeyed that she left without further instruction.

Boil water first, eat second. Surely this was a task Miranda could handle.

Sarah walked her through the steps while the other girls laughed behind their hands and whispered rude remarks.

In the firelight, Miranda noticed bright-red blisters on Sarah's over-worked hands. She was no longer a prestigious lady's maid but a maid of all work—left to complete the tasks the other maids were too busy to accomplish, until the housekeeper could find a specific place for her. Her normally tidy bun was coming undone, and her dress was smudged. Miranda looked down to see that her own dress, which only this morning was a pretty day gown of yellow, was far worse. Tears pricked her eyes. How had she fallen so low? No one would marry her after this.

"Now, watch the spit, mind you." Sarah pointed to the roasting goose. "His Lordship won't like his food dirtied."

Miranda managed without incident. Finally, she could eat. She leaned against the fireplace's stone encasement and sighed.

"Well, that was not too hard, now, was it?" As soon as she said it, a thin wisp of smoke trailed up the side of her. She looked toward its source and gasped. The hem of her dress was on fire! She screamed and started dancing to keep the small flame from reaching her skin.

Sarah was smarter than Miranda and grabbed the barely warm pot on the hearth and dumped it on Miranda's dress. The small flame disappeared, leaving behind wet, charred fabric.

"You were never this clumsy in London," Sarah said, melting against the table in relief. Several kitchen maids burst into laughter. Their humiliating cackles echoed around the room.

Miranda threw up her hands. "I'm cursed. I'm doomed to live the rest of my life as a miserable lout."

The door banged open, and Mrs. Guttridge gasped. "What now? I swear, if ye burned the dinner—"

"The dinner is well. It's the lady who's burnt," a young kitchen maid with plaited hair said. She snorted, and the others dissolved into peals of laughter once more.

Tears teased Miranda's eyelids, but she blinked them back. She stuck her chin in the air proudly. "I refuse to help in the kitchen, the garden, or anywhere else. I am not doing any more work. I demand to speak with my uncle immediately."

Mrs. Guttridge surprised Miranda by nodding in agreement. Miranda followed her up the servants' stairs into the corridor and toward Lord Aldington's study.

After a knock and a request to enter, Miranda found herself facing her uncle far sooner than she'd hoped. He sat behind his desk with his pen held to a ledger. A wine bottle and a nearly emptied glass lay next to his work. The whole room seemed to carry a fruity odor from the drink. Her courage waned. She knew she was more outspoken than most, but her intimidation by her uncle had only grown since their first meeting.

"Go on now, say your piece. I do not have all day," he growled. He looked tired and his skin more yellow than white.

"Yer Lordship," Mrs. Guttridge began, "the miss don't have any notion of work. She's caused a heap of trouble, and I don't have time for the likes of her."

Lord Aldington's frown deepened. "I told you to do whatever you wanted with the girl."

"I want her out of my kitchen and away from the help." Mrs. Guttridge's eyes were wide, her mouth set in a firm line.

Miranda had to press her lips together to keep from gaping in surprise. She'd been preparing to perform a speech of her own, but she'd rather her uncle turn his anger toward his housekeeper than her.

"I am sure you can find something she can do or let her look after herself." Lord Aldington turned his beady eyes on Miranda. "I will not tolerate any more interruptions from you. You are here on a trial basis, and you are not putting your case in a favorable light by inconveniencing myself and Mrs. Guttridge. I suggest you learn to get along, or I will have to ask you to stay elsewhere."

Miranda blustered, but words could not form. Where did he think she would go? She never would have come if she hadn't been in the direst of straits. She had to make peace. "I will look after myself. You need not worry about any more interruptions."

"Good. You are both excused," Lord Aldington said tersely.

Mrs. Guttridge scowled at Miranda and waddled out the door. Miranda took a daring stance and waited to speak with her uncle privately.

He looked up, and his glare turned icy. "I said you were excused."

Miranda saw more than just his seething anger. Lines of fatigue were etched around his brown eyes. With no wife and no children to give him purpose, he had nothing. A weariness of life settled around him like a determined companion. Before her sat a very sad, lonely man. The sudden perception engulfed her with new awareness.

Her temper diffused, and she yearned to bridge the gap between them. "Please, Your Lordship, I do not understand why you hate my father, and I will not ask you to tell me. But why extend those feelings to me? We are all the family we have left in the world."

Lord Aldington looked at her as if seeing her for the first time too. Then he blinked away the connection and poured himself a drink. A dark ring where the bottle was set remained on the table as if from years of bottles being in the exact same position. He tipped the glass to his lips, and the red liquid disappeared, along with any hope Miranda had.

"I do not have any family," Lord Aldington said. "Now, get out."

"You are right," Miranda snapped back, feeling her defenses rise. "Drink yourself to death, and see if I care." She slammed the door behind her for good measure and then heard the piercing thud of glass upon wood. She shuddered. Her uncle despised her, and she knew there would be no second chances if she dared provoke him again.

CHAPTER 7

THE SUN HID BEHIND A few dense clouds, but the day was warm enough for a comfortable walk around Stonebrook's vast estate with Miss Withers. They, of course, were only walking toward a small pond a half mile from the house. Jane had been all too willing to walk with Hannah ahead of them so Ethan might have a few minutes of private conversation with their lovely guest. It was a thoughtful gesture, since she had never been willing to leave him and Miranda alone without a great deal of obvious hinting.

"Do you walk this way often?" Miss Withers asked.

It had been only a few days since their last meeting, but he appraised her before answering, not sure he'd even really looked at her in such a close proximity. She wore a scarlet pelisse, and several brunette braids by her neck were pulled up into her bun. It was an odd hairstyle—one Miranda would probably think was fetching. "I usually ride, actually," he finally said. He almost mentioned his morning runs, but they did not know each other well enough for him to talk about his strange habits. "Are you fond of long walks?"

"I am."

Ethan anticipated her to say more, but she didn't. Lud. Now he would have to think of a topic of conversation. Knapweed, red clover, and ragwort spread a rainbow of color across the grassy downs and left a faint, sweet aroma. He bent and picked a knapweed bloom and handed it to Miss Withers.

"Thank you." She took it and promptly sneezed. "Forgive me; weeds make me sneeze."

Weeds? He was an idiot. He saw them as beautiful wildflowers. "It's my fault. I thought it was pretty. I shouldn't have pressured you to hold it." He quickly accepted it back and tossed it into the field. Another two sneezes followed. Miranda adored flowers, or so she had led him to believe since she'd gushed over everything he did for her—as if he were the ultimate gentleman. It would take time to learn Miss Withers's likes and dislikes. He handed her his handkerchief. "Come, the pond is just around this bend. There is a wood bench on the shore, where you can rest."

A few moments later, he took her hand and assisted her over some uneven rocks to the bench. Down the way, they could see Jane and Hannah attempting to skip rocks. When he released Miss Withers's hand, he bent into an elaborate bow. When he looked up, she was frowning at him like he was utterly ridiculous. He straightened. Perhaps he was. Whenever he broke from character and did something lighthearted in front of Miranda, she had always laughed with him. He wasn't sure if he could go back to being serious all the time. But that wasn't his real concern; his real concern was that he could not cease comparing everything Miss Withers did to the woman he'd walked away from. He needed to focus on Miss Withers alone.

He sat down beside her just as she pulled out her fan from her reticule hanging from her wrist. Ethan narrowed his eyes. Not the fan. How was he to avoid thinking of Miranda now? She had made sure he was well-versed in the language of the fan, and they had both laughed themselves to tears on more than one occasion. It had proved to be a useful skill when they had not been capable of conversing privately.

"This spot is perfect," Miss Withers said.

Ethan smiled. "I'm glad you like it."

Miss Withers ran her fan through her hand, and Ethan sat straighter. Her action said she hated him. Could she be holding something against him because of the card party and his association with Miss Bartley? Or maybe she just hated that he'd given her a flower.

He decided to test her with a story. "My friend and I spent many hours here as boys, building rafts. We managed a few successful designs but even more unsuccessful ones." He watched to gauge her interest.

"What an industrious child you must have been." She put the tip of the unopened fan against her left ear.

She wished to get rid of him. Ethan folded his arms across his chest. Maybe she didn't know the language of the debutantes and was perfectly imitating the actions simply by accident. "Ah yes, I was quite an active child. What were you like in your youth? I can't imagine anything remotely mischievous."

Opening her fan, Miss Withers began gently wafting air toward her face—with her right hand. It meant he was being too eager. Well, there was no denying that. "When I was a child, I liked to embroider long verses of scripture," she said. "I was quite good at it, or so my mother said."

Scripture? What an odd child. "I'm sure you were quite adept."

"I'm jesting, Mr. Roderick." Miss Withers snapped her fan shut. "I would have likely been here making rafts with you, but my mother insisted I keep my dresses clean. I did like to mix water with berries and spices to make watercolors for painting rocks. It's not as quaint as embroidery, but it passed the time."

Ethan relaxed. "How inventive. If we had known each other in our youth, you could have painted our rafts for us."

"You would have loved the hearts and swirls I perfected."

Ethan chuckled. Maybe Miss Withers had some personality after all. He enjoyed the diverse natures people possessed, but it was the selfishness he could not stomach. Miss Withers was proving to be a happy combination of both sweet and amusing.

She dropped her fan in her lap—a sure sign she wished to be only friends—or to begin as friends. "Shall we join your sisters in skipping rocks? I have always enjoyed the simple sport."

"If it pleases you." He stood and brushed off his backside. They just needed more time to get to know each other. He could not let his impatience to get over Miranda—or a silly fan—ruin a perfectly good opportunity.

CHAPTER 8

DURING HER MONTH AT GRAY House, Miranda had stumbled upon her uncle only on a few occasions, but each time he carried a glass swirling with wine or brandy. As a child, she'd adopted a hatred of her uncle from her father, but now she feared him. The constant drinking turned him into an unreal person—one with glassy eyes and a heavy countenance.

Lord Aldington lacked presence of mind during his drunken stupors, leaving the control of the house to Mrs. Guttridge, who domineered even the butler. Miranda found Mrs. Guttridge to be the lesser evil during times such as these, as she and the housekeeper had come to an impasse. Miranda was no longer treated as a maid but as an outcast. Mrs. Guttridge kept her away from all the staff, but she would not have Miranda idle. So Miranda spent the majority of her time on the monotonous task of sweeping and mopping the many corridors in the manor, staying out of the others' way. Unlike the days slowly passing, the repressive feeling at Gray House never faded. Miranda was tired, always hungry, and fiercely lonely.

After another long day of chores, fatigue pulled at Miranda's eyes. She finished her supper at a table by herself in the kitchen, then climbed the stairs to her small corner bedroom that was isolated from the rest of the house. She pulled open the door to her room to discover two footmen, Alan and Kurt, neither of whom she knew well, tossing her expensive gowns into her trunk.

"What is happening? I demand you release my things."

The two looked at her and returned to packing.

Panic ripped through her. "Stop! Stop this instant! Why are you doing this?"

Alan, who had more freckles than his fair share, cast her a disinterested gaze. "Mrs. Guttridge ordered your dresses sold."

Shock nearly knocked Miranda's feet out from under her. A wave of emotion came with such a rush that it expelled from her mouth in a sound of unfettered rage. She ran forward and attacked the men with her fists. "Get out of here, you scoundrels! Get your filthy fingers off my things. I hate you! I hate you horrible, ruthless people."

The men laughed at her but retreated, leaving her trunk spilling over with her things and slamming the door in their wake. In a feverish fervor, Miranda rushed to her trunk. She threw the gowns aside and located her writing box. Her tired fingers, flustered from emotion, fumbled for the penknife. She took it to the corner of the room and used the knife to pull up a floor panel. The tip broke, but she cared not for the damage. Down in the small hole went her jewelry—buried where no one could steal it. She had a few fine pieces, including a lovely garnet ring, and not a one would find its way into Mrs. Guttridge's hands.

When her precious things were safe, Miranda leaned her head against her bedpost. A candle flickered from somewhere in the room, likely left from the footmen, but she did not register where. All she saw and felt was darkness pressing into her. A wail slipped from her lips, followed by sobs. She cried for the loss of her father, for her comforts, for the life she once had. She cried for the destruction of her hopes and dreams. And she cried because no one in the world cared at all. It seemed that even God had abandoned her.

Hugging herself, she wondered, if she disappeared right now, whether anyone would even notice. With her eyes pressed closed, her heart conjured an image of Ethan wrapping his arms around her. She recreated his smell in her mind and imagined his soothing words calming her frightening thoughts. As unworthy as she was, thinking of his goodness—his gentle smile—eased the torment inside of her. She focused on the memory of his smile and curled up on the floor.

Hours later, she moved to her bed. Fully clothed, with only a nub of candle still burning, she awoke to the sound of Sarah's voice. When Miranda opened her eyes, only Sarah's head and one shoulder were visible behind the barely open door to the room.

"Forgive me for waking you, but are you all right, miss?"

"I am not myself." Miranda blinked slowly, her heavy lids swollen from a river of tears.

She expected Sarah to leave her alone again, but she didn't. "I heard about your clothes. Everyone is saying Mrs. Guttridge wished to sell them and pocket the money." Sarah motioned to the disarray on the floor. "Would you like me to help you put the room to rights?"

Perhaps someone would have noticed after all if Miranda disappeared. Sarah would have noticed. Relief gave Miranda the strength to pull herself into a sitting position. "Why would you even offer? You do not have to help me anymore. I am not the one paying you. You should leave this forsaken place while you can."

Sarah looked over her shoulder as if searching for eavesdroppers. Then she entered the room and closed the door behind her. "Miss—"

"Miranda. Call me Miranda. I am no different from you now. I do not deserve any respect in your reference to me."

"Perhaps you don't deserve it," Sarah said. "You've never been kind to me."

The truth pierced Miranda. She cringed as she remembered all the rude, flippant words she had thrown at Sarah over the years. Never had she said thank you or inquired after Sarah's well-being. For the first time, she felt embarrassed for her behavior. Though, she would take back her past life in an instant.

Sarah shrugged. "You cannot help the life you were born into."

Miranda stared at the threadbare quilt on her bed. "It is true experience is a great teacher. Still, a person always has a choice." She thought of Ethan and squeezed her eyes shut. "I wish I would have thought twice before making mine."

Sarah nodded. "I'll keep calling you miss, but only because I think you've got the stuff in you to be a real refined lady. A dignified one, too, if you have the heart to try a little harder."

Miranda yanked her head upward. "Try? I have been slaving away like a common servant. I am sick of trying."

Sarah stared at her with sad eyes. "Perhaps, but you still sound the same when you talk."

"Of course I do. I am still the same person."

"Never mind." Sarah folded her arms across her chest. "You're right. I don't have to stay here. It's not the best money or work." She stared at Miranda for a moment, then threw her arms down to her side. "Very well, I'll stay a little longer on one condition."

"Tell me." Sarah was the only person who cared at all. Miranda feared life without her, for then she'd truly be alone.

"I want you to *keep* trying."

"What other choice do I have?" Miranda huffed. Only in death could she truly escape her suffering, but if God gave her a reason—proved He cared—she could endure.

Sarah gestured at Miranda with a wave of her hand. "Just attempt to be nice for a change."

Nice? Why? She had lost her entire world, and Sarah wanted her to be nice? How much would a person have to suffer to justify fits of despair? Sarah's soft smile halted her complaint before it could be uttered. There was compassion in her expression, and it felt like a breath of hope.

"I will try," Miranda finally said in a small voice. She cleared her throat. "Would you please help me put to rights this mess?"

"Ah, *please*, that's a new one. Yes, *miss*, I would gladly help you."

As they folded and hung dresses, Miranda's deepest yearnings resurfaced. It was out of desperation that she confided in Sarah. "Losing my dignity is not as defeating as realizing not a single person in the world cares for me."

Sarah eyed her. "What of your father?"

"I keep thinking about him. If he loved me, he would not have been able to leave me behind so easily."

"It won't do any good to doubt your father's love, miss. He was only trying to protect you."

"You are probably right. After everything that has happened, after being with my uncle, I am not sure I even know what love looks like anymore. But you are thinking clearer than I am. I will do as you say and not think ill of him." Miranda's eyes hurt from the hours spent crying, and new tears stung as they filled her lids. It was Gray House. Here, love and light were absent. What she wouldn't give to feel both again.

CHAPTER 9

ETHAN WAS MAKING A LIST of things he planned to bring with him on his trip to visit his good friend. Stephen was Lord Meredith now, the Earl of Radnor, but they had been friends since university, and it was still hard to think of him in such a role. They had been corresponding about the current conditions of the poor boys' school they both sponsored in Folkestone, spurring Ethan to add a few last-minute additions to his list.

He paused when he wrote about having a maid gather spare quilts. Quilts reminded him of the brightly colored ones spread on the lawn during his recent picnic with Miss Withers—a success, to say the least. Since the picnic, there had been a succession of pleasant encounters, some planned, some unexpected. Their relationship was progressing rather nicely. He wasn't officially courting her yet, but she could not be mistaken about his intentions.

"What are you doing today?" Hannah stepped into the library and leaned over the back of a chair near him. Her hair was pulled up off her neck, and she looked years older than she was.

"When did you grow up?"

"Really, Ethan. If you didn't want to tell me what you were doing, you could have just said so."

His pulled his lips between his teeth while he added another item to his list. "I am just making plans for a trip to the boys' school."

"Why can't you make a school for poor girls?"

Ethan sighed. "Timing is important, Hannah. Someday, perhaps I can be an investor for such a project. As it is, my funds are tied to Father's, and I can only do so much."

"Can I help? I'm dreadfully bored."

"Are you?" Of course she was. Jane had not been her usual self this summer. She had been surly and despondent, and Hannah was not one to seek out the company of other young girls.

She picked at the embroidery in the chair's upholstery. "When is Mother coming back?"

"Mother and Father will return in a few months."

"I already know that. I want to know the day. Why can't I know the exact day?"

"Because there is no definite return date."

"So I am to be at the mercy of you and Jane for an undetermined amount of time? Excellent. Just excellent. You are far too busy, and Jane is far too dreadful."

Ethan pushed his papers back. "Come, I will play cribbage with you."

"Thank you!" Hannah said. She went directly to the small library table and pushed aside the chess set.

"Well, if you wanted to play a game so badly, you could have just asked." Ethan mimicked the tone she had used on him only a few moments before. He grabbed the cribbage game from a nearby shelf and carried it over.

"All right. If I need only ask, why not tell me about Miss Withers?" Hannah cut the deck of cards and handed them to Ethan to deal.

Ethan shook his head in exasperation and took the cards from her. He had walked right into that trap. Taking a seat opposite his sister, he asked, "What do you want to know?"

"When is the wedding?"

"There is no such understanding . . ."

She gave him a dry look. "I have eyes."

"I don't have any immediate plans." He gave them each six cards, then flipped the card over on the remaining deck. "I am taking things slow and doing things just right."

"Because of Miss Bartley?"

Ethan scratched his head, then leaned forward on his elbows. "Love is like mathematics. The components need to add up. If one end comes out short, well, it can't be a balanced equation."

"Are we still talking about love?"

A stream of air escaped his lips. "Well, I'm trying to."

Hannah thought on his words for a moment. "Miss Withers balances you?"

"She is the same as I am in nature and character."

"And that is a good thing?"

"Yes. It's exactly what I want."

Hannah nodded like she wanted to understand but didn't. "It's been your move for several moments."

"Oh." Ethan quickly laid down a card and pegged his point.

A knock sounded against the frame of the open door. Ethan turned and saw both Jane and Miss Withers standing on the threshold. Heat seared the back of his neck and the tops of his cheeks. How long had they been standing there?

Miss Withers was grinning.

Ethan's lips turned up as well, but only because this meant less time to play games, and he was thinking of courtship, not cribbage. When he returned from his trip to the boys' school, he would make things official between them. Miss Withers finally seemed just as interested in him as he was in her.

※

Sarah found Miranda scrubbing the floors outside the dining room. "Need a hand?"

"I do not know why Mrs. Guttridge keeps punishing me," Miranda growled. "If I even so much as breathe while she is around, she thinks I am being idle. She is a housekeeper, not a governess! She has robbed me of my self-respect."

"I didn't ask to hear all your problems—just to help you mop." Sarah motioned to the bucket of suds.

Miranda threw her dirty rag at Sarah, who deftly caught it. "All right, I am sorry. And you do not have to help me. I know you have your own chores."

"Yes, I do five in the time you can do one," Sarah said with a sharp laugh.

Miranda stuck out her tongue.

Sarah threw the rag back. "I thought you were a fine lady."

Miranda snagged the rag and shoved it into the bucket. Her back ached, but she bent forward and began scrubbing again. "The past and present are having a bit of a tug-of-war. I think the present is winning." She motioned to her bucket. "Come now, don't just stand there."

"Please?" Sarah prompted.

"Please, Your Highness," Miranda said with a large flourish of her arm.

"Yes, Your Lowliness," Sarah responded.

Miranda laughed. It felt like years since she had heard the sound come from her mouth. Sarah seemed oblivious of Miranda's triumph and joined the mopping.

"Do you ever dream of a different life?" Miranda asked after a few minutes.

Sarah didn't lift her eyes from her task. "My sister has a half dozen babies and is always fretting about one thing or another. But still, I like the idea of someday marrying and having a brood of children."

Miranda smiled at the image Sarah conjured. "I've never thought much about children."

"Well?" Sarah asked. "What do you think of them now?"

"I think they would make a great deal of messes, and I would be stuck cleaning up after them."

Sarah stared at her with disappointment.

Miranda snorted when her laugh came out. "Your face!"

"My face?" Sarah exclaimed. "Your snort!"

Miranda nodded. "I know! It happens once in a while, to my dying shame."

Sarah shook her head and went back to scrubbing. "Tell me what you really think about children."

"Well, I want to start with getting married first," Miranda said, "but then I would like to have children."

"So it doesn't bother you at all about your own mother dying with a babe?"

Miranda would be lying if she said otherwise. "I don't know the first thing about motherhood. That is what scares me. Still, sometimes I think I imagine an adorable little girl with dark hair just like—" Miranda had to stop herself.

Sarah grinned. "Like who? Mr. Roderick?"

"You remember him?" Miranda asked as an image of his dark brows and Roman nose came to her mind.

"You floated around the house after he called on you and made me retwist your hair over and over again on nights you were to see him. I'd say you were quite enamored."

Miranda bit back her own grin. "I was, wasn't I? To my disappointment, he saw right through to the real me."

"You weren't so very bad," Sarah said, then stopped herself. "Never mind. You were horrible."

Miranda glared at Sarah but knew she was right. "Well, it was enough to scare off Mr. Roderick for good. Right from the start, I knew he was different from the others. It was the way he looked at me, as if he saw only my eyes and nothing else."

"He respected you," Sarah clarified.

"Yes," Miranda said sadly. "And I ruined everything. The more we were together, the more ridiculous I acted. I wanted to keep his attention. I wanted to show him I was better than all the others. I wanted to impress him."

She stood to mop the bottom of the staircase but tripped on the hem of her dress and heard a rip. "Blast!" She had lost too much weight since arriving at Gray House, and her gowns hung looser than she was used to.

Sarah hurried over to see the damage. "No use stitching it back together. The fabric has gone to shreds."

Miranda heaved a sigh and bent over to keep scrubbing.

"Surely you can change into another dress."

"I am saving them," Miranda said a little too forcefully. The idea of waltzing back into Society as the old her was ridiculous, but still. She couldn't bring herself to destroy the fantasy.

The two worked in silence for a spell after that, each lost in their own thoughts. Finally, Sarah asked, "What exactly ended things between you and the Honorable Mr. Roderick?"

Miranda would never have had this conversation months ago, but Sarah was not just the maid any longer. "It was a summation of things, really, with a spectacular performance for the finale."

"Your performance?" Sarah asked.

"It was a card party with loads of boring people. I was in royal form."

"Oh dear," Sarah said.

"Let's see. I offended a group of philanthropists, Miss Withers, and Miss Karlson. Then the hostess, Mrs. Grantham, grew upset once she discovered it. And I likely offended Mrs. Jones, too, because when she spoke to me about her illusions of poor health, I told her how to dress better." Miranda used the back of her hand to push back her mobcap. "Not all of my mistakes

were intentional, I would have you know. I blame Mr. Roderick for introducing me to Miss Withers, his new neighbor. A switch just flipped inside of
me. I am sure his interest was greater than he admitted, and I had to let him
know how I felt about her. Besides, at the time, I thought both her and Miss
Karlson so beneath me that it would not matter to anyone."

She moved to clean the next step and continued. "Judge me as you
want, but it was self-preservation. I only accepted the invitation in the first
place because Mr. Roderick encouraged me to."

She would have continued to pour out her soul, but a wet rag to her
face stopped her. She gasped and peeled the smelly, dripping cloth from her
hair and face. She scowled at Sarah. "Why did you do that?"

"Mr. Roderick is not a rake! Even someone blind with only two teeth
could decipher that much about his character."

"Two teeth?" Miranda blustered. "You have never even met the man!
Gentlemen often have wandering eyes."

"Servants stoke the fires, bring in the tea, open and close the front
door. Servants are everywhere. We know a great deal more than you think."

"That is most disturbing," Miranda said, even though she was embarrassed by her obvious ignorance.

"You thought we were all too stupid to pick up on anything." Sarah
stood to leave.

"Wait," Miranda pleaded. "I think a dirty rag to the face is punishment
enough. You don't have to keep helping me, but please, stay and talk."

Sarah folded her arms but remained in place.

"Truly," Miranda said, "I am sorry for my many character failings. I
know I was wrong and have suffered for it." Her list of regrets seemed only
to grow. "Perhaps a person does not have to be the same as always. Perhaps
a person can change and be different—better, even." Maybe this was a
greater fantasy than being able to wear her dresses again.

"I believe people can change," Sarah said, her features finally softening.
"I even believe you can."

Gooseflesh erupted on Miranda's arms, and she blinked back tears.
"Thank you, Sarah. I am not promising any miracles, but I do want to better
myself. I still want pretty things and people to wait on me though. I cannot
erase those longings." Ethan's hurtful words about her vanity haunted her.

"It's natural to want more than you can have," Sarah said as if there
were something in particular she herself was dreaming about, "but there is

a dignified way to go about it. For example, if a lady is in want of shade, she need not wallow in the mud like a pig. She simply uses a parasol."

Miranda wondered at the wisdom a young maid could possess. "I do not like being compared to a pig."

"You do snort."

Miranda glared.

"I meant you can still have all the things in the world, but you don't have to be greedy about it. You can be grateful. You can be humble."

Miranda sat down on the dry step above where she was working. "I simply wanted to stand out. To be noticed."

"You were noticed, but likely not in the ways that reflected well on you." Sarah came and sat down next to her. "It is good that you are being honest with yourself—a worthy trait."

"Did you just admit I have some virtues?" Miranda put her hand over her heart.

"Not some, just one."

Miranda stuck out her tongue again.

"You snort, and you have bad manners. Perhaps you are a pig."

Miranda adopted a saucy tone. "Perhaps some rich, handsome man will pay a fine shilling to have this little porker for a wife."

This time Sarah snorted. "You're too thin. Lean meat isn't worth much to the rich."

They both laughed, but there was an underlying truth to their joke. What worth would Miranda possess after her time at Gray House? Would any gentleman want her? The idea of dying a spinster in an unhappy place such as this left her fearful and uneasy.

✳

Ethan was just about to mount his horse when he saw Jane crossing the grounds toward him.

He held off until she reached him, not anticipating the letter she extended.

"I don't want to detain you from your trip to the school, but I thought you should see this before you left."

Ethan accepted the letter and unfolded it.

"It's from Mama," Jane said. "The second paragraph is what I wanted to show you."

Ethan easily found the second paragraph and began reading.

> *When Mr. Bartley lost his fortune, I was terribly concerned about Miss Bartley's welfare.*

Ethan's stomach clenched. "Mr. Bartley ruined?" He did not wait for Jane to answer and read on.

> *Just this morning, I have had word from our friends the Bradshaws. They have discovered that Miss Bartley has been sent to live with her uncle in Kent. I am greatly relieved, as I remember he was a man of some means.*

Miranda was safe. Thank the stars! Ethan knew little about her uncle, only that he was titled and estranged to the family. What was his name again?

> *It is a shameful thing for a young woman to have to bear the disgrace of her father. I hope, in time, she can recover a portion of her reputation and secure a decent marriage. Sadly, there is little hope for her father's future or for either of them to rejoin our circle of friends.*

His eyes flashed to Jane's. "This is . . . unfathomable. A tragedy. Mr. Bartley was extravagant, but I had not even heard rumors of his situation."

"He duped us all."

"You don't seem upset," Ethan said. Jane lowered her gaze, and realization dawned. "Did you know something?"

"By the time I heard, it was too late for the family. All was lost. I wasn't sure if you would care to know—I know you hate to hear any mention of Miranda—but at the end of the letter, Mama said to be sure to tell you."

"Of course I would want to know." Ethan handed the letter back to her. "I still have respect for the family. Mr. Bartley is a good man, despite his misfortune. Perhaps a little misguided about his finances and unrestrained in his parenting, but he is amiable nonetheless. When did this happen?"

"Before we came to Stonebrook."

"Nearly six weeks ago? I forget how slow news travels to the country." He blew out a long breath.

"I thought the rumors would reach you sooner. I am sorry I did not tell you myself." Jane shifted, avoiding his eyes.

"Now I know why you have encouraged my attachment to Miss Withers. I appreciate your support, but I am sorry to hear your dear friend has suffered. It is no doubt a loss you feel just as keenly as Mir—Miss Bartley does."

Jane nodded and stepped backward. "Safe journey to you."

Ethan swung up into his saddle. He had not expected such news. Miranda had been dealt quite the blow. The thought of her hurting made him sick to his stomach.

CHAPTER 10

WHERE GRAY HOUSE SMOTHERED HER enthusiasm for life, being outside filled Miranda with a sense of freedom. Mrs. Guttridge did not care for her presence in the house and had begun to send her on errands to town. This was one task Miranda did not complain about. Despite the occasional strong winds, wet roads, and chilling rains, unusual for the summer season, the fresh sea air revitalized her soul.

"What is it today?" Sarah asked Miranda once they were on the dirt path that led to town.

"Cardamom," Miranda answered. "I am unfamiliar with the spice, but fortunately, my ignorance ensured me of your company." Her friendship with Sarah grew stronger every day.

"Your timing is excellent," Sarah said. "I was to hang the rugs with the other girls. I despise beating rugs. The dust chokes me."

Miranda grimaced. The very idea of such a chore made her want to rescue Sarah. "I will have to keep claiming ignorance so you and I are forced to walk to town more often."

Sarah paused in her step. "Lately, I forget who you used to be."

"I know the feeling." Miranda gave her a small smile. The easy comradery between them usually began with teasing and laughing about Miranda's past indiscretions, but more and more, it turned into deep conversations.

The more distance they put between themselves and Gray House, the more she felt parts of her soul creep back. The place seemed to drain all the happiness out of a person. The road to town was long, but they detoured to walk along the rocky beach to see the white fingers of the ocean curl upon the sand. A hard rain had bathed all of Kent the night before, and they frequently had to hop over large puddles of mud once they returned to the path.

At the edge of town, Miranda paused before a large puddle straddled between two hedgerows.

"Oh, go on." Sarah nudged her.

Miranda scowled, but she was never one to shy from a challenge. She took a deep breath and lunged over the puddle. The mud on the other side was thick, and her feet slid upon contact. Her body propelled backward into the watery brown slime.

Miranda opened her eyes and blinked away the drips of dirty liquid. She sputtered and wiped her mouth with her arm as she sat up. Sarah hitched up her skirts and took dainty steps around the edge of the puddle, where it was not so very deep.

"Here," she said. "Give me your hand."

Miranda gladly accepted the assistance and stood. "Why did you not suggest I walk around the side like you?" She wiped at the grime dripping from her dress, but it was useless since her bare hands were just as filthy.

"I only just thought of it," Sarah said with a straight face, which suddenly crumpled into a humorous grin. "Oh, come now, it was just a bit of fun."

Miranda grimaced. "I guess I do owe you a little merriment after dragging you to Gray House."

"Maybe a little."

Miranda linked arms with her, and Sarah recoiled against the dripping sleeve. "Ugh!"

Miranda giggled. "Just sharing the spoils of my battle."

"You probably won't even change your dress when we get home," Sarah said, sticking out her tongue. "You wouldn't want to risk smelling decent."

"Carrying water to my room to wash in is a great deal of work!"

The two were laughing and pushing each other as they entered an outside market where people bought and sold food. Only, not many seemed to be buying—just milling about, arguing.

"Mama," a boy who couldn't have been older than five or six said from across the way to his mother, "we can't go home yet. We forgot to buy food."

"Hush," his mother said, urging her son home.

Miranda's smile dropped.

"The food prices have increased again." Sarah pointed to a sign outside a shop that always smelled of tantalizing meat pies, but Miranda's attention remained on the boy.

"Poor dear," she murmured.

The child glanced back at Miranda, then hugged close to his mother. Miranda must have looked a fright. Still, the thought of the boy hungry bothered her. She understood poverty on a different level now. Her own stomach suddenly gnawed in sympathy. At least Lord Aldington's kitchens were well stocked and Miranda had the potential to meet her own needs. She and Sarah began walking again to their destination, but Miranda took one last glance at the hungry little boy before he disappeared behind a corner.

When she dragged her gaze forward again, it was in enough time to keep from barreling into a gentleman. Sarah pulled Miranda out of the way before they shared a muddy encounter.

Miranda looked sideways at the man as they passed him, and the blood drained from her face.

Ethan.

His eyes met hers.

For a split second, she was a deer, stunned in place. Her shock quickly spurred her to action, and she ducked her head, pulling Sarah as fast as she could away from him. There was no way he would recognize her like this, but she would not take any chances.

"Wait," she heard Ethan say.

Her gut clenched. "Move faster!" she said desperately to Sarah. Her new world could not collide with her past. No one could know how low she had fallen.

⚜

Ethan knew those sky-blue eyes as well as he knew his own. Without stopping to think, he chased after the two women. They were moving quickly, despite their long skirts. He followed as they turned between two houses and reached a dead end. The one he thought was Miranda stayed facing away from him, and her companion tried to shield her.

"Excuse me." His heart thumped in his chest. "Miss Bartley?"

The hidden woman turned to face him with great reluctance. *Miranda!* It was her! He could hardly believe her physical transformation.

"No, sir. I'm 'fraid ye are mistaken." Miranda hid her face beneath the folds of her hood, and her uneducated accent caused him to hesitate. He took one step closer and then another, his brows furrowed. Underneath all that mud, her identity was indisputable. "Miss Bartley, what has happened?" Her once full cheeks were hollow. "Are you well?"

Miranda kept her head down. The Miranda he knew would have kept her superior nose in the air with a smile so wide the world could not think less of her. This Miranda was novel to him. "Sorry, sir. Yer mistaken, sir."

Ethan closed the last of the gap between them and gently placed his hands on Miranda's shoulders. The cloak was dirty, and she felt frail beneath his grasp. "Can you not spare a few minutes for an old friend? Truly, I am astonished to meet you here."

Miranda cowered before him, her gaze downcast.

"Please, at least let me buy you and your companion a hot meal." His lips pursed with concern. This was the woman he had once dreamed of spending the rest of his life with. To be so near her felt natural, and yet, it made a part of him ache.

Miranda faced her friend, a fair-headed woman, and shrugged in defeat. Miranda's stomach growled, answering for the both of them.

"Come," he said, motioning with his head. "There is an inn down this street, and they have delicious fish stew and sandwiches. The owner is a good man. And, well, I think you'll both find the food satisfactory." How could he convince her? He wasn't letting go of her until she said yes.

"But my cloak . . ." Miranda waved her hand down the front of her.

"Is stunning. I know you to be particular in your style, and I must say I'm impressed." He hoped to make her smile, which in the past was always her role toward him. To his great relief, it almost worked. Her expression softened, and the fear left her eyes.

"You neglected to mention my hair," Miranda said, motioning to her golden-brown hair, streaked with mud and hastily tied back. She had always been witty, but this was said without her usual spirit.

"My compliments to your maid," Ethan said, trying to keep his tone light. He had never imagined what meeting Miranda again would be like, but this would be hard to forget.

He dropped his arms from her shoulders and extended his gloved hand toward her. Would she take it?

The dainty hand that connected to his was entirely blackish brown. Something soft and wet squished between his fingers.

Her eyes widened as she saw the mud transferred from her hand to his, and she ripped her fingers from his. "Blast!" she muttered.

Ethan had to bite his cheek to keep from laughing. Miranda was the only lady he knew who uttered such a phrase. "Of course, out of respect to the innkeeper, I will see that you are given a chance to wash your face and hands before we eat. His sensibilities are not as refined as yours and mine. Surely that is an acceptable arrangement?"

Miranda met his gaze full-on, and the connection made his heart trip over itself. "Thank you," she said softly.

He cleared his throat. This wasn't him rekindling a smothered flame between them. This was just like finding one of his lost boys. He clasped his hands behind his back, where they were safe.

The three of them walked in silence to the inn. Miranda kept her chin down, and her friend, clearly a servant by her subdued manners, looked anxiously between them. Before long, Miranda was cleaned up, and she joined Ethan in the dining room. She took a seat across from him, next to her maid.

Miranda's gaze flitted to his. "You were always a generous man."

"You have not even tried your food yet," Ethan joked, glad now that she was at least comfortable enough to look him in the eyes again.

Miranda lifted a corner of her lips into a half smile. "It smells wonderful."

There was a glint of her old self in there, but Ethan reeled with what was missing. It was more than her sunken features; it was like seeing a completely different person underneath. Was poverty always so soul-crushing?

"Where are you living?" Ethan asked.

Miranda glanced around her before answering. "With Lord Aldington at Gray House."

"Gray House? Your uncle has subjected you to this squalor?" He blurted the words with little tact.

"You know him?" Miranda asked, giving him a furtive glance.

"My mother mentioned you had gone to live with your relation, but I could not recall his name." Ethan stared at her in disbelief. Her eyes were telling him one thing, but his mind reasoned against it. "Surely your own uncle—"

"No." Miranda stopped him. "He has no use for me. Please, I do not care to talk about it. You have seen me as I am, and we must leave you now."

Miranda stood, and Ethan motioned for her to return to her seat. "Please, you must eat first. I did not ask you to come simply to gawk at you. I am merely startled to find you have been so mistreated."

"Tell the Society papers, will you? I would hate to surprise anyone else." Her sharp voice was more in line with the spirited Miranda he knew, but the harshness was not so familiar.

He thought she would bolt from the room, but a maid with a tray of steaming bowls blocked her path. Miranda begrudgingly retook her seat. Her companion nudged her in the shoulder.

"I apologize," Miranda said with emotional reticence. "Thank you for the meal."

"You are welcome." No matter how he tried, he could not reconcile the skittish woman in front of him with the overconfident debutante from London. "Please, eat as much as you'd like. I can order more."

"We are not pigs, Your Lordship." Miranda might have been disconsolate and humbled, but she still had a little fight left in her.

"No, of course not," Ethan said. He didn't want to argue with her—just help her. "Pigs have more meat on their bones."

Her companion giggled and then coughed to cover it up.

Miranda did not even attempt a retort. The rest of the meal continued in silence. When the bowls had been emptied and all the rolls devoured, Ethan followed the two women back to the street in front of the inn.

He didn't know how to say goodbye. He tugged awkwardly at his gloves. Could he leave her like this? What choice did he have? "It was good to see you again."

She nodded in agreement

"The wind is picking up. Can I call for a carriage for you?"

"No, we will walk, thank you."

"You must hurry, then, before you catch a cold or worse in those wet things. I've never seen such severe weather in late August." Why was he bringing up the weather? He hedged for a moment. "I will be in town for a few weeks more. Perhaps our paths will cross again." As he said it, he realized he wasn't just offering platitudes, and he relaxed his posture. He wanted to see Miranda again—as her friend—to reassure himself of her well-being.

"That would not be wise," Miranda said simply, tucking her cloak closer. "Good day, sir."

The two women hurried off, and Ethan resisted the temptation to follow. Not so very long ago, he had thought himself in love with Miranda, so he reasoned it was natural to want to care for her. Thankfully, he had Miss Withers to think of now. With his feelings in check, he could honestly admit that his run-in with Miranda was no coincidence. She would not be in this current situation if he had not walked away from their relationship. If they had been engaged, he would have been duty bound to marry her no matter her circumstance.

He adjusted the tightness of his cravat, unintentionally yanking it to the side.

He would have to tread lightly. Very lightly. The cold humidity left behind from the rain made him shiver. Or was it his body warning him? An instinct to run as far away from Miranda as possible? She was a hard woman to forget, and that alone made her extremely dangerous.

CHAPTER 11

MIRANDA WOKE WITH A SCRATCHY throat and a cough, no doubt from her restless night consumed with thoughts of Ethan. Questions nagged at her. Had he heard her family name bandied about at every party? She blushed further at the thought of Ethan seeing her dressed as a vagrant. It had taken hours to wash the mud from her clothes, and her hands were still red from the lye. She tied an apron about her waist, noting how easy it had been to exchange gloves for aprons. What must Ethan think of her? Was he relieved he had not attached himself to a woman connected to a scandal? She would have to imagine the answers, because she would be sure to never run into him again.

She made her way down to the kitchen for breakfast and noticed more than one servant coughing. It seemed her malady was not from emotional strain but a passing illness. She took a seat at the table, away from the others, and grimaced at the watery porridge set in front of her.

"How is it that I eat worse than the servants?" She lifted the gruel into her spoon and let it drain back into her bowl. A few other maids at the other end of the room turned and stared at Miranda oddly. She had begun talking to herself the week before. And why not? Besides Sarah, the other servants took great pains to avoid her. The loneliness was utterly consuming at times.

"The hot liquid will ease the throat pain," Miranda muttered. "You will see." She took a bite and nearly choked. They may as well be feeding her glue now! She swallowed before she could gag it back up and gulped the water from her glass. "Insufferable! My tongue just died a thousand deaths." She didn't know if it was her throat or if there was something different about today's fare, but it was not worth a second bite to formulate a proper guess.

Maybe Sarah would know a remedy for Miranda's throat. She pushed back her chair and went to the dish bucket to wash her bowl. When she finished, she quickly wiped her hands dry on her apron, noting a smear of blood. Another knuckle had cracked and was bleeding. Sighing at the thought of more laundry, she slipped away from the kitchen to search for Sarah. Guessing she was still in the library finishing her early-morning chores, Miranda moved in that direction. The clanking of a metal shovel in the coal bucket first alerted Miranda to Sarah's presence, and sure enough, there she was on her knees next to the fireplace. Her movements were sluggish, and her cheeks blazed with a fierce redness.

Sarah looked up from her position on her knees by the fireplace. "Oh, it's you. Are you still thinking about the handsome Mr. Roderick?"

"You know I never think of him anymore."

Sarah's laugh turned into a coughing spasm.

Miranda took the bucket from her hands as Sarah struggled to catch her breath. "It seems the whole house is coming down with something." Sarah should have been in bed. Miranda crouched down next to her. "Let me finish your chores."

"Now, why would you do a thing like that?" Sarah pushed sweaty tendrils of hair back into her cap, her skin pallid.

"Because you need your rest." Miranda's resolve hardened.

"So do you," Sarah said.

Miranda shook her head. "I have a bit of a cold. You, on the other hand, are flushed and weary." She put her hand to Sarah's head. "Sarah, good heavens! You are burning up."

"I have had a fever or two in my days, and I have a strong constitution that always sees me through."

"Please," Miranda said, her voice soft and sure. "Let *me* help *you* this time."

Sarah gave a faint smile, the fatigue lines around her eyes deepening with the gesture. "Oh, very well."

When Sarah left the library, Miranda bent over and finished dumping the coal for her. She finished Sarah's chores, along with her own, faster than she thought possible. Mrs. Guttridge glared at her every time she entered the kitchen, and the other servants turned their backs as if she were not even there, but Miranda felt a sense of peace in her decision.

The next morning, Miranda woke in the same gown she had worn the day before, the smudge of blood on her apron still apparent. She had been too tired to change into her nightgown. She voluntarily skipped her glue for breakfast—Mrs. Guttridge had won this battle—as her throat was too sore to attempt it. Despite her throat, she wasn't coughing, and she had more energy than the day before. She was ready to take on Sarah's tasks once again, but first she would see how Sarah fared.

At the sight of Sarah in her bed, Miranda's heart fell into a pit in her stomach. The color in Sarah's cheeks matched the white-blonde of her hair. She moaned and tossed in her bed covers as if experiencing a nightmare.

"Sarah?" Miranda went to her bedside and reached for her shoulder. Sarah batted Miranda's hand away without registering who Miranda was. "Don't worry. I'm going to get you help."

She pulled back and hurried down the corridor.

"Mrs. Guttridge!" Miranda called out. She ran to the kitchen and found the wrinkly, round woman bent over with pen and paper. "Mrs. Guttridge, Sarah is very ill. She needs a doctor!"

"Humph." Mrs. Guttridge slapped a menu in front of the cook, ignoring Miranda.

"Please, Mrs. Guttridge!" Miranda said, invoking the obliging word that always worked on Sarah.

"Doctors are too expensive. Tell Sarah she must work or leave us."

"I'll ask Lord Aldington, then."

Mrs. Guttridge chortled. "His Lordship left day before yesterday. Escaped just before the sickness hit, he did."

"See reason. Sarah is very ill," Miranda repeated. "She needs help."

"I have too much to do. You, however, lead a fairly useless life. You help her."

"I will." Anguish squeezed Miranda's heart. She could not lose Sarah, her only ally left in the world. "I will see the apothecary in town." Even as she said it, she knew it would be impossible to buy medicine without money. She had no pin money left, but she could sell her pearl necklace.

Racing to her room, she dug up the floorboard and pocketed the necklace. She half ran all the way to town, hardly noticing the wind biting at her skin.

If ever she needed God to hear her, it was now. "Dear Father in Heaven, please help Sarah." She prayed out loud, not ever remembering doing so before. She looked up at the gloomy sky, her voice trembling. "I will commit my life to being better if thou wilt but spare her."

※

"The roof is in terrible shape with all these winds," Ethan told the local thatcher. "I will pay you extra if you see to the school right away." He couldn't risk further damage to the building and supplies.

"Very good, sir." The man accepted the job, and Ethan paid him.

Ethan stepped out of the thatcher's shop and hesitated as a carriage passed in front of him. When the carriage moved, he saw Miranda exit the apothecary shop across the street.

"Ho, Miss Bartley!" Ethan called from across the street. Some of her hair had pulled free from its bun, causing it to cover one eye as she took one glance at him, pulled her thin, dirt-streaked cloak tighter, and hurried to get away. Something wasn't right.

He jogged over to her. "Miss Bartley, are you well?"

She heaved a sigh and halted her escape, slowly turning to face him.

He motioned to the brown vial she held in her hand. She appeared to have been up half the night. A gust of wind parted her cloak, revealing a dirty, wrinkled dress.

"I am well enough." She stole a quick glance at him. "A few of the servants at Gray House have a fever, and I was sent for medicine."

"Your companion from the other day?"

Miranda nodded. "She was my lady's maid and traveled with me to Gray House out of the kindness of her heart. I never should have insisted she come."

Ethan masked his surprise over Miranda being friends with a maid. "You must be anxious to return to her. Might I walk you there?" She was far too beautiful, even in her harried state, to walk alone. She might be accosted by someone of low morals. She eyed him warily, and he did not blame her for hesitating after how they had parted in London. He wished he could forget the way he had treated her, even if he was still resolute in his decision that they were not meant to be together. "Please, I cannot let you walk alone. Especially not this close to the docks."

Her shoulders drooped, and she acquiesced. "Very well, but you will have to keep up."

He fell into step with her swift pace, and they weaved their way through town in silence. The wind pushed her dress around her feet, and without her bonnet, he had a clear view of her profile. Her distress urged him to speak up. "My parents are in Bath for my father's health," he supplied. He wished he could ease her concerns, but maybe talking of his family would at least provide a distraction. "My brother, Richard, was with them for a time but has just returned to school. Jane and Hannah are residing at our estate in Sussex. My great-aunt has been with them, and they have been shopping to prepare my youngest sister for her debut."

They passed around a man bartering for goods at a booth.

"I am sorry to hear your father is unwell," Miranda said. So she had been listening.

"Yes, his gout continually troubles him. I do hope Bath will be good for him—if nothing else, a change of scenery might help."

He was afraid she would not speak to him again and was surprised when she asked, "How did you find yourself in Folkestone?"

"I am staying with the Earl of Radnor while I look after some business." Ethan sidestepped a puddle that Miranda plowed through in her haste.

"Business?" Miranda was the one surprised now. "The only thriving business here is fishing. I thought you detested handling fish. Jane loves to tease you about it."

Ethan chuckled. Miranda remembered that? He had yet to have such rapport with Miss Withers, but it would come with time. "I actually didn't mind catching the fish, but my friend Harry took them off the line for me. I think I ought to try it again sometime. I daresay I would not be as squeamish as I was as a boy." He glanced at Miranda, who gave him a knowing look. "I did not distract you from your question, did I? Very well, I will admit why I am here. I am a benefactor for the Harvey Grammar School, a free school for poor boys."

"Oh?" Miranda lifted a curious brow. "I did not realize. Have you come to make sure they are spending your money well?"

"Not at all." Why did he feel embarrassed about his admission? Before, he had only helped here and there, but after he had ended things with Miranda, he had put his mind to doing more than ever. "I have come to bring them a student. I met a young chap while in London and have arranged to have him educated here. I also volunteered to see to the school's immediate needs. I was just securing a thatcher to repair the roof of their garden shed when I happened upon you."

Miranda paused abruptly and stared at him with an expression unlike Ethan had ever seen on her face before, as if she were seeing the real him for the first time. "How very gallant of you."

Heat touched the back of his neck. He reached up and covered the redness with his hand, only to find that his cravat and collar hid it from view. "Anyone in my situation would do the same."

"You are wrong. Most would do nothing. You are truly kind." She started walking again, intent on the path in front of her.

"Thank you." Her sincere words brought him a great deal of pleasure. And it served a dual purpose, as Miranda no longer seemed on the brink of despair. Perhaps sharing his motivations for helping at the school would continue to distract her until they reached Gray House. "My father's steward's son was my best friend growing up. When I had to go away to Eton, my father instructed me to set my sights higher. I was to make friends with boys who could elevate my status once I became an adult and later a baron. I grew obsessed with the idea of making my childhood friend good enough in the eyes of my father."

"You were a true friend, then," Miranda said.

"I wanted to be, but in truth, we have drifted apart because of distance and time." Ethan shrugged. "It opened my eyes to a world of people who would and could never be my equal. The natural segregation between classes of people, simply because of their birth, has never sat well with me. When I heard of Harvey's school, I latched on to the idea. I have sponsored only a few boys' educations, but it has been a worthwhile endeavor."

At the edge of town, a man called out to him, asking if he wanted to buy bread.

"When was the last time you ate?" He stopped walking, and Miranda reluctantly did as well. Her gaze stayed longingly on the path ahead.

"Have you eaten anything since your meal with me?" She was in too much of a rush to answer him, but he persisted. "You cannot help your friend if you are not well yourself. This will take only a moment." Ethan bought a slice of buttered bread for her and one for himself.

"Nearly five shillings for a pound of bread." Miranda shook her head. "Highway robbery, if you ask me."

Ethan nearly choked on his bite, utterly surprised that Miranda would notice or even care about such a fact. "Yes, I agree with you completely."

"Gray House is this way." Miranda steered him out of the village, her bread disappearing in only a few bites. The sounds of the ocean faded, but Ethan could still feel the chilly, salty sea breeze urging them to hurry. Miranda's energy waned the farther they walked, fatigue lining every feature and movement. He should have called for a hackney, but this was not London, where drivers waited all day for someone to pay them to get around, and he'd not thought to even fetch his horse.

He was relieved for Miranda when they finally caught a glimpse of their destination. But the consolation quickly abated with each step nearer Lord Aldington's forbidding house. There was nothing obviously wrong with the structure, rather a feeling. Cold. Uninviting. Lonely. It was likely born of Ethan's imagination after seeing Miranda so altered.

He cleared his throat and turned to say goodbye. "My best wishes to your friend."

"I will let her know you said as much." Miranda clutched the vial to her stomach and took a few steps from him toward the house.

"Can I see you tomorrow?" Ethan's desperation surprised him. What if she construed his concern for a renewal of affection? Nothing could be further from the truth. It was the feeling about Gray House that had spurred his request.

"Tomorrow?" Miranda turned back, her eyes wide with surprise. "Why would you want to see me again?"

She would not take kindly to his desire to give her charity. He thought quickly. "I would like to know if your friend is better."

"I . . ." She seemed to debate her answer. "My time is not my own."

The weariness behind her eyes told Ethan she was telling him the truth. "I will be in town a few more days. I will walk this way each day around noon. If you happen to be able to get away, then I would consider it a great favor—as an old friend, of course."

She nodded, but Ethan wasn't sure if she meant it or not. He hoped she did. He turned to walk back to town. His motives weren't wrong, were they? Following his conscience sometimes led him to uncomfortable situations, but this was by far the most perplexing. He had just begun courting Miss Withers, and he rather liked her too. As unexpected as finding Miranda had been, he could not simply walk away while she suffered unjustly. Miss Withers would still be there once he saw to Miranda's needs.

CHAPTER 12

SARAH HAD WORSENED SINCE MIRANDA had left her. Dread filled her belly, which was no longer empty, thanks to Ethan Roderick.

"How are you?" Miranda dipped a cloth into the basin of water by Sarah's bed, draping it across her forehead.

Sarah moaned in reply. Sweat soaked through her shift, but she shivered like she was cold.

"I saw Mr. Roderick again," Miranda said, hoping to distract Sarah. "He said he wishes you well. You should have seen how handsome he looked in his sage-green waistcoat and crisp black greatcoat. Not that I noticed."

How she wished to see Sarah smile.

Miranda combed the damp hair away from Sarah's cheek with her fingers and smoothed it across the pillow. Then she sat down beside her on the thin mattress. "I am sure anyone looking on would have thought us a curious pair. Me, contrasting his elegance with my dowdy, grease-stained apron and my hair sticking out in every direction." When she received no response, she sighed. "But never mind that; it is time for your medicine."

Miranda stood and brought the vial over along with the watered-down tea she had made downstairs. Mrs. Guttridge would not spare anything more for a mere ill servant. Miranda lifted Sarah's head against her arm. Then she tipped the warm liquid into Sarah's mouth. It was a relief to see her swallow the tea until it was all gone. Miranda helped her settle back down on her pillow and smoothed her hair again.

"Thank you, miss," Sarah whispered, her eyes opening for a moment.

"You are welcome," Miranda said with a soft smile. She let Sarah sleep, but the ball of anxiety in her chest remained. Her life at Gray House was only tolerable because of Sarah. Without her, Miranda would have nothing to live for.

She could not bring herself to leave Sarah's side and go to bed. She administered to her off and on through the night, sleeping in a wooden chair for a few hours and then awkwardly curling up across the foot of Sarah's bed. By morning, Sarah was little improved. Miranda left the room, needing a respite and some fresh air.

Kurt, one of the footmen who had ransacked her room, stepped into the corridor with a cloak on. She put aside her reservations and asked, "By chance, are you going to town?"

He grimaced. "Yes, miss."

She wanted to sigh with relief. He was a great deal humbler in her presence without Alan or the other servants. "Sarah needs a doctor. Please, will you send for one? I will pay his fees, so you need not trouble Mrs. Guttridge."

She hoped she had enough to barter for such services. She had no idea what fees a doctor charged.

"I . . . don't know," Kurt said.

Miranda's temper flared. "If you don't help me, Sarah could die. I don't dare leave her side as it is."

"Very well," he said, though he shook his head as he walked away. Did he fear the others would mock him if he showed compassion toward Miranda?

Too tired to think on it, Miranda returned to Sarah's side. Hours passed, and finally Kurt returned.

"Many in the village are sick. The doctor's wife said he will come when he can, but we must wait our turn."

She nodded her thanks, her voice stuck in her throat. It was late before Miranda finally made the long walk from the servants' quarters back to her room. Exhaustion overpowered her anxiety, and she fell into a deep slumber. She did not know how long she slept, but the gleam of the sun's rays piercing through the gap between dusty curtains caused her to wake with a start. She jerked up in her bed and pushed back the bedraggled hair by her face.

Sarah.

Miranda threw back the covers and bolted from her room. Running the length of the passageway, she nearly collided with a disgruntled maid. "Sorry!" she called as she flew by. When she reached the open door of Sarah's room, she had to grab the door post to slow her pace before propelling herself into the small room. What she saw forced her heart and feet to still instantly. Mrs. Guttridge stood over the bed, blocking Sarah from view. Miranda heard the unbending woman sniff. Was she crying?

She would only cry if . . .

No, Sarah could not be dead. *No, no, no.*

Miranda pushed past Mrs. Guttridge's hefty form. Sarah lay there with her eyes open. And she was breathing.

"Oh, blessed girl!" Miranda cried. "You are alive!" God had heard her. He had delivered Sarah from death's grasp.

"Yes, but she will be leaving us yet," Mrs. Guttridge's voice was altered, as if she had caught the same illness as the rest of them, and her annoyance was a far cry from the emotional one Miranda had imagined.

She ignored Mrs. Guttridge and stared in disbelief at Sarah. She put her hand on Sarah's head to find it blessedly cool. "Her fever has broken. I hate to disappoint you, but Sarah will be on her feet by tomorrow."

"Tomorrow ain't soon enough. Lord Aldington always says that if the servants don't do their chores, they're dismissed."

"You did not dismiss the other sick servants! Sarah cannot work, not in this state. You have no right!" Miranda could not stop the storm of words she threw at Mrs. Guttridge. She yelled complaint after complaint, not caring how many meals she would miss because of it.

"As the housekeeper, I am in charge of the servants. I do as I please."

If her uncle were here, Miranda would appeal to him. She would beg him to listen.

"All will be well, miss," Sarah said, her hand pulling on Miranda's. "I will go to my sister's house until I find work."

Mrs. Guttridge pulled her lips into a tight line. "See that ye do. I want ye gone by morning." The housekeeper left the room, and Miranda jumped to slam it in her wake.

A flood of tears engulfed Miranda. "Oh, Sarah!" It was like saying goodbye to her father all over again.

Sarah pulled herself into a sitting position, and the small effort winded her. "You can get along now without me. Mr. Roderick will soon whisk you away from here; you will see."

Miranda sank to her knees and laid her head on the edge of the bed. "I can see his intentions very clearly, and they are not romantically inclined. Besides, I did not even know he rescued poor little boys. I don't deserve him."

"Does he now? I told you he was a good man."

"He sees me only as another person he must rescue." Miranda sniffed and wiped her nose on her sleeve—she had lost all refinement. "No one has ever cared for me like you have, Sarah. No one else in this wretched world has an ounce of your kindness. Now you are to be cast out, and I shall be all alone."

Sarah put her hand on Miranda's head. "Do not borrow trouble. Take it one day at a time. And promise me this: promise you will keep trying."

Miranda lifted her head so her eyes met Sarah's. She remembered the prayer she had whispered and the promise she'd made. "I will try."

Sarah grinned, which did little to soften her sickly pallor. "Then, you and I shall see each other again. And when we do, you will be a different person."

"Yes," Miranda said with all seriousness. "My clothes will be in tatters, but Mrs. Guttridge will have made a decent servant out of me."

"There's the spirit!" Sarah said with muted enthusiasm.

❈

The next morning, Miranda shivered against the cool air as she said goodbye to Sarah in front of a traveling coach. "Are you sure your sister will take you?"

"I wrote to her after we moved here with my forwarding address, and she offered to have me anytime. I just couldn't bear to leave you in such a place until you could manage on your own."

"Why would you do so much for me? I was a horrible mistress back in London."

Sarah smiled, her features still a little haggard from her illness. "There, I had the comradery downstairs along with decent wages to keep me going." She looked up at Gray House. "Living here is like wishing for the sun to come up after a tempest, but it never does."

"I am thrilled you have such nice things to say about my home," Miranda quipped.

"It's true staying here has been difficult, but I had faith in you."

"I will never understand why."

"You were like the good silver in the house—of great worth but tarnished by Society and indulgence. All you needed was a bit of polishing to make you shine. And who polishes silver best but a maid?" Sarah's brows raised with an expectant smile.

Miranda couldn't return the smile. She sniffed and blinked back tears.

"Keep your chin up, miss. One sighting of Mr. Roderick, and you'll have your skip back in your step."

"Mr. Roderick?" Miranda groaned inwardly, but it was better for Sarah to think Miranda would be taken care of, even if it was a stretch from the truth. "Oh, very well. Just so you have something to warm your carriage ride with, I will confide in you. When he walked me home from town the other day, I nearly swooned to have him so near me." Sarah's lips pulled upward, and Miranda decided to forgo any mention of the complete fear and anxiety she had suffered during that long walk as well. Instead, she added, "How could I not? His eyes are the color of melted chocolate."

Sarah giggled.

Miranda would miss the sound of her laughter. She threw her arms around Sarah and squeezed her tight. "I won't forget you!"

"And I you, miss. Stay out of Mrs. Guttridge's way."

"I shall endeavor to do just that." Miranda released Sarah. Then she pulled a present out of her apron pocket. "This is for you."

The present was not wrapped in paper but in a pretty oriental silk scarf. Sarah cooed, recognizing it immediately. "Oh, miss, you love this scarf."

"So do you," Miranda reminded her. "I have seen you look at it often. I want you to have it . . . and what is inside."

Sarah unwrapped the scarf to reveal a garnet ring. "I cannot take this."

"You can." Miranda pushed Sarah's hands back. "I should have sold it when we had so little to eat, but I had too much pride to let go of anything." She clasped her hands together in front of her stomach. "I am ashamed of the failings in my character. Yet you did not abandon me when everyone else did." She looked up again, meeting Sarah's surprised and tearful expression. "If you never wear these things, I want you to sell them. Take the money and let it sustain you until you find another position." Miranda pulled a second item from her pocket. "And this is a letter of recommendation. If my reputation does not serve you well, write to me, and I will have Mr. Roderick find you a place. I know he will help if I ask."

"He will, will he?" Sarah asked with a gleam.

Miranda bit back her smile. "He has a good heart, and I promise to put aside my pride if you but ask."

"For what it's worth, I do care about you." Sarah squeezed Miranda's hands.

Emotion lodged in Miranda's throat. "Thank you." More than money and food, she wanted someone to care. She finally had a true friend. It warmed her and made her ache at the same time. Why now? Why did Sarah have to leave? At least she could be comforted to know Sarah would be happier somewhere else. Wiping her tears, Miranda waved goodbye to her only friend.

※

Dealing with Mrs. Guttridge over the next few days was like ordering a dress from the last roll of fabric only to have it cut too small. No amount of alterations would ever make it fit, just like nothing Miranda did could please Mrs. Guttridge. It was quite impossible to meet Ethan, though Miranda had already decided such an act was pointless and would only serve to torture her. Instead, she'd focused on what would improve her situation. As soon as she was sent to town again, she'd sell off the rest of her things until she'd raised enough money to flee to Scotland or maybe catch a boat to the Continent. There she would look for work as a servant, if anyone would hire her. Nothing was beneath her now. She wanted to work for someone who had no connection or knowledge of her past. Her uncle would no doubt celebrate her departure with a toast of his finest brandy wine.

With nothing to keep her at Gray House, Miranda decided to write her uncle a letter of farewell. He had still not returned from his trip, and she would not wait to speak to him. She pushed aside her toiletries on the small table in her room that doubled as a desk and dressing table. Opening her writing box, she pulled out her pen and ink and a sheet of paper.

> *Dear Lord Aldington,*
> *I am leaving to seek employment elsewhere and will no longer burden you with my presence. Please do not be angry with me for my sudden departure. While I regret not making peace between us, this seems for the best. It is my wish that our family will someday repair our relations. I beg you to put aside whatever harm was done in the past. My father does not hate you and has long regretted this rift. He never told me what came between you, but I must believe there is a chance to heal. You might not ever care for me, but please try just the same.*

Miranda wiped away a tear as she wrote *try* at the end. There was power in that tiny word. Sarah had taught her that. Miranda folded the letter and crept down to her uncle's study. She pushed open the door, noticing immediately that the room had not been aired for several days. Hopefully, it meant no one would stumble upon her or her letter. She slipped inside and closed the door.

The faint musty odor of alcohol made her nose itch, but after a moment, she no longer noticed it at all. She glanced at a few papers on his secretaire and added her folded one on top. She heard footsteps and froze. The sound approached the door, then kept going past it. Miranda clutched her chest and exhaled. She counted to one hundred before letting herself out. She returned to her room and began to pack her things. It was time to say goodbye again—this time, to Gray House—a home without a heart.

CHAPTER 13

UNIQUE CIRCUMSTANCES CALLED FOR UNIQUE solutions. Ethan rested his head on the floor in the earl's billiards room and put his hands on either side of his head. He took a deep breath and pushed up on his arms and kicked his legs upward. He swayed for a moment and then carefully balanced his legs and feet against the wall. Blood rushed to his head, but he ignored it and tried to think through his problems.

A moment passed and nothing. The world upside down seemed equally as confusing as the world aright.

The door opened, and after a few footsteps, Ethan had a perfect view of the earl of Radnor's hessian boots. "My compliments to your valet, Stephen. I can almost see my reflection in your shoeshine."

Stephen chuckled. "I can't take you seriously like this."

Ethan bent his legs and rolled his feet back to the floor. He lifted his head slowly, releasing the built-up pressure. Stretching his neck, he raised himself to his full height.

"Dare I ask what you were doing?" Stephen had a reputation for being arrogant during their time at university, but it was a front to hide his soft side. Ethan knew that when Stephen asked about something, he intended to listen.

"Clearing my mind," Ethan answered. "Doesn't everyone stand on their head while they think through their problems?"

Stephen's brow rose under the wild curls that fell across his forehead. "You should get your money back from the sawbones who told you to do that."

"Very funny."

Stephen held up a key and unlocked the ivory balls from the box at the end of the room. "We can play while you tell me what's been on your mind all week."

"It's an awkward situation," Ethan said, grabbing a wooden mace off the billiards table.

Stephen's thin lips curled into a catlike smile. "My favorite sort."

Taking the white ball from Stephen, Ethan spun it around with his fingers and leaned against the table. "Imagine courting one woman only to find another who suited you better. You sort out the dilemma, only to have the first woman come back into your life. You feel obligated to assist her because of your complicated history together. How do you keep both women from drawing unnecessary conclusions about your efforts?"

"Is the first woman beautiful?"

"She has the kind of beauty that haunts a man's dreams."

Stephen chuckled. "But you prefer the second woman?"

"The first is trouble." Ethan dropped the white ball onto the table, blinking away Miranda's image from his mind. "More so in her current situation than ever." No use getting into things about how her father had destroyed all her chances at a decent marriage.

"And you want to help her?"

How to explain what he himself had trouble rationalizing? "Could you pass up the last boy you handpicked for the school?"

Stephen shook his head. "At only twelve, he could do mathematics better than my solicitor without any formal training. He deserved a chance." He bent over and pushed the ball toward the net. "Sounds like you have a problem on your hands."

"Made more complicated by the fact that she doesn't want me to help her."

"We can't help everyone. It's impossible. We do our best, and we must leave the rest up to heaven."

Ethan leaned against the table and dropped his head. "Every day I've ridden from here to Gray House and have not had any sight of her. She could be sick."

"Half the town has been struggling with illness. My butler just succumbed to it."

"I'm tempted to storm the house and demand she leave with me."

Stephen studied his next shot. "You will ruin your chances with the second woman if you lose your head."

"I know, I know. I'm not thinking clearly."

"Did standing on your head help?"

Ethan took a turn, but his concentration was not there, and he missed. "Physical exertion often does the trick for me, but not this time." He blew out his breath.

"I'd give you a drink," Stephen said, "but it sounds like you need your wits about you."

"I do. I wish you would tell me more about Lord Aldington. I can't seem to learn much about him."

"The man has no life to tell about." Stephen connected his mace with another ball and made a clean shot. "He doesn't make or accept calls. He is often out of town, but as far as I can tell, it's an immoral life he leads—all drinking and debauchery."

"That doesn't bode well for Miss Bartley," Ethan said. "She was like a shiny gem back in London; she stood out everywhere. Her appearance now is quite altered. I hardly know her anymore. Whether it's because of her father's misfortunes or her uncle's treatment of her, I do not know."

Stephen's shrewd gaze unnerved him. "Miss Bartley, is it? I can't say I know her. I *should* urge you to forget her, of course. I get enough ridicule from my peers about my measly efforts to help others that I know the consequences. Instead, I will offer my assistance in whatever way I can."

Ethan's lips twitched. "You are too soft."

"I just whipped you at billiards, and you're insulting me?" Stephen's eyes narrowed.

"Very well. I'll hold my tongue in case I need your help. Right now everything is largely up to Miss Bartley. If I am ever to help her, it'll be because fate throws us together. I'm planning on returning home the day after tomorrow, so fate will have to work quickly."

❋

Providence either smiled upon Miranda or served to tease her.

With her trunk packed in her room, she went to town on her last errand for Mrs. Guttridge and to check the schedule for the traveling coach. It felt strange to be alone, without Sarah by her side. After finishing with her purchases, she exited the shop and saw Ethan again. There he stood, as if he had been waiting in that very spot for her all week. Their eyes met, and the connection seemed to draw him directly to her.

Then he went and asked a question that made her knees shake.

"Forgive me," Miranda said. "Could you repeat yourself?"

"I want you to come stay at Stonebrook Hall with my family." He put his arms out as if to showcase his brilliant idea, his eyes gleaming with boyish excitement. His crooked cravat only added to the silliness of the image.

Miranda could not resist grinning. "I cannot just come live with you."

"Not live. Just visit."

Embarrassed by her mistake, Miranda turned her gaze away from him. "Oh, well, it makes little sense. Your idea is generous but not one your family would support."

"Miss Bartley, it is clear you are suffering here." He stared at her, his brow creased. "Please."

Miranda almost gave in. She waited until a man passed them on the road before she answered. "If I did visit, I would simply have to return to my uncle's. Why bother?"

Ethan was unfazed. "You must come. Jane, at least, will be glad to see you."

"Jane? No. My presence will make her uncomfortable." Miranda would not forget Jane's hurtful dismissal. Could Ethan want her to come for another reason? Did he finally feel something again for her? If she came with him, it would be like an announcement to the world that he intended to marry her.

"Say yes," Ethan begged. "It will give me time to try to help you. I do love puzzles, and your situation is as complicated as they come."

In the time it took to blink, a wistful dream vanished into reality. She could not bring her tired lips to smile again. "Thank you, but I am all right here." *At least for today.* Tomorrow she would be entirely on her own.

"You are not all right," Ethan argued, stepping closer to her. "You are clearly fatigued. Your dress and cloak are filthy, and your hair—"

"I take your point," Miranda said, fingering her hair self-consciously. She did not want to go into details about her cracked and aching hands from the laundry and the exhaustion that came from heating and hauling her own bath water across the large house. "I have my things still. I am simply trying to preserve them . . ." Dare she tell him how she wanted to sell her things? He would never understand. With Sarah gone, Ethan was the closest thing she had to a friend, and she couldn't afford to lose that.

"See reason, Miss Bartley. I could find you a position as a governess or, if need be, a lady's maid. They are respectable situations, and surely anything is better than the life you have now. I can buy you time until something different can be arranged. You're an old family friend, and it would be easy to explain away a visit with Jane."

How could she say no to those beautiful dark eyes? His words made so much sense, and yet she was suspicious. She had relied on him before and been brutally disappointed. "Why would you help me? I'm still the same person as before. You could barely stand to remain in my company a second longer than needed, as I remember."

Ethan shook his head. "Circumstances change."

Miranda shook her head too. "People do not. Trust me, I have tried."

His stance was determined. "You will have to have faith in me, and I you. We will depend upon each other and see if we cannot bring a little joy back into your life."

Miranda stared at the busy harbor town, and between two shops, she could see a glimpse of the endless ocean not far beyond. Despite the cold wind nipping at her cheeks, Folkestone was beautiful. Strange how, after all this time, she could finally see the beauty in her surroundings. Was it because Mr. Roderick was back in her life and she saw a glimmer of hope? Or, perhaps, discovering herself and making new goals for her future had slowly begun to remove the veil of discouragement from her eyes and allowed her to appreciate new things.

While both of these reasons seemed likely, only one was undeniable. God had brought her to Folkestone to learn a few lessons, and now He was letting her leave. But could she trust Mr. Roderick after all that had transpired? Was she worthy of his assistance? "What do you get for helping me?" she finally said.

Ethan rubbed his chin. He seemed to be looking everywhere but her. He sighed and finally met her gaze. "Do you not know me well enough by now?" His voice sobered. "I find satisfaction in helping people."

Moisture gathered in her eyes, but she blinked it away. What choice did she have? She knew relying on Ethan was the quickest means of escaping Gray House. She took a fortifying breath and nodded.

"Yes?" Ethan asked.

"Yes," Miranda said. "I will come for a visit."

Ethan clapped his hands together. "Let's not waste another moment. I will send you in my carriage to retrieve your trunks. My footmen are at your disposal. I will ride ahead to prepare my sisters and my housekeeper."

Miranda laughed in disbelief. "Very well." How very like him to have a plan all set to execute.

The carriage ride back to Gray House was faster than Miranda would have liked. She relished the bumpy feel of the conveyance. It had been too long since she had enjoyed such a privilege. Unfortunately, there had not been ample time to formulate her own plan by the time she arrived.

The butler opened the front door with raised brows. Ethan's footmen followed her upstairs, and within minutes, her things were being carried back down.

"What on earth do ye think yer doing?" Mrs. Guttridge bellowed down the corridor.

Miranda put her hand against the wall to steady her trembling legs. After a quick breath, she did her best to shake off her fear and rally her courage. "I have been invited to visit Mr. Roderick's sister and her family."

Mrs. Guttridge howled, and for a moment, Miranda thought she might be hurt—or mad. But after a few knee slaps, Miranda ascertained the woman was laughing. "A friendly visit? There's only one reason a man would want the likes of ye to stay with him, and it has nothin' to do with meetin' a sister or a mother. Ye ain't smart enough to know Satan's hand when his fiery fingers are wrapped around ye. Well, no virtueless woman will be allowed back here, and I can promise ye that! Just wait until yer uncle hears about this."

Miranda rubbed her hands over her arms to warm them. "You can condemn me all you want, but God is my judge, not you." Then she fled out the door. Threats chased her all the way to the carriage.

In the quiet safety of the conveyance, Miranda knew she was one step closer to freedom. She had not told Ethan about Sarah's departure, but she was not afraid of the consequences of traveling alone. Not when she was finally free. Pulling a blanket folded on the floor of the carriage up over her lap, she was surprised to find a hot brick at her feet. She was indebted to Ethan for all of this. He would ride his horse to Stonebrook, and then they would be together. A mixture of hope and hurt whirled inside of her. Could she make him love her again?

Out her window, Folkestone slowly passed farther from view. Her hands still shook from her encounter with Mrs. Guttridge, and she was reminded that there were some things she could not run from. She must keep her head. Ethan had rejected her even before her father's disgrace, after all. He was unlikely to change his mind. She would show a repentant heart and her gratitude for his invitation to visit. His kindness would have to be enough for her.

CHAPTER 14

"YOU CANNOT REALLY THINK WE would let *her* stay with us," Jane said rather forcefully.

"You once begged me to marry her, and now you do not even want her in your home?" Ethan's eyes widened as he stared at her from behind his father's desk. Surely his sister was jesting. "Come now, you will warm to the idea. She arrives this afternoon in our carriage, and I expect you to welcome her."

"What would people think if they knew we still associated with her after her father's disgrace? What would they say about us?"

Ethan's fingers stilled on the ledger on the desk, and he dropped his head. She was right, and it gnawed at him. People would inevitably talk. All his life he'd avoided unnecessary attention, but he had willingly brought this to his doorstep. But he could not argue his conviction. Even if he didn't harbor a measure of guilt, rescuing Miranda was the right thing to do. Some things in life were worth a personal sacrifice, and he had to believe this was one of them.

"It doesn't matter," he finally said.

"Really, Ethan." Jane narrowed her eyes, in true Jane form, and folded her arms across her chest. "You cannot be simple enough to pretend otherwise."

"I do not pretend. There will no doubt be whispers from anyone who is aware of the Bartley family's situation. But not from us. Would you give up a dear friendship so quickly?"

"I did not give it up." Jane huffed. "She changed into . . . into . . . someone different."

"Someone in need of our help?" This was the argument he'd used to win the war waging inside himself. He tapped a pen against the desk while he waited for her response.

"Yes, and I cannot respect someone who needs my help. I pity them, yes, but I could never attach myself to them."

Ethan tilted his head and pinned Jane with his stare. "What if the tables were turned?"

"I would die or hide myself. I would never come crawling back to Society and invite their scorn."

He had not counted on his sister acting like a warrior guarding her castle. "Beware of pride, Jane. It is an invitation to be humbled."

"Ha!" Jane turned to the window and pushed the curtains aside. "Are you so very perfect? The man who could not marry her because she was beneath his personal ideals? Who was judgmental then?"

Ethan remained silent as the point hit its mark. She was right. He had dropped Miranda in a most ungentlemanly manner. He had trifled with her affections, leading her to believe they would marry, then left her to resurrect her own reputation. The truth made him uncomfortable, but this was his way of clearing his conscience and repairing a wrong. He cleared his throat and pushed back his guilty thoughts. "I am not perfect, but I will not turn my back on someone I can help. Miranda needs us. She needs you. She will never make it in this world without our support."

"She will not have mine," Jane said. "The only reason I do not write to Mother and Father this very minute is because I dare not let a single word leave town about your folly." She whirled around and marched from the room, slamming the door behind her.

Ethan blew out his breath and flicked his pen. It skidded a few inches and rolled to a stop. Jane had once been kind. She had been generous, even. Not anymore. Society had flogged out any goodness in his sister with the whip of vanity and pride. She was much like Miranda had been—heaven help her.

Jane, however, did have a good point about one thing. Helping Miranda could hurt his own family if he were not careful. He would start putting out word to some of those who'd associated with the Bartleys to make them aware Miranda was protected by her titled uncle. They need not know of his neglect. Thankfully, Lord Aldington had isolated himself, and the locals were unaware of whom he was housing. A few simple letters to the right people, and Lord Aldington's station would lessen the severity of Miranda's circumstance.

But there were still aspects of her life that Ethan did not have the power to remove. Her path would still be a hard one to walk—as would his, if he did not handle things just right. He would accomplish nothing, and would even go backward, if he could not maintain his emotional distance toward Miranda. The execution of his own life plan depended upon it.

⚜

Walking across the threshold of Stonebrook Hall felt to Miranda like stepping into a safe haven. The cool September air seemed to nudge her farther into the entry hall. The door shut behind her, and she took a deep breath, one more freeing than any she'd taken since leaving London two months before. A footman led her into the drawing room. Miranda's heart thudded in her ears. She had expected an empty room, not to find Jane standing so near the door. Jane froze, just as off-centered.

Her old friend was quite regal, even with such a deep scowl on her face. Miranda had not given Jane credit often enough for the lovely young lady she was. The hint of uncertainty in her otherwise hardened eyes glimmered like hope to Miranda.

She dipped her head and curtsied. "Hello, Jane."

"Miss Roderick, if you please."

Miranda felt the verbal slap. She had been wrong about the glimmer of hope. Jane could never overlook Miranda's disgrace. She steadied herself. "Stonebrook Hall is as beautiful as you claimed." She motioned to the expansive room decorated in a soft peach color, searching for safe conversation.

Jane raised her brow. "Why would I lie about such a thing?"

Annoyance replaced the shock of seeing Jane's rudeness continue. "To lure in innocent bachelors? I don't know, Jane. Why this charade? No one is here but us. Can we not sit and have tea like old times?"

"There is no charade." Jane sniffed, clearly refusing to lower her guard. "Unless you are referring to you in that dress. Where did you get it? It's hideous."

"Why, thank you." Miranda gave a small, awkward laugh. "I did not spare a minute to change before fleeing my uncle's."

Jane squirmed, looking at the door as if she wished to escape. "Was it as bad as all that?"

An imaginary cold seemed to seep into Miranda's bones as she tried to think of the best way to describe Gray House. A lump rose in her throat. "I am afraid I am not ready to share my experiences just yet. They are too fresh. You do understand?"

"I don't know if I understand or if I care to." Jane shrugged. "Ethan is attending to some urgent business and won't be home for some hours. I will have a maid come show you to your room. Excuse me." She turned on her heels and scurried from the room.

Miranda could not blame her. Jane had never known real hardship, and it was a shocking, ugly thing. Miranda's gaze dropped to her gown covered in soot and dirt. She smiled in spite of herself. What a sight she made. A little laugh bubbled out of her throat as she realized there was a smell about her too. No wonder Jane had fled.

Despite her smile, tears began to trickle out. Tea. She needed tea. She settled into a soft chair by the fireplace and proceeded to drink every drop in the pot and devoured four almond cakes. No use letting them go to waste. The fullness in her stomach chased away her sadness, and she heaved a happy sigh. She might not have the friendship she craved, but she was never going to take such luxuries for granted ever again.

Once settled in the guest room, Miranda requested a hot bath in water she did not have to carry or heat herself. Vanilla and lavender filled her senses as she washed away the last traces of her former life. A maid helped her dress for dinner in one of her nicer gowns, and her scalp seemed to sing from the attentions of having her hair fixed. Heaven knew no bounds.

"Will you save that dress for me?" Miranda asked the maid Jane had reluctantly shared with her.

The tall, gangly maid held up the tattered gown she had collected from beside the tub. "Are you sure, miss? You have all those lovely gowns, and this one is better fit for the rag box."

Miranda had not the faintest idea why she would want to keep it either. "For sentimental reasons."

"Yes, miss."

Feeling quite pampered, Miranda went down early for dinner to avoid a run-in with Jane and to poke around Ethan's home.

As far as houses went, Stonebrook Hall nearly reached perfection. She had imagined some sort of Gothic setting since Ethan and Jane came across so seriously at times. In contrast, Stonebrook was light and spacious. Wood paneling painted white lined the corridors and staircase.

She stepped outside the house, once again entranced, as she had been when she had first caught sight of her destination. The outside was red brick with white pillars stretching to the first floor and plenty of chimney stacks for the plethora of rooms.

She turned away from the house to view the vast yard and the overgrown trees casting shade along the sides of the lawn. Tomorrow she would walk the perimeter. She was used to walking back and forth from Gray House to town, and the fresh air had served her well.

Miranda slipped back inside and wandered past the sitting room and dining hall toward a third door. This could have been her home, had things played out differently. A wistful sigh sailed through her lips as she trailed her hand along the smooth trim on the wall. She was just about to peek into the closed room when she realized it could very well be Ethan's study. She had not seen him yet and was not ready to barge in on him unannounced had he returned without her knowledge. She moved toward a door that was open at the end of the corridor. A young lady stepped out as Miranda approached.

"Oh, hello," Miranda said. "I did not mean to intrude."

"You were not intruding. That is the library. No one is in there, and you are welcome inside."

"Thank you." Miranda smiled at the soft sweetness about the girl, who could be no older than sixteen and had the same dark-brown hair and eyes as Ethan and Jane. "And I know we have not been introduced, but I can easily guess your name. Are you Hannah?"

Hannah nodded, wrinkling her button nose that was so unlike her siblings' long, straight ones. "Did Jane tell you about me?"

"Yes, she and your brother have spoken of you, your brother most especially. He speaks with such tenderness when he discusses his family." Miranda stepped into the library, and Hannah followed her back into the room.

Only the inside wall had bookcases, but they were from floor to ceiling and held a great many books. A round table sat in the middle of the room with two Sheraton chairs tucked neatly around it. Between the bookcases was a prominent fireplace, with no less than four sofas in the rectangular room.

"How do you like the room?" Hannah asked. "With the east wing under renovation, I hope it is quiet enough for you." At a closer look, Hannah did not resemble Ethan quite as much as Jane did. Miranda had never met their brother, Richard, before, but she imagined Hannah to look like him since it would make the family picture more balanced in her mind.

"I like it very much," Miranda said, although she was more interested now in Hannah than exploring. "I am so glad to finally make your acquaintance." She gave the girl a friendly smile.

Hannah blushed sweetly and looked away. "I've heard your sad tale."

Miranda hesitated and nodded. Had she also heard how Ethan had once cared for Miranda? "I do not think there is even a church mouse who has missed the scandal around my family's name. I hope it does not keep us from being friends." It was too much to ask for so soon, but Miranda still felt a longing for someone's acceptance.

"I . . . I will try." Hannah looked up and gave her a shy smile. The girl's bashfulness was endearing.

"Have you enjoyed having your brother and sister all to yourself this summer? Or do you miss your parents terribly?"

"I miss my mama a great deal." Hannah clasped her hands in front of her. "Jane has done her best to prepare me for my coming-out this Season, along with my great-aunt, who left us a few days ago. But according to Jane, I am to be a royal failure."

"Nonsense," Miranda said. "You'll be every bit of a success as Jane."

"I do have several ball gowns being made that I think are quite flattering," Hannah admitted almost to herself.

"Surely they are as beautiful as you are." Miranda resisted a strange urge to hug Hannah; after all, she'd only just met her. Did Ethan know how insecure his sisters were?

Doubt clouded Hannah's features. "You are much kinder than Jane said you were, and even more beautiful."

Surprised, Miranda took a step backward and turned to look out of a large bay window at one end of the room to hide her emotions. "I am not kind. Jane was telling the truth about me."

"She does exaggerate on occasion."

Miranda gave a self-deprecating laugh. "Don't we all?" She turned again and faced Hannah once more, blinking away the threat of tears, and gave her a careless smile. "Exaggerating is a great ally to humor, which can help you in your Season. If you are going to exaggerate, always include silly things . . . like snails or mud."

"Snails or mud? You mean a lady can discuss those sorts of things?"

Miranda's teaching surely went against everything Hannah's governesses had taught her. "It is a great secret. Playfulness diffuses awkward situations. I will demonstrate later, and you will never worry about conversing with anyone ever again."

"Truly?" Hannah's tentative smile finally emerged. "Snails and mud. I will remember."

❈

Dinner proved uncomfortable, to say the least, as Ethan had still not returned. After eating, Miranda slipped into the oversized drawing room.

She took a seat near Hannah and opposite Jane. Silent ticks of the clock on the mantel marked the prolonged silence. She was about to excuse herself when Ethan surprised them with his arrival.

"Well, aren't we a merry lot?" Ethan's joke fell flat, and he shuffled his feet before finally sitting down in an armchair. "Miss Bartley," he began, "I am happy you arrived safe and sound. I wanted to greet you, but I had some business that required my immediate attention."

She gave him a half smile, relieved to have him there. She did not realize how much she had needed to see him.

"Jane planned a dinner party for the day after tomorrow," he said. "She is hoping for enough couples to attend for a dance afterward. I hope you will find yourself comfortable enough to join us."

Jane groaned, and Ethan cut off any potential complaints with a sharp look.

Miranda glanced between the two of them. "I . . . ah, am not sure I am ready to be thrown back into Society." The skin on her cheeks warmed. It shamed her to admit her feelings. She finally looked normal again on the outside with her dress and hair styled just so, but no one would care about her appearance once they knew she was a penniless charity case.

"See?" Jane said, folding her arms like a stubborn child. "We must not rush our guest."

Hannah surprised Miranda by placing a hand on her arm. "Oh, do come. I should love to have someone there to talk to."

"How do you like that?" Jane guffawed. "Your own brother and sister will be there, yet you act like you will be entirely without support."

Hannah let the silence speak for her.

No one knew more what it felt like to be alone than Miranda. Hannah was innocent to the cruelty of Society, and Miranda couldn't hide in her room while the poor girl suffered. Besides, she couldn't imagine disgracing herself any more than she already had. "I shall come if it will make you feel more comfortable, Hannah." She turned to Ethan. "Unless it will make your guests uncomfortable."

"You underestimate our friends," Ethan said, giving Jane a significant look. He relaxed back in his seat and stretched his legs out before him. Miranda had never seen him so at ease before. "I assure you they will be more accepting than those in Town. You will be our guest of honor."

His pronouncement did not reassure her in the way he might have hoped. "Wonderful. I shall feel like the prodigal debutante."

Ethan chuckled, but if glares could kill, Jane's would have done him in.

Miranda's analogy was more fitting than she cared to admit. If she could go back and live her life differently, maybe she would have more allies than merely Ethan and Hannah.

CHAPTER 15

MORNING CAME LIKE A SILENT gift, blessing Miranda with new surroundings and a chance to be a new person. She pulled back the bright-yellow quilt entangled around her legs and breathed in the hint of vanilla and lavender from her bath the day before. Ethan had invited her to join him and his sisters on a ride, and after an indulgent cup of hot chocolate taken in bed, she decided to do something brave first.

Miranda pulled out her writing box and spread out a paper, some ink, and a pen on the small table in the corner of her room.

Dear Lord Aldington,

She paused. The man did not care one wit about her. Why was she doing this? She knew the answer as surely as she knew her reservations for writing him. She would always loathe her time at Gray House, but the hope she harbored for her uncle encouraged her to put pen to paper.

I arrived safely at Stonebrook Hall, where I am visiting Lord Gibson's children. I am well. I do not know when, if ever, I shall see you again, but I hope this letter finds you in good health. I intend to find a position somewhere but am enjoying my time with old friends until something can be arranged.

Would he even read her letter? She knew he would not demand her to return, but would he care at all if she were safe or not? With a flick of her pen, she signed her name and blotted the ink. When she was sure it was dry, she folded and sealed the letter. She gave the missive and some coins for post to a servant in the passage and made her way to the stables.

Wearing her riding habit again thrilled her to no end. It was a robin's-egg blue made of gabardine wool, with white braided frog clasps and matching ruffles around her wrists and neck. One of life's pleasures was beautiful clothes. Riding, of course, brought its own source of satisfaction. Miranda had wondered if she would be given the opportunity to ride again with her new circumstances. Once on the lawn, Ethan, astride his gray gelding, led a lovely roan-colored mare with a white stripe down her nose toward Miranda.

"This is Starstreak. I thought she would make a good match for you. She has just enough spirit to make the ride enjoyable."

"She is beautiful." Miranda accepted a lift up from the groomsman. The familiar feel of reins in her hands made her sigh with pleasure.

"I know you rode often with your father while in London," Ethan said, pulling his horse up beside her. "You have a good seat."

Jane groaned from atop her horse.

"I mean . . . a good seat on a horse," Ethan corrected, followed by a short cough.

Miranda bit back her smile.

Jane turned to her sister. "Come, Hannah. I will race you to the tree line."

The mention of racing made Miranda squirm. No doubt betting on races had been part of her father's financial downfall. She tried to think of another source of conversation, but there was an undercurrent of awkwardness between her and Ethan. How did one transition from marital prospect to charity case? It was simply too difficult to find her footing. Perhaps she should make plans to leave sooner rather than later.

"What do you make of Stonebrook Hall?" Ethan finally asked.

Miranda nudged her horse in the direction Jane and Hannah had taken. "It is bright and cheerful." She paused. "My, that sounds rather doltish, does it not?" She used to be cleverer with words. The new her was too introspective and unnatural.

"Not in the slightest." Ethan seemed pleased enough with her answer. "Then, you are comfortable here?"

"Certainly," Miranda said, hiding a grimace. It was hard not to focus on the fact that she might have been the lady of such a fine house. Thankfully, she was distracted by ridiculous thoughts like how long it would take to scrub the floors in the gallery. "You must write and give my compliments to your parents. When do they return from Bath?"

"I plan to see my parents in London for the Season and not before then."

"Oh." Such a pronouncement brought immediate relief. Perhaps they were ignorant of her presence in their home. She imagined they would be as angry as Jane should they discover it. Miranda and Ethan passed underneath a large tree, and the hundreds of leaves shook in the slow breeze. It gave her sudden perspective. She was just one of many shaken by adversity, struggling to find a place in this world. Realizing this helped her to relax in Ethan's presence, allowing for a comfortable silence to fall between them as they rode.

They had nearly caught up with Jane and Hannah when Ethan asked, "Do you have any plans for your future now that you are free from your uncle?"

"I . . . I have not taken time to think about it." Not unless he wanted to hear about her plans to become a maid in Scotland. "I assure you I will put my mind to it right away."

"Excellent," Ethan said. "I hope you will let me be of assistance."

"Thank you." His gaze warmed her, but she still had to force a smile. How wonderful it would be for the man she loved to help her find *employment*. How quaint. Miranda did not want to lose the peace she felt inside, but there were some aspects of being with Ethan that would not settle in her mind. Perhaps she could spend her time at Stonebrook Hall trying to prove she was a better Miranda—too irresistible to send away. Only, if it did not work to her advantage, wasting her hopes on such an idea could crush her even more. She pushed away her conflicting thoughts and said, "Shall we catch up with your sisters?"

"Race you there?" Ethan gave her a mischievous smile and spurred his horse to a gallop.

Any discomfort Miranda had for racing disappeared with Ethan's teasing smile. It was familiar, comforting, and confusing all at once.

※

Ethan paced back and forth in his father's study. He was walking a fine line. Miranda had been there only two nights, but by keeping her at Stonebrook, he was clearing his conscience of any obligation he might have owed her. He was also sleeping better than he had since he'd jilted her in London. However, the image of Miranda that first night—thinner, yes, but dressed in finery with her golden hair curled just so—kept pressing upon his mind.

Now, seeing her through the window, finishing her walk, with her cloak wrapped tightly around her small form, tugged at his heart.

He dropped his arms to his sides and shook them as if to rid her from his thoughts. Tomorrow night would be their dinner party, and Miss Withers's beauty would dispel any thoughts of his houseguest from his mind. The front door opened and closed. Ethan cleared his throat and rallied his courage. He exited his father's study and smiled all too readily at Miranda.

"Ah, you were out walking, I see," he said, acting as if he had not just been spying on her.

"Yes," Miranda answered. She smiled unabashedly, dispensed of her cloak to the butler, and just like that, Ethan's cheeriness dissipated.

Her dress and appearance were not so altered from yesterday in style or comeliness, but he recognized the aubergine-colored gown. It sent him mentally back to a moment when he had been trying to win her over and brought his conflicting feelings right back to the surface. Her beauty did more than rival Miss Withers's, and her confident smile was back. It was hard-fought for him not to openly admire her. He had spent too many months hoping to secure her as his bride before their unfortunate parting.

Oblivious to his tortuous thoughts, she added, "I find walking, even in this early-autumn air, quite refreshing."

Ethan cleared his throat and attempted to continue the conversation. "It's far too cold for this time of year. If I may advise you, as perhaps an elder brother would, I encourage you to take every precaution to bundle up before you go out." *Elder brother* was a bit thick, and even he knew it.

"I will do just that, thank you." She eyed him suspiciously. "And what tasks have you been about this morning? Surely not planning Hannah's debut with the same eagerness as Jane?"

"Ha!" Ethan said, already searching for a reason to retreat. "I am compiling a few notes for a meeting with my father's land steward. I hope to spare my father as much work as possible while he is away."

"I am impressed you would so easily think of how to ease his burdens. You have had a taste of your future responsibilities, then," Miranda said. "Do you enjoy managing an estate?"

"I do, actually," Ethan admitted. He enjoyed overseeing the tenants and refiguring numbers in his father's record books. All sorts of ideas about risk and profit played in his mind even now. "I only wish my father was alongside me and I could benefit from his experience."

"Are there any challenges you are facing in his absence?"

Ethan found himself motioning for her to sit on a bench in the entry hall that usually sat more for decoration than use, but he made sure not to sit by her. He had lost his opportunity to retreat, but her questions had distracted him, and he was suddenly eager to talk. No one else seemed the least bit interested, and he felt his mind could explode with his thoughts if he did not speak of them to someone.

"This cold front—it has caused all sorts of havoc. My father would know exactly what to do, and yet I am reluctant to write and ask." He began to pace in front of her. "The last thing I want is for him to rush back here. I assured him he need not come to Stonebrook Hall this summer. It took months to convince him I was capable."

"I see your dilemma." Miranda pursed her lips as if she were thinking of a way to help. "Have you tried chocolate?"

Ethan put his hand on his hip. "You would suggest that. I heard you asked for a glass of chocolate only this morning."

"You heard?" Miranda said, raising a brow. "Does the role of host include monitoring your guest's choice of drink?"

Ethan chuckled. "The role of host includes listening to his exasperated sister complain about absolutely everything. I think she is creating complaints about you. But that being said, I do not think chocolate the cure for my troubles."

"Well, I will show my appreciation for your service by helping you. I insist you start your day off tomorrow with chocolate, and I defy you to not have a better outlook on your situation."

Ethan bowed deeply and waved his arm in front of him, as he had done many times in the past for her. "Your challenge is accepted."

"Marvelous!" Miranda laughed. "If only I had a wealth of knowledge on the subject to help you further."

He stared at the vacant spot next to her and willed himself not to sit down. If he sat, he would want to touch her hand, and such a gesture would open ideas to him that he needed to smother.

She stood, catching him off guard and ending his mental debate. Her smile rather dazzled him. "I am afraid I am more chilled from my walk than I thought and must retrieve my shawl. My elder brother would not want me to catch cold sitting so close to the door."

He knew he would regret that elder brother comment. She breezed by him, unknowingly saving him from himself. He put his hand on his head and groaned.

CHAPTER 16

THE LAST THING MIRANDA WANTED was for Ethan to think of her as a sister. She sat at her dressing table, fingering her jewelry, wondering what she could wear that would make Ethan view her differently. She was already dressed for the dinner party in a Pomona-green evening gown with her hair pulled low at her neck and loose curls spilling out. The effect was pleasing but a little simple. Strangely, the longer she stared at her jewelry, the more she was content with her unpretentious attire, which was not like her at all. She couldn't help but think of Sarah as she fingered what pieces she had left. How she ached for an ally who knew her past as well as her present.

She picked up a beaded comb. This had been one of Jane's favorites from last Season. It would mean a great deal to have Jane's friendship back. Miranda wrapped her fingers around the comb as an idea formed in her mind. She stood and left her bedchamber. With the guest wing under repair, she was staying by the family rooms. Through observation, she had learned where everyone slept. Miranda found Jane's door and knocked.

A moment later, a maid opened the door, and Miranda breathed in her friend's honeysuckle scent permeating the room.

Jane sat at her dressing table and glanced up. She quickly faced her mirror again and pursed her lips. "Come in."

Miranda made her way to Jane and extended the peace offering. "I remembered how you favored this and thought you might like to have it."

Jane's gaze rested on the comb. Her brow creased, and for a moment, she did not say anything. Miranda glanced at the white-and-pink floral quilt on Jane's bed and the charming blue curtains on the window. It was a happy room, but Jane's mood toward Miranda did not match it. Miranda struggled not to squirm.

"I cannot accept your offering," Jane said, though her tone was gentle and absent of any ill will.

Miranda pulled the comb back to her stomach. Unsure of what to do, she turned to leave.

"One moment," Jane said. Miranda wondered if she would accept her gift after all, but what Jane said shocked her. "I must warn you. There will be a guest at dinner who is destined to be my brother's wife."

Miranda froze. She pivoted to face Jane, but Jane was busy with her toiletry, and her guarded expression cut off any further explanation. She had done Miranda a favor by revealing this ahead of time, but the news was still soul-crushing. She left Jane and hurried back to her room. Once inside, she put her back to the door and took several deep breaths. This was not the end of the world. Jane could be exaggerating. Hadn't Hannah said Jane often did as much? Miranda easily recalled many times when Jane had been overly dramatic.

It took nearly a half hour before she could gather her courage to go down for dinner. She brought her fan with her in case she felt faint and required air. Each step felt like walking back home to Gray House, robbing her of any happy thoughts. No matter how many encouraging talks she gave herself, she was completely unprepared to meet the woman who would succeed where she had failed.

Then she saw her in the drawing room—Miss Withers. Her lungs refused to fill with air. Dinner was announced a moment later, allowing Miranda to breathe again and find her equilibrium in the bustle. She watched helplessly as Ethan led Miss Withers in to dinner, his eyes riveted to her face. Miranda could not blame him. Miss Withers's beauty could capture a blind man's attention. She wore a stylish pale-pink crepe gown far nicer than the one she had worn at the card party, and her russet-brown locks were expertly coiled on her head. There also wasn't a scandal attached to her name. Jealousy ran down Miranda's back like cold water, and she shivered with bitter disappointment.

She put her hand to her empty throat. Perhaps the jewelry would have helped her confidence after all.

The seating arrangement at dinner set Ethan next to Miss Withers, and Miranda as far away as she could possibly be, with at least a dozen others between them. Jane had no doubt been behind it, as she was the acting hostess, and Miranda could not quite blame her. Still, her eyes remained on the couple. From the snatches of conversation around her, Miranda learned Mr. and Mrs. Withers were the couple sitting near their daughter. An officer, one other married couple, and a few others of eligible age were also in attendance. Dinner went long, and no matter how she tilted her head, Miranda could not overhear a word spoken between Ethan and Miss Withers. She did, however, catch their mutual smiles. Was it just an invention of her mind, or did they suit each other?

Miranda took a bite of her chocolate dessert to help her swallow her disappointment, grateful that at least the menu made sense. She pulled her spoon from her mouth and frowned. Bland. Utterly bland. She pushed her dessert aside. It was a monumental moment when chocolate did not bring her pleasure—a sure sign something was not right in the world.

At long last, dinner concluded. They all drifted into the oversized drawing room, perfect for entertaining a large group. Miranda located an open chair by an arched window at the end of the room, discreetly hidden by the pianoforte. She set a course for the chair, but Hannah chose that moment to step up beside her.

"Hannah." Miranda smiled amiably, although hiding was still on the forefront of her mind. "How are you making out with all this company?"

"I could not think of a thing to say to the gentleman next to me at dinner." Hannah's pale lips turned down into a frown. Timidity seemed natural to her. Miranda looked closer and realized Hannah wasn't truly upset but was likely just disappointed.

"At least the food was excellent," Miranda lied, thinking of her sorry dessert. "When the company is poor, always appreciate the next best thing."

Hannah giggled. So did someone else across the room. Both turned toward the source. Ethan stood not too far from them, entertaining Miss Withers with a story.

"Georgina Withers is perfect, you know," Hannah said. "Not a blemish on her skin."

Miss Withers laughed again, and the sound was almost musical.

"No one is perfect," Miranda said, her tone a touch condemning.

"Miss Withers is a benefactor for underprivileged women. While in London, she personally nursed several unwed mothers who were ill."

Miranda shrugged as if the news meant nothing to her.

"She saved a cat from a tree only last week."

Miranda turned on Hannah. "I could save a cat from a tree. Anyone could save a cat from a tree."

"Yes," Hannah said carefully. "But have you ever done so? Miss Withers has."

Miranda pinched the bridge of her nose. "Come, it's time for me to demonstrate the secret to conversation I promised you when we last spoke."

"Now?" Hannah's eyes lit with excitement.

"Yes, all I need is an introduction." This would be the perfect opportunity to work on keeping her promise to Sarah. She was going to undo some of her wickedness by giving those she cared for a little helping hand. Hannah would be her first victim—er, patron. Of course, if she happened to interrupt the happy couple before them, she could not help such a circumstance.

Hannah led Miranda over to her brother, and Ethan moved to make room in their otherwise intimate circle.

"Miss Withers, you remember Miss Bartley? She is visiting us for a time." Ethan glanced at Miranda, then flicked his gaze back to Miss Withers.

Miss Withers smiled with her incredibly straight teeth. Miranda groaned inwardly. Maybe this woman was perfect.

"I hope your stay has been pleasant," Miss Withers said. "Stonebrook Hall is full of charm."

"Indeed." Miranda's tone bordered on sarcastic. She felt a surge of her old self returning—the part of her that never let anyone else take what she wanted. She repeated Hannah's name like a mantra in her head to help her stay focused on her true goal. "I hope your family is enjoying the neighborhood. Do you find time to come to Stonebrook Hall often?"

"All the time." Miss Withers smiled prettily at Ethan and then looked at Miranda again. "It's beginning to feel like a second home."

That was exactly what Miranda would have said had she been battling for Ethan's affections, which she was not. She put on a benign smile. "And you wish to live here, of course? Who wouldn't adore such *charms*?" Her eyes turned to Ethan, suggesting him to be the real charm.

Miss Withers blushed, and Ethan cleared his throat.

And Miranda was back at the card party. She needed to fix her blunder. This was not the person she wanted to be anymore. She opened her fan and started beating fresh air onto her face. "I, for one, could live here forever," she said, then drew her fan across one eye. Ethan caught the slight cue, and his eyes widened almost imperceptibly. She was telling him she was sorry and hoped to fix things. "Because I adore snails."

"Snails?" Miss Withers asked, confused.

"Yes, Stonebrook has them in excess. Please tell me you have noticed the snails, Mr. Roderick."

Ethan eyed her strangely. "We do have snails, yes, but I would not say—"

"See? That is exactly why everyone wants to live here. And snails remind me of shells. Do you collect shells, Miss Withers?"

"When I was a child, I used to keep a linen bag full of them." Miss Withers smiled at the memory.

"Did you? And surely you had a favorite?"

"Why yes, it was a beautiful cockle shell. My brother fashioned it into a necklace for me." And just like that, Miss Withers was off sharing stories about her childhood.

"Exhibition one. How to get yourself out of a mess," Miranda whispered to Hannah.

Hannah giggled. Miranda looked up, thinking Ethan would be hanging on every word Miss Withers uttered, but he was looking at Miranda. He raised his brow in question. She wished she could tell him all of her thoughts, but not even a fan could communicate what she felt, nor should it.

She was all too grateful when a freckled Miss Van Helsing stepped up to the pianoforte and the first strains of music poured into the room. Several couples lined up to dance, and Miranda stepped to the edge of the room.

Hannah came up beside her once more. "How did you know Miss Withers collected shells?"

"She lives near the coast. Of course she collected shells," Miranda said. "The trick word was *snail*. I merely used the term to change the subject. It isn't complicated. You will have to try it sometime."

"I will," Hannah said with a grin.

It was by far the biggest smile Miranda had seen from the sweet girl. Miranda hated to ask, but she had to know if what Jane had said was the truth. "Can you tell me if your brother is courting Miss Withers?"

"Why yes," Hannah said. "That is, everyone says he is."

Miranda's heart sank like an anchor. She had seen it with her own eyes but still hoped for it to be otherwise. Ethan deserved to be happy, and she owed him a great deal, but was Miss Withers right for him? Did she make him happy? Happier than Miranda had made him?

"Miss Bartley," Ethan said behind her.

She turned, afraid he had overheard her conversation with Hannah. "Yes?"

"Might I introduce Captain Grant to you? He recently bought an estate in the neighborhood and is renovating the place." The man standing next to Ethan was of similar height, with hair streaked blond from the sun, and was dressed in a blue uniform with gold epaulettes on each shoulder. "Captain, this is Miss Bartley, a houseguest of ours."

Miranda extended her gloved hand, and Captain Grant, with rigid posture, bowed over it. "You did not mention you were entertaining such a lovely guest tonight," he said to Ethan.

Miranda blushed. It had been too long since someone had paid her a compliment. Captain Grant's smile was a little crooked, but his features were pleasant.

She felt someone else's eyes on her, and she glanced over to see Jane scowling. Ah. Jane liked the captain. Jane's mother, Lady Gibson, insisted on a family pedigree that could be found in Debrett's book and likely would not approve of such a match. Even if Miranda stepped aside, Jane would not so easily be won over. Perhaps if Miranda did more than just remove herself from the equation.

"You are too kind, Captain. I am not used to being praised by someone in uniform. Though, I admit I am easily impressed by men who give their lives to the service of their country."

Ethan eyed her, and Miranda hesitated. She was not flirting—not exactly. He would understand her motives later. She smiled coyly at the captain.

He chuckled modestly. "It is an honor to be a soldier, though it is a hard path to walk."

"Walk?" Miranda laughed lightly. "Who said anything about walking? It is dancing we need you for tonight."

"And that I will gladly endure, if you will partner me."

Jane glared daggers her way, but Miranda ignored her and let Captain Grant lead her to where a few others danced.

The small line of couples was perfect for conversation. "You are so young to be a captain," Miranda said, assessing the sun lines on a face absent of any wrinkles. He could be no older than thirty.

Captain Grant shrugged. "When you cannot inherit, you must secure your own living. I was fortunate enough to have an uncle buy my post. I like to think I have earned it since that time, but all I can truly claim is to have survived the title where others have not."

"Napoleon wreaked havoc on too many lives." When the words were out, she was struck by the reality of them. Shame filled her at the thought of dismissing all the stories told about the war—pretending as if it never existed so she could keep up her frivolous lifestyle. She knew about suffering now and would not make that mistake again.

"That he did." Captain Grant nodded, and a shadow cast over his eyes.

"Which is why you must not let him steal your spirit along with the rest of his acquisitions," Miranda said rather plainly. "I have the perfect solution."

"Do you?"

"Why yes." And just like that, a hint of light returned. Perhaps helping people was her true talent. "As you will soon learn from our host, I know the secrets of Society."

"Mr. Roderick never told me," Captain Grant said, amused. "Please, enlighten me."

Miranda laughed, despite her attempt to hold a straight face. "Happiness comes in the form of a treasured relationship." This was no lie. It was exactly what Miranda herself was looking for. She leaned forward and conspiratorially whispered, "We must find you a wife."

Captain Grant put his head back and laughed. The sound boomed from his mouth and carried above the music. Every head in the room turned to stare at them.

Miranda used to love when this happened. Tonight was a different matter. She bit back her smile, but it was too late. The song ended before she could finish explaining her plan.

Captain Grant led her straight back to Mr. Roderick. "Where have you been hiding Miss Bartley? She is full of life and yet appreciates the more delicate aspects many of our friends turn up their noses at." He gave Miranda a warm look.

She swallowed uncomfortably. Ethan narrowed his eyes, and his deep frown reminded her of the day he'd cried off their almost-engagement. He only thought her selfish. His disappointment in her stung. How could she explain that she'd meant to bring Jane into the conversation? She certainly could not beg another dance with the captain.

She had to do something though. She turned to Captain Grant. "I am none of those things," she said, her voice heavy with remorse. "Mr.

Roderick's sister—now, there is a fine woman. She is the one who taught me to appreciate the things in life you mentioned." She lowered her gaze. Lying in order to help someone was not a sin to Ethan, surely. If only talking of snails could help her now.

"Humble too," Captain Grant said, flashing her his adorable crooked smile. No wonder Jane liked him. "Might I call on you tomorrow, Miss Bartley?"

Miranda lifted the fan that dangled from her wrist and tapped it against her left cheek to signify no.

Ethan caught the message but nodded anyway to the captain. Wasn't Ethan supposed to be her friend now? He had rescued her, but apparently Ethan was more loyal to the captain.

"I will look forward to it," Miranda said. She would, too, and that fact did not ease her conscience one bit.

She fell into her bed that night exhausted and plagued by her shortcomings. She had managed to embarrass herself in front of Miss Withers and might not have taught anything of real value to Hannah. She'd butchered any chances Jane had with Captain Grant and even disappointed Ethan. She would keep trying as Sarah had suggested. Effort had to be good for something. Though, at this point, she wasn't sure of anything. She missed Sarah fiercely and yearned to feel loved again.

CHAPTER 17

ETHAN TRIED TO SEE THE best in people; only once had such an endeavor brought him ill will. Being kind to Miranda had awakened his attraction for her, making him vulnerable to her manipulative ways. He only wanted to help her, but without realizing it, he had found himself in an awkward position.

While her silly declaration about wanting to live forever at Stonebrook Hall was said in jest, others were whispering. And why not? His own parents would surely object to an association with Miss Bartley. Heaven forbid they discover the identity of their houseguest. Fortunately, those in their neighborhood seemed unconnected with the Bartley family, buying them all a little time to rectify the situation.

Not that he hadn't begun to entertain ideas of his own. The woman was far too beautiful for her own good—or, rather, his. He was a fool to think she had changed because of her reduced circumstances. The night before, Miranda had acted much like she had at past parties—like a diamond of the first water—primarily concerned with her own well-being.

Ethan groaned, realizing how easily he had been sucked in. Back in Folkestone, he'd believed Miranda to be different, but apparently one's character needed far more time and opportunity to change than she had been given. His friend Stephen had hinted that their peers had mocked Ethan for his generosity. He could see now why a soft heart could be construed as a weakness. He had even begun to crave chocolate with his breakfast.

"Dear Brother, you seem ill at ease this morning," Jane said, waltzing into their father's study, where he had been hiding. "Might I guess the source of this dark mood?"

Ethan scowled at her. "Not today, Jane. Are you not needed elsewhere?"

"I am needed in a great many places. You are fortunate I choose to be here, eager to hear your woes." She floated into the seat across from him and tossed the long, thick curl that hung from her bun over her shoulder.

Ethan gave her a bored look and drummed his fingers across the mahogany desk. "*Fortunate* would not be my word choice. Perhaps ill-fated?"

"How dare you!" Jane drew up her shoulders. "I'm going to write to Father and tell him straightaway of your rudeness!"

"And I shall write and tell our parents of your haughtiness," Ethan countered. Then he heaved a great sigh. "Come, let us not do this right now. As you have said, I am in a mood."

"This is all Miranda's fault." Jane folded her arms across her chest. "You never should have welcomed her here. She has put you against me. She ruined the party last night. I believe she is beginning to get to Hannah too. Really, she must go."

Ethan didn't meet her gaze. "Very well."

"What?" Jane blinked rapidly. "Did you just agree with me?"

"I never agree with you," Ethan clarified. "I simply meant that it would be prudent for Miranda to leave."

Jane's expression turned almost gleeful, and she clapped her hands. "Wonderful! I want her gone by teatime."

Ethan was already exhausted by this conversation. "I am not pushing her out the door and throwing her trunk out after her. Give me a little time to look for an alternate situation."

Jane stood with a pout. "Very well, but please hurry. Captain Grant just left here, and I will expire if a romance develops between them."

"Gladly. Now, leave me in peace for a while. I need time to figure this out."

Ethan dropped his head on the desk and moaned. He had rid himself of Miranda once before, and now he must do it a second time.

He lifted his head once the grain of the wood felt like it was making an impression on his forehead, and he caught sight of a piece of stationery addressed to him. Ah! Here was the solution to not just one but two of his problems.

✴

"I have found a position for you," Ethan said to Miranda a mere two days after the dinner party. His expression was guarded, but Miranda observed his heavy-handedness with the salt on his eggs as a sign of his discomfort.

She had prepared herself for this, but still she had to school her features. "What sort of position?"

"A lady's companion. I think you will find the position offers many of the comforts you enjoy—Society, pretty dresses, and even a chance to secure a reputable husband."

His aloofness rubbed her wrong.

"You have thought of everything," Miranda said. She had been foolish to think he had softened toward her at all. Like the boys he helped at the reform school, she was just another project.

Ethan scratched at the back of his neck. "Not everything, just the position and the carriage ride to deliver you there."

"Where exactly is it?"

"Not five miles from here, at Crowfield. My mother wrote to me explaining Lady Callister's need for a companion. She is a widow of some years, and her children are often too far away to be of assistance. I think you will take to each other with time. In fact, I think the situation is quite providential."

Miranda wanted clarification. Was it providential she was leaving Stonebrook Hall or that she would be only five miles away? Relief battled worry, and the worry won.

Hannah entered the dining room and huffed. "Jane just informed me Miranda is leaving." She took a seat beside Miranda. "You cannot abandon us. You have been here only a week."

A glorious and terrible week, Miranda wanted to say. Instead, she simply nodded.

"It will be an opportunity for her, Hannah," Ethan said, tucking in to his food.

"How could you say that?" Hannah sent him a cross look. "You're acting like you're her father, not her friend."

Miranda did not like the tension between the brother and sister, as she knew from Ethan that their relationship was a treasured one.

"Ethan, was that mud on your boots last night? I can't imagine you've been climbing trees again."

Ethan's spoon slipped from his grasp and clanged against his plate before he snatched it back up. "Ah, er . . . I don't remember any mud. And trees, well, I never . . . um . . ."

Hannah started laughing. "You said *mud*! I've been waiting and waiting for your next exhibition!"

Miranda bit back her smile. Ethan's confusion made the moment even more entertaining.

"Mud?" Ethan shook his head, confused. "I find myself relieved we are not about to discuss climbing trees. Do either of you care to let me in on the humor here?"

Miranda turned to Hannah, but they both shook their heads.

Ethan finally cracked and gave them a small smile. "I see my presence is no longer needed here, and I will excuse myself." He took a long drink from his glass and pushed back his chair to stand.

Hannah cleared her throat. "Um, Ethan. You have chocolate above your lip. Just here." She pointed to the spot on her own face.

Ethan met Miranda's gaze with a disgruntled look and wiped his lip clean.

Miranda held back her smile, wishing for an excuse to beg him to stay. But he wanted her to leave, and she needed to respect his wishes. She knew he meant to help her, but the hurt left in his wake made her regret ever coming. Some moments after he left the room, she realized she was still staring at the door where Ethan last stood when Hannah broke the silence.

"Jane said Ethan courted you in London, but . . ."

"He cried off, so to speak." Miranda took her napkin off her lap. "We were not an equal match."

"Was it the money?" Hannah asked curiously. The girl was practically bursting for information.

"It was before my circumstances changed," Miranda said, feeling her cheeks color. "I once told you that I am not a very nice person." It was her turn to leave. She was growing too attached to Hannah as it was. "You must trust your family's judgment where I am concerned." Miranda stood and hurried from the room and did not stop until she reached the front door. She needed fresh air to clear her head.

*

Meeting Lady Callister reminded Miranda of all her failings. Not a hint of desperation lined the older woman's face, so it seemed safe to assume this interview would be short and fruitless. No one else wanted her, so why would Lady Callister be any different?

"You are rather skinny," Lady Callister observed. This woman was all classic elegance. Her white hair was swept under her lace-fringed mobcap, and her black dress crinkled over her own small frame as she shifted in her seat to get a closer look at Miranda. "Never mind that. Tell me of your accomplishments."

Miranda sent a silent plea to Ethan, who sat rather expressionless in a chair not far from her. "I, ah, am well-informed on the latest fashions and converse easily with others." It was difficult to sell herself for a position she did not want.

Lady Callister scowled, rippling the age lines in her face. "Talents. What are your talents? Do you play the pianoforte?"

"No, Your Ladyship," Miranda replied.

"Do you paint or sing?"

"I have never excelled at music or art, and before you ask, I am not well-read. I can embroider if there is a minimal amount of stitches. I haven't the patience for anything of intricacy."

"Good heavens!" Lady Callister said as she leaned forward in her seat. "What *can* you do?"

Miranda glanced at Ethan one last time, but not for help. The man was useless. His form of help extended only so far. "I can boil water."

"Boil water? What use do I have for that?"

Should she mention the possible hazard of catching something on fire? Miranda decided it was better not to say anything more.

"I employ plenty of servants. I have need of a companion."

Before, Miranda had always relied on her beauty and money to secure her happiness. Mrs. Guttridge and now Lady Callister had illustrated her uselessness with ease. Miranda thought she might be sick on the woman's oriental rug, but then she'd probably be asked to clean up the mess. And that she could do. She had Gray House to thank for that.

"Mr. Roderick, I am not sure Miss Bartley and I will be a good match."

"I think you have misjudged Miss Bartley." Ethan gave Lady Callister a calming smile. Miranda did not think his charms would work here, but he continued. "Her humility is a credit to her. She is an amiable young woman, and I would not have brought her here if I did not believe her capable of assisting you. She has a unique ability to make others smile. Any loneliness that might afflict you will be lost forever with her around."

Miranda's lips parted in surprise. Her gaze connected with Ethan's, and Miranda felt her cheeks warm. She could melt into a happy puddle with this sort of attention. He seemed sincere, but could she trust it? Was he so desperate to be rid of her that he would cast aside his honesty?

"I trust Mr. Roderick's opinion. Miss Bartley, you can stay." Then Lady Callister added, "On a trial basis."

Ethan nodded and stood. He bowed and said, "We appreciate your generosity. I will bring Miss Bartley tomorrow morning with her things."

Miranda stood and crossed to Lady Callister. She wanted to retract all the things Ethan had said, but she wanted to believe them even more. "Thank you for giving me this position. I hope you will be frank if there is anything I do that does not suit you."

"I am nothing but frank." Lady Callister's shrewd stare unnerved Miranda. "There is something about you I find refreshing. Come tomorrow, and we'll see if we can't mesh our lives together."

Miranda curtsied and left with Ethan. They found Hannah waiting outside for them. She had wanted to get out of the house, but Ethan had refused to let her join their meeting, saying it wasn't her place to participate in Miranda's interview.

"Well?" Hannah asked.

"I am to return tomorrow," Miranda said.

Hannah resembled a sad puppy with the way her bottom lip protruded. "I want to be happy for you."

"That is the worst happy face I have ever seen," Ethan said, handing Hannah into the carriage. Then he turned to help Miranda up.

It was like going back through time. Suddenly they were back at Gunter's eating their ices. His touch on her gloved hand still turned her legs immobile. She held on a moment longer than necessary.

"Miss Bartley?" Ethan's voice revealed the awkwardness of the moment and snapped Miranda back to the present.

"She saw a snail," Hannah said for her. "You know how she adores them."

Ethan eyed them warily but seemed appeased enough by Hannah's explanation.

Miranda let herself be helped to her seat, and Hannah gave her a knowing look. She seemed to understand more about what had just happened than Miranda did.

CHAPTER 18

LADY CALLISTER'S HOME SMELLED LIKE an old person—slightly floral and musty. Oh, the servants did clean—Miranda noticed that right off. However, the smell remained and hovered mostly about Lady Callister herself. It wasn't just the adjustment to her new surroundings that bothered Miranda; she doubted her ability to please her new employer too. She had never learned to appreciate her elders. They repeated themselves, talked as if they knew everything, and were entirely too bold in their opinions. It did not bode well to drop Miranda, outspoken as she was, into the mix with Lady Callister.

"You must begin every morning with an hour on the pianoforte," Lady Callister said.

"But—" Miranda sputtered.

"No buts. You must prepare yourself to be presented into our society here."

"I have already experienced a London Season, and I was a smashing success, if I do say so myself, and without any musical talents to recommend me. Not that any of that matters now."

"Yes, well, success is a matter of opinion. The London set has apparently lowered its standards. Here you must practice."

Miranda sighed, weighing her options. "If it pleases you, then I will." Her life was no longer her own, and she must remember that. She was in service now. If she was paid to practice the pianoforte, then she would be thankful for it. Anything was better than Gray House.

"Good. After you practice, you will take exactly three turns about the garden with me. Each morning, we will either entertain visitors or make visits, except on Thursdays. Thursdays we take around charity baskets. In the evenings, you will read to me. My eyes are not what they used to be, and since you mentioned you are not well-read, we will attempt to eradicate such a weakness from your character."

Miranda's eyes bulged. "Reading is important to my character?"

"Essential," Lady Callister said emphatically.

Miranda melted back into the stiff embroidered chair where she was assigned to sit while in the morning room. It allowed her to be close enough for Lady Callister to peer at her. The woman was likely critiquing every flaw. "Might I get a shawl for you?"

"Why would I want a shawl? It's stifling in here. You can open a window."

Miranda stood and made a face as soon as she turned away. She had been desperate to make an escape, but the shawl idea had not been brilliant enough.

After opening the window, Miranda asked, "Shall I ring for tea?"

Lady Callister glared. "You know perfectly well the hour marks the time you must practice your music."

Miranda huffed and dragged herself to the piano. She stretched her fingers like an animal with claws trying to keep from attacking its prey until exactly the right moment. She must restrain her thoughts. Winning over Ethan and staying away from Gray House were motivation enough.

Over her painful notes, Lady Callister kept on a running monologue. Not that Miranda could catch every word even if she wanted to, which she didn't.

"Such a handsome man . . . might be interested in a rich widow . . . have to bide our time . . . not getting any younger."

Miranda's hands froze on the keys. Finally, a conversation she wanted to participate in.

"Keep playing," Lady Callister said sharply. "You are worse than I thought."

Miranda sighed and plunked away, one ugly note at a time. When her practicing mercifully ended, she moved to her designated chair beside her employer. As soon as she sat down, a question nagged at her.

"Lady Callister," Miranda began, picking at an invisible thread on her chair.

"You might as well have it out. No use picking apart my furniture."

"It's only that . . . well . . . are you aware of my background?" Miranda never stumbled over her words. She always said plainly what she had to say. What was wrong with her?

Lady Callister's frown lines smoothed, and a barely discernible smile touched her lips. "Mr. Roderick presented your case to me in a complete and honest fashion. I am aware of your father."

Miranda's cheeks burned with shame. She thought she had accepted her fate, but having someone so far above her acknowledge her family's folly did not sit well. "Then, truly, you have my gratitude for taking me in."

Something akin to pity crossed Lady Callister's face. Miranda deflated beneath her gaze. Not long ago, she had only received looks of admiration or jealousy. Time had a way of stealing one's best self.

⁂

Ethan arranged for Captain Grant to join him for a morning hunt for waterfowl. Their tall boots sloshed in the wet grass as they each restrained a German shorthaired pointer on a leash. They reached their destination—an undisturbed pond—and set their guns down so they might untie the dogs.

"Nice spot, this one," Captain Grant said.

"I like it." Ethan picked his gun back up. The two of them walked side by side as the dogs raced forward and dove into the water.

"It's almost as pretty as a certain debutante you introduced me to at your dinner party," Captain Grant said.

Ethan's jaw clenched just as a few ducks flew into the air. Both he and the captain knocked off a shot. Their second round rewarded Captain Grant with a kill, and Ethan sighed, slapping the captain on the back. "Good aim."

"Thank you. Yours, on the other hand . . ."

Ethan laughed off his poor performance. It was not his aim but his mind he was worried about. How was it possible that the mention of Miranda Bartley still drove him to distraction? He knew the captain had paid a call on Miss Bartley before she had left Stonebrook to stay with Lady Callister. It was none of his business how the call had gone, but it was infuriating not knowing what had transpired.

After an hour, the two filled their game bags and started making their way back to the horses.

"How are you settling in at Laurel Manor?" Ethan asked.

"It's a glorious heap of emptiness," Captain Grant replied. "I want my mother and sisters to come live with me, but my mother insists she is perfectly comfortable where she is. The only other solution is to marry."

Ethan adjusted the bag on his shoulder and tried to smother a sudden wave of disgust. He could guess who the captain had in mind for a suitable marital prospect, but Ethan couldn't countenance the idea. He had done his best to include this newcomer in their community's social calendar, but he was beginning to regret it.

"What about your tenants?" Ethan asked, eager to move to a new topic. "You have a few on your estate, yes?"

Captain Grant nodded. "There are whispers about laborers meeting about their wages. They are all hotheads with not a brain between them. But I am not worried. I can handle my own."

"I have heard such rumors as well," Ethan said. "It is one thing to say you can protect yourself and keep your men in line, but you do not have your sisters with you like I do. My concern is greater there. I am starting to worry every time they walk out together."

"It sounds as though you have your hands full with all those women about."

Ethan chuckled. "I suppose I do. I only wish I could design a way to keep the peace in our community. I do not like the stories I hear of hungry farmers revolting in other parts of England."

Captain Grant agreed. "They must have not gone to war, or they would be sick of bloodshed by now."

They reached their horses, and Ethan tied his game bag to his saddle. "I have never gone hungry, but I imagine I would do just about anything to feed my family."

Captain Grant hesitated, then nodded. "I do believe I would do the same."

They both mounted their horses and parted ways back to their respective homes. Surprisingly, Ethan's thoughts were not on the social and economic problems facing their country; they circled the idea of Captain Grant choosing a wife. It would be a simple solution to Ethan's problems, but he had never known anything to be simple where the fairer sex was involved.

What was wrong with him? People were starving, and he was distracted by two females. Where was his head? It was time to set his agenda in order— as well as his heart. As soon as he tied up some tenant issues, he would meet with Mr. Withers about his daughter.

❧

Lady Callister was in the running with Mrs. Guttridge for who could make Miranda more miserable. Nothing she did was up to scratch. Miranda's tongue almost split in half with the number of times she bit it in order to remain pleasant.

"Put down the Psalms," Lady Callister said one night after dinner. Miranda had been ordered to read the Psalms out loud for six nights in a row. It often put them both to sleep. "Fetch me the book from my yarn basket."

Miranda glanced to the corner of the room at the yarn basket she had seen many times with apparently no book inside. Was Lady Callister going senile?

"It is just there. Go ahead," Lady Callister prompted.

Miranda crossed the room and dug through the basket only to find a gothic novel. "This?"

Lady Callister smiled in an innocent, never-do-wrong manner. "Yes, start at chapter three, won't you? Training you is rather tedious business, and I need something more lighthearted tonight."

Miranda flipped to the designated page and cleared her throat. "Rafe's heart dashed against the rocks like the roaring waves before him. His wet ebony hair clung to his neck in clumps, and damp sand made his skin itch. He took a deep breath and searched the salty water with renewed desperation. Without his hard-won pearl—the finest specimen in size and color he had ever seen—there would be no life with his beloved Desiree."

"Rafe's a pirate," Lady Callister clarified. "Chapter one was a little too gory for my taste, but in chapter two, he meets the dignified Lady Desiree. She won't have him, of course, because she thinks he is a ruffian like all the others."

Miranda blinked in surprise. Lady Callister looked ready to swoon, even though this sort of story was completely frowned upon by most matrons. "Shall I continue?"

"Yes please," Lady Callister said, leaning forward with enthusiasm.

Miranda could not resist. She stood up and put some feeling into her words. "Behind Rafe, he could hear his men drawing close. If they discovered the pearl was lost, they would mutiny. They knew he owed them a share of their greatest booty yet. His fingers combed the gravelly sand, bringing up a lackluster handful of broken shells. His glossy gem was naught but a dream, cast away at sea with the last hope of his heart."

"Poor Rafe," Lady Callister sighed.

Miranda bit back a smile. Perhaps there was hope for the stodgy lady and herself after all. Lady Callister was clearly a romantic. Miranda stifled a yawn. "Oh, look at the time. I should retire if I am going to be alert enough to give adequate attention to my music tomorrow."

Lady Callister's smile drooped. "Hmm, perhaps your practicing could be put off for a day. That is, if you think you are up to reading a few more pages."

Miranda lifted her hand and, with an artistic flair, read through a lively sword fight, a haunted cave, and a lovers' tryst. It was late by the time Miranda closed the book. Lady Callister complained, but Miranda could tell the woman was exhausted.

"We can read another few chapters tomorrow afternoon," Miranda suggested hopefully. "Although, it would break my heart to have to skip our visits."

"Nonsense," Lady Callister said. "Tomorrow is Thursday, and I never miss bringing our charity baskets around. People depend upon it."

Did they? Miranda wondered. It no doubt shamed the receivers and did so very little to remedy their situations. The subject was nonnegotiable, however, and Miranda wished she had attempted a more pliable topic. At least she was excused from her practicing in the morning.

The reading had proven a great distraction, but as she climbed the stairs to bed, she found herself missing her father. Was he well? It worried her that he had not written. She hoped he had made it safely to Spain. Though it was late, she knew she would not sleep. Before she climbed into bed, Miranda decided to pen another letter to her uncle. If she could not write her father, she would keep sending letters to Lord Aldington.

> *I am a paid companion now to Lady Callister. She is doing her best to improve me, and I think even you would agree with her tactics. Have you considered the contents of my first letter? Is there any hope for a familial reconciliation? I shall not ask for anything more. I am content here with Lady Callister— even if I do tire of reading Psalms.*

✳

Several baskets heaped with preserves, fresh bread, yards of folded fabric, and other items littered the floor of Lady Callister's carriage. Their driver stopped in front of a shoddy tenant's cottage nearly hidden with weeds. Miranda reached to grab the closest basket.

"Not that one," Lady Callister said and pointed to a basket with jars of broth. "That one."

Miranda was not Miss Withers. She did not regularly give charity. Her most charitable acts had been different from the kind delivered in a basket. She had favored ladies with advice on fashion, whom to avoid, and who would be a good match. Lady Callister knocked on the door, and Miranda shifted awkwardly beside her. The door slowly opened.

"Good day, m'lady." A middle-aged woman dipped her head only to start coughing.

"I thought I told you to stay in bed," Lady Callister said, using the same tone she did when ordering Miranda about.

"Yes, m'lady," the woman replied once she recovered. She made her way back to her bed, which was no more than a lumpy tick mattress covered in rags.

"Is your son still checking on you regularly? We have soup for you and a poultice that will help with that cough. Did the doctor come yesterday like I requested?"

Miranda did not remember Lady Callister sending for a doctor.

"My son has heeded your guidance. The doctor came and gave me medicine. I thank ye for paying for him, Yer Ladyship."

Lady Callister dug out a bowl from a single cupboard and poured the broth from the jar. The savory smell drew a smile from the sick woman. Lady Callister draped the napkin across the woman's lap and set the bowl upon it.

"There, drink up. You need your strength."

"Oh, bless ye," the woman cooed and sipped down the still-warm liquid.

"I want regular reports on how you are faring."

"Yes, m'lady."

The second home they stopped in was completely different and yet the same. A poor family humbly accepted the bolts of fabric for their growing boys. Another home was in need of nails and raved about them and the cakes as if this were Twelfth Night. Each recipient exuded gratitude and looked at Lady Callister as if she were a saint. Miranda was beginning to look at her the same way. How did her employer know the families' needs before arriving? When did she have the time to think of such kindnesses when she was so busy keeping Miranda occupied?

Lady Callister insisted upon introducing Miranda at each stop. The tenants all treated her with kindness and respect. Would they still if they knew Miranda was as destitute as they were? Such poverty twisted at her heart like it had at Gray House. She had seen it time and time again on the congested streets of London and in Folkestone, but this was an uncomfortably close view. She wondered, if not for Ethan, whether this would have been her future.

Thoughts of their visit plagued her sleep and occupied her mind well into the next day. She had to satisfy her curiosity on the matter. As soon as Lady Callister was settled after tea, Miranda was ready to pelt her with questions.

"How did you do that yesterday?"

Lady Callister didn't miss a knot in her knitting. "Do what?"

"Figure out how to help all those people."

"I simply observed."

"You spied on them?" Miranda snapped her fingers. Who did the woman employ for the task and why?

"Nonsense, child. I don't have to spy on people. I talk to them. I ask them questions directly. Then I give them what they need. Nothing too outrageous, of course."

Miranda's forehead crinkled as she thought. "And then they love you for it?"

"Are you inferring I buy their love?" Lady Callister laughed. "What a notion."

"But they do love you. It is on all their faces." Miranda had never had anyone look at her that way. Not even Sarah when Miranda had given her the scarf and ring.

"They do love me, do they not? I suppose people care for those who care for them. When you are a mother, you will understand the concept. It is hard for a small mind like yours to grasp."

Miranda made a face. "I do not imagine I will be a mother."

"And why not?" Lady Callister squinted. "You have an excuse for that just like you do for your lack of ability at the pianoforte, I suppose?"

"No, it is because I am your companion. I have to earn a living."

Lady Callister shrugged her bony shoulders. "My cook has to earn a living, and she is a mother."

"She is?"

Lady Callister raised her gaze to the ceiling as if she were uttering a prayer for Miranda's ignorant soul. "Sometimes you say the most ridiculous things."

"I know servants get married," Miranda said. "I just did not know your cook had children. Where are they?"

"They are tended during the day by the oldest. There are six in all. Overfed, the lot of them. Happy and round."

"Well, she is a good cook."

"I hire only the best."

"Does that imply I am the best?" Miranda was tired of solely hearing about her faults.

"I took you on as a favor. There is quite a difference."

"Yes." Miranda slumped her shoulders. "I suppose there is."

"Now, Reverend Giles is coming for dinner. Wear something plain— no jewelry. He is a pious man and very particular."

"Yes, my lady."

"And don't ask any of your infernal questions."

"Like what color hair did the Virgin Mary have?" Miranda asked with a straight face.

Lady Callister bristled. "Exactly like that. And absolutely no mention of our favorite pirate story or the fact that your oral reading skills rival the actresses in London. By the way, I borrowed another book today about a ghost story set in Italy."

"Who loaned it to you?" Miranda asked.

"I do not share my sources. You will have to find your own."

Miranda really had to bite back her laugh this time. She would be the picture of perfection at dinner, for Lady Callister's sake. Though, she wished Ethan was to be their guest. She had glimpsed him across the pew at church but had not spoken with him since she had arrived at Crowfield. Any hope she harbored for a renewed connection between them grew slimmer with every passing day. No doubt the perfect Miss Withers was taking advantage of every moment Miranda missed.

CHAPTER 19

REVEREND GILES WAS NOT QUITE the pious man Lady Callister had described. Old, yes, with white hair and crow eyes, but much more relaxed than he was over the pulpit. His crinkly smile reached his ears every time Lady Callister said anything. Even as trite a phrase as "Pass the salt."

"I thought your sermon last Sunday on guile very thought-provoking," Lady Callister said. Her eyes took on the same gleam they had when Miranda read to her . . . and not from the Psalm passages either.

"Yes, guile is an interesting topic, and I thoroughly enjoyed studying it. A person cannot pretend righteousness in the least degree without subjecting themselves to pride and vanity."

Miranda's head whipped up from her meal at the mention of vanity. Reverend Giles turned at her sudden interest in the topic of conversation.

"Miss Bartley, do you agree?" he asked.

"Oh, most definitely," Miranda said, though she wasn't sure if she even understood his full meaning. She had always thought vanity meant she enjoyed looking nice, not that she thought herself better than others. She might not have been capable of it before, but with her changed perspective since Gray House, she freely admitted she was no better than anyone else. Thankfully, she was currently without guile. This do-good business was quite the thing.

Reverend Giles seemed appeased and turned back to Lady Callister. "Imagine a society without guile—no envy or strife. No lying or contention."

Well, Miranda was still guilty there. She envied Miss Withers. She had strife with Jane. She had caused problems for Ethan and his friends. While she wanted to hate him for his honesty so many months back, he was without guile.

"I believe there are good people in the world," Miranda said, surprising herself by joining the conversation. "Lady Callister, for example."

Lady Callister blushed a light shade of pink. Miranda had never seen her embarrassed.

"Oh, come now. What a silly thing to say," Lady Callister said, brushing off the compliment.

"Lady Callister is the utmost example in our community." The reverend's affectionate smile caused Lady Callister's blush to deepen.

"Thank you. I do try to involve myself where I can be of assistance."

"Then, you might be as concerned as I am about a recent piece of news." The reverend dished himself some more peas. "I learned yesterday of a man who gambled away his fortune and left his daughter destitute. I have reason to believe that woman is now in our midst, and a few families are expressing their concern. Mrs. Godfrey's niece is visiting, and I cannot help but wonder if it is her. Such a scandal will disrupt our harmonious congregation. I hope to speak with Mrs. Godfrey soon and encourage her to send her niece to reside elsewhere."

Miranda's heart raced. She met Lady Callister's eyes, unsure whether the woman would call her out in front of the reverend. This was the end. Gray House was calling.

"Oh, I do not think it necessary." Lady Callister sent a reassuring glance to Miranda. "The poor girl deserves our sympathy. Besides, Mrs. Godfrey's niece is staying only a fortnight."

"Oh, excellent," Reverend Giles said. "A fortnight ought not be long enough to make any permanent impressions on any person."

"Mrs. Godfrey is mostly housebound and such a sensitive soul. Let's not speak a word of it to anyone."

Mr. Giles put his steepled fingers to his mouth as if sealing his lips. "Your wisdom astounds me as always, Lady Callister."

Lady Callister smiled, and there was no denying the two were besotted with each other. Miranda observed them carefully. More than ever, she wanted to know what it took to make a relationship work. Moments like this made her wish she had a mother to teach her.

＊

Miranda never received visitors, which made one particular visit a rather thrilling occurrence.

"Captain Grant to see you," the butler announced.

Lady Callister raised her brows and turned to look at Miranda expectantly. Would Lady Callister allow her to receive callers? Miranda, who sat in her same embroidered chair in the drawing room as always, stood and clasped her hands together.

Captain Grant entered and gave a perfunctory bow, followed by a delighted smile directed at Miranda. "Good morrow, ladies. How are you faring on this lovely afternoon?"

"We are well," Lady Callister responded for the both of them. "Please, sit down."

Captain Grant flipped up his coat tails and took a seat on the edge of a chair. He resembled a soldier ready for battle. "When I last visited Stonebrook Hall, I was informed of Miss Bartley's change of accommodations. I thought I might ask after her welfare and pay my respects to you, Lady Callister, as well."

"How delightful," Lady Callister said, although she did not sound quite delighted. Odd, since she enjoyed at-home hours during which a number of callers frequented her door.

Captain Grant directed his next question solely to Miranda. "How are you enjoying your new role as a companion?"

"I find it suits me," Miranda answered honestly. The truth of her words struck her as odd since she had not noticed that she had adjusted to her position. Lady Callister was not pointing out as many failings now, and Miranda no longer resented her. Equally strange, she still had hope her future would take a different course. Right now, however, her future was out of her hands, and she was enjoying her current direction. "Lady Callister tolerates me well enough, I think."

Lady Callister nodded as if she were considering the idea. "Miss Bartley is an acquired taste, though I think you would disagree with me, Captain."

"I do disagree," Captain Grant said. "I found Miss Bartley absolutely charming from the moment we were introduced."

No wonder Jane loved this man. His sincerity and kindness reminded Miranda of Ethan. Lady Callister, however, seemed to study the captain with an astute stare—not disagreeing with him, nor agreeing, but measuring his every word.

"How long have you been in the neighborhood?" Miranda asked, sensing the need to direct the subject away from herself.

"I bought Laurel Manor, which had been empty for some years. I am attempting to have several rooms redecorated, but I am finding it a little out of my realm of experience. Perhaps the two of you might come for tea and offer your advice?"

Miranda nearly gave her immediate acceptance but remembered her place and looked to Lady Callister.

"I would gladly advise you," Lady Callister said, "but our social calendar is filled for the foreseeable future. Perhaps you will be content to hear our opinions at a later date."

"Or if you cannot wait," Miranda added, avoiding Lady Callister's eyes, "Miss Jane Roderick might be of assistance. She has impeccable taste."

Captain Grant raised his brows. "I appreciate your recommendation and will take her into consideration. As far as my timeline for redecorating, I will gladly content myself in my current situation until you both are free to bestow your generous opinions."

How impressive. The man had glibly managed to be both genteel and assertive. Lady Callister might not approve, but Miranda smiled shamelessly his way. He deserved something for his efforts today. Then a thought struck her, making her smile disappear. Since her chances with Ethan were all but lost, could she open her heart to someone new? The very idea alarmed her, and yet, Captain Grant seemed liked an eager recipient.

She studied her lap, smoothing her skirts while her thoughts tormented her. If she loved Ethan, she should want him to be happy with whomever he chose. It wasn't like Miranda expected to feel the same fervor of devotion to Captain Grant, because that seemed impossible, but her spirit was weary of chasing a dream. Besides, Miranda was not in any position to turn down an offer—especially from a man who was as good and kind as this one. Her last thought was for Jane. Such a decision would permanently sever all hope for a renewal of friendship. Would she ever be free of this hold Jane and Ethan had over her?

⚹

The light caught on the rose-gold ribbon weaved through Miss Withers's hair, and Ethan found himself staring at it. He was fortunate to have her attention. She was everything a man in his position could want. He simply wished his interactions with her did not feel so forced.

"Tell me, what is your favorite pastime?" Ethan had made a list of questions in his mind before calling on her, determined to push past this mental barrier. Miss Withers's mother was deep in conversation with the housekeeper at the other end of the room, which he could not have planned better.

"Sketching," Miss Withers answered easily. "I love drawing people and trying to capture the personality beneath the face."

Charming. Absolutely charming. "I would very much enjoy seeing some of your work."

"Next time you call, I shall have my sketchbook to show you."

Oh, she was good. Almost as good as Miranda, who always roped him easily into returning.

"I will depend upon it." He grinned at her. "We do not have much longer before the *ton*'s exodus from the country toward London. Are you looking forward to the Season?"

Miss Withers shrugged her dainty shoulders. "Are you?"

Ah, she wanted to match her response to his. Cunning. Ethan tugged at his cravat. He was acting remarkably suspicious. Miss Withers was not trying to stake him through the heart. He was supposed to be enjoying himself. "I am not quite ready for London," he said. "I left with a bad taste in my mouth, and though I am eager to rid myself of it and give London a second chance, it does give me pause."

"Was it a matter of business or the heart?"

Ethan's gaze drifted to the window. What could he say to that?

"The heart, then," Miss Withers surmised.

Ethan returned his eyes to hers. He knew she hinted about his time courting Miranda. "Thankfully, time has a way of covering the past with so many cobwebs we cannot see backward." Except the cobwebs he spoke of were rather translucent lately, and he felt himself subconsciously comparing Miss Withers once again to Miranda. He flashed her his most sincere smile, admiring the way she tilted her head sideways to study him. "You are looking at me strangely," he said. "Perhaps I will find myself a subject in your sketchbook."

Miss Withers pursed her lips to hide her smile. "I have never sketched a young man before. I would hate to disappoint you if I got it wrong."

"It depends on how perceptive you are," Ethan said almost warily.

Miss Withers's expression was frank. "I think you have touched on my greatest strength."

It was Ethan's turn to study her. If she was as perceptive as she said, then he was in trouble.

Their visit concluded, and Ethan said goodbye to Miss Withers, left her home, and steered his horse toward his own, his hands clenching the reins as frustration seeped through him. Mr. Withers had been away on business, and Ethan had not had the opportunity to make his courtship with the man's daughter official.

Once back on his family estate, he saw Mr. Dalkins, his land steward, riding away from one of their tenant houses. He raised his hand in greeting.

"Hello there, Mr. Roderick," Mr. Dalkins called out, the ends of his yellow mustache curling upward as he smiled. He pulled his horse up to Ethan's. "I have been meaning to come to the house to have a word with you."

"This is as good a time as any. Follow me, and we can discuss whatever it is that needs discussing."

"Very good, sir."

After they reached Stonebrook Hall, they dismounted and sent their horses off with a young groom. Ethan led the way to his father's study and slid into a chair across from Mr. Dalkins.

"You know what tomorrow is?" Mr. Dalkins asked.

"Of course. It's Michaelmas. I've been looking forward to the horse race for weeks. After the entertainment, we'll be eating goose like everyone else in the neighborhood. You are welcome to join us, if it is an invitation you are fishing for."

"No, I will be dining with my family this year, but I thank you all the same. I was referring to quarter day and the rents I will be collecting."

"Oh." Ethan chuckled. "Yes, of course. How can I be of assistance?"

Mr. Dalkins's mustache drooped, and he smoothed it away from his lips. "You are aware of our meager harvest. There are several families that will not have enough for both rent and food."

"Surely this has happened before." Ethan enjoyed the responsibility of overseeing things in his father's absence, but he did not like the weight of such heavy decisions. "What would my father do in this instance?"

Mr. Dalkins sighed. "There have been plenty of rough seasons, but this is the worst I have seen. Your father runs his estate with a firm hand, which keeps the tenants in check. I have never known him to give an extension for rent. I fear such rigidness will mean the expulsion of many loyal and hardworking families."

Ethan drummed his fingers on his leg. There had to be a simple solution, but he was lost to it. "What is it you suggest, then?"

"Merely that you determine whether the loss of rent is greater than the value of the tenant. There are plenty in need of work, but a dependable man is hard to come by."

"You have made several excellent points," Ethan said grimly. "I will accompany you to collect the rents. I would like to see how bad things really are."

"That won't be necessary, Mr. Roderick. You should be at the horse races."

"I insist, Mr. Dalkins. When we are finished, we can see where our accounts stand. I am sure we can come up with a reasonable extension for those who need it. I believe my father is a fair man and would agree."

Ethan saw Mr. Dalkins out and stood at the window for a moment. It was awfully cold for a family to lose their home this time of year. An image of Miranda, half-starved with her dirt-stained cloak dancing in the wind, came to his mind. The thought of such hardship left him greatly unsettled. Then another image came to his mind. He could almost see Miranda finishing her walk just outside the window where he had watched her only a few weeks before. He pressed his eyes closed.

CHAPTER 20

"I HAVE INVITED MR. RODERICK and his sisters for dinner tonight since we did not see them as planned for Michaelmas," Lady Callister told Miranda over breakfast. "The man cuts quite a dashing figure, would you not agree?" She flicked open her fan and started fanning her face.

"Um, yes," Miranda answered, wondering if the room was too warm or if she merely felt annoyed with Lady Callister's flippant compliment about Ethan. Her employer had a soft spot for all things romantic, and her comment about Ethan was nothing different from her comments about the heroes in her novels. Miranda smoothed her dove-gray muslin skirt, wishing Lady Callister had given her more notice about their company. How would she dress for dinner? Should she wear her hair higher on her head or lower, by her neck, with a few tendrils framing her face? Which would Mr. Roderick prefer?

"I asked if you would finalize the menu with Cook," Lady Callister said, interrupting Miranda's woolgathering. "I was planning on a crumble for dessert, but Mr. Roderick prefers—"

"Trifle," Miranda finished. "Or so it was when I last visited," she amended. "I will inform Cook."

"Thank you, dear."

Miranda stumbled through her music, hitting more wrong notes than usual. Lady Callister excused herself, saying she had to lie down because a splitting headache had formed. This left Miranda to do whatever she pleased for the afternoon, which would have been nice had she not needed a distraction. She put on a spencer jacket and bonnet and took a long walk. The fresh air reminded her of her last walk with Ethan. How should she act when he came? When she had seen him last, he'd been eager to be rid of her. He bounced from friendly to cold, and predicting his mood toward her was as useless as wondering when her father would return to England.

When the dinner hour came, Miranda trembled with nerves. From the drawing room she heard a commotion at the front door and imagined a footman collecting hats, Ethan's greatcoat, and his sisters' cloaks. How could Lady Callister act so calm? There she sat, pulling at the threads in her sewing box, trying to untangle a mess of knots. The voices came nearer, and Miranda stood. She took several shallow breaths and forced her arms to relax at her side.

Ethan stepped into the open doorway, his cravat nearly straight and his hair glistening from a light sprinkle of rain. Butterflies danced in Miranda's stomach. His eyes met hers, and he dipped into a bow, his expression serious. Miranda searched for a sign of his pleasure to see her, but Hannah stepped around him and stole her focus. She, at least, smiled at Miranda, reminding her to breathe. Hannah's eagerness was exactly the prescription Miranda required to endure Ethan's presence.

"We have missed you at Stonebrook Hall," Hannah said, rushing toward her.

Miranda looked up and saw Jane's scowl. Perhaps Hannah ought to have employed the use of a singular pronoun in her declaration. It seemed no one else had missed Miranda at all.

Taking Hannah's outstretched hands, Miranda squeezed them. "I have longed to see you as well."

"No use starving ourselves," Lady Callister said. "Come, Mr. Roderick, walk me in."

Ethan extended his arm, and Lady Callister rested her gloved hand on his. Jane came next, and then Hannah, and Miranda followed last. She was seated at the middle of the long lace-covered table, but because of the configuration of seats, she was on one end while Ethan and Lady Callister were on the opposite. Hannah sat between Miranda and Ethan, and Jane across from her brother. So much for concerns over dinner conversation.

"Miss Bartley, please inform your friends of the progress we have made this past month. I do not want Mr. Roderick thinking our time unproductive."

Miranda almost laughed. She had just convinced herself silence would be best. "Gladly. Lady Callister runs a tight household and could give our mutual acquaintance Captain Grant a lesson or two."

Hannah giggled but slapped her hand over her mouth when no one else laughed. Jane's scowl deepened.

"Miss Bartley, I was referring to your progress, not my own." Lady Callister's mouth was firm, but her eyes revealed her amusement.

Miranda warmed to the opportunity to speak freely. This was not some dry group she need endure, after all. These were her friends—Ethan, Jane, and Hannah. They knew her, and she need not slave over impressing them. She could be herself.

"I am learning to play the pianoforte and could rival any seven-year-old future debutante. I take my exercise in the garden daily and have successfully prevented any new freckles. And I am thoroughly enjoying reading—"

"Enough!" Lady Callister said, nearly choking on her pea soup. "Perhaps dear Miss Jane might tell us how her sister's wardrobe preparations are coming. Hmm?"

Jane moved her mouth as if trying to hold back a laugh. "Certainly," she said, finally managing a somber expression. "Hannah has had all her fittings, and we are awaiting two last dresses. My mother's counsel of a complete set of gowns for every occasion possible has been met, and I pride myself in having stayed well within budget. I feel economy necessary for young ladies these days." Jane's eyes trailed to Miranda's. "Indulgence breeds wantonness."

Miranda took her point but did not appreciate it. It had been a long time since she had indulged in anything. Why did Jane feel the need to sever their relationship again and again? Miranda smiled, however, refusing to be baited. Someday Jane would see that Miranda merely wanted her friendship.

"Yes," Ethan interjected. "Economy is an important consideration when purchasing an entire wardrobe." He gave his sister a silencing stare. "I would not be surprised if both my sisters met with successful Seasons this year. After all, they will have me frowning over their shoulders at every uninspiring or remotely unworthy gentleman."

"You are an excellent brother," Lady Callister said. It was clear the woman held Ethan in high regard. She took another bite and then wiped her mouth with her napkin. "Mr. Roderick, perhaps you would do well to focus on obtaining your own marital luck. I thought you would be married before your youngest sister ever made her debut."

Miranda watched Ethan squirm. He avoided her gaze and turned his head completely in Lady Callister's direction as he answered. "And leave my sisters without an escort? As charming as the ladies might find me, they must wait their turn."

Miranda's smile was tight. Ethan was terribly charming, but they all knew the real reason he wasn't jumping back into the marriage mart was because he had already picked out Miss Withers.

"Surely," Miranda said, her thoughts finding voice, "when you find someone special, you will discover you can simultaneously love your sisters and secure happiness for yourself." Under her social smile was a grimace. Part of playing the game was not being the obvious, desperate one. She had meant to imply Miss Withers, but for some reason, her comment made it seem like she had been selling her own case. She really needed to filter her words.

"He has found someone," Jane said. "Miss Withers. And we all adore her."

"Jane," Ethan scolded.

Jane laughed off his concern. "I heard you commissioned her to draw your portrait."

The tips of Ethan's ears turned red. "Nothing has been determined."

Miranda's stomach soured at the direction the conversation had taken.

"The actual proposal is simply a formality," Jane said to her brother. "There is no secret the two of you are smitten."

"Mud!" Hannah practically yelled.

Everyone turned to stare, especially Miranda. Hannah met Miranda's anxious gaze.

"Mud pie!" Miranda laughed awkwardly. "You misheard me. I was trying to whisper we are having trifle for dessert, which always reminds me of the mud pies I used to make as a child with all the layers of sticks and rocks . . ." Everyone stared at her now, and Lady Callister the most viscerally. "You would not believe it now," Miranda lied, "but I used to love to dig in the mud. Mr. Roderick, perhaps you enjoyed such merriment as a young boy."

"No mud pies for me," Ethan said, willingly taking her bait, "but I did dig in the mud for worms to fish with. Jane used to help me, actually. She always found more than I did."

"I absolutely did no such thing," Jane said, indignant.

"You did so," Hannah answered and then turned and grinned at Miranda.

Miranda needed to tell Hannah to forever forget the code words. The girl couldn't go around blurting the word *mud* at the top of her lungs during her first Season. People would think her mad.

After dinner, the company migrated to the drawing room, and Miranda excused herself to freshen up. She closed the drawing room door and walked a few feet down the corridor. She stopped in front of a portrait of a very ornery-looking gentleman.

"Not you too," she said. "Can't I please anyone?" She marched several feet away from the portrait and put one hand on her forehead. "Mud? What will I think of next? I am supposed to be a changed person. Why can't I even pretend such a feat? Where are the acting skills Lady Callister spoke of? If I had a scrap of intelligence, I would be acting now."

"Acting on what?" she heard from behind her. Ethan had his head out the drawing room doorway.

"Pardon?" Miranda whirled around, her mind going blank. Those brown eyes of his were finally looking her way for the first time all night.

"I was not aware you talked to yourself," Ethan teased, stepping into the corridor, leaving the door open a crack.

She hadn't done so since leaving Gray House, but the stress of the night was getting to her. "Sane people do it all the time." Miranda flicked back a curl from her eyes and tried to compose herself. "You should try it. I'm sure it's how the great philosophers solve the world's problems."

"Oh? I thought they stood on their heads." Ethan gave her a lopsided grin, stopping a foot away from her.

"What?"

"Never mind. What problems weigh on your mind?"

"That is a very probing question. I thought a gentleman is never to ask what a woman is thinking." Miranda didn't intend such a harsh tone, but she wasn't about to admit to thinking of him and only him.

"You're right. I apologize." He leaned one shoulder against the wall, clearly not scared off. "Do you mind if I share my thoughts?"

She shook her head. She loved to hear his perspective and was eager to hear anything he had to say.

"I think you and Lady Callister are getting along famously. I also think Hannah has taken quite a shine to you."

"Perhaps that is because they did not know the London me."

He pulled at his cravat, an old habit, and tugged it into its perpetually crooked state. "Many thought you likeable in London."

"Not everyone." She dropped her gaze, her heart thudding. "Even Jane is done with me."

"She will come around. Speaking of Jane, she wanted me to have the carriage readied. She declared a headache, but we both know . . ."

Miranda finished for him. "We both know she can't stand to spend time in my company."

Ethan shrugged. "She doesn't show it as she should, but she is grieving the loss of your friendship. She doesn't understand your new station and her place in it."

"I do not know how to categorize myself, so I cannot presume she would," Miranda said dryly.

"That didn't come out the best," Ethan said. "But you do understand why we are still finding our footing."

We. He had finally included himself. "I do understand, more than you realize."

"I'm truly sorry about your father. About everything. But you are content here with Lady Callister?"

"Yes. I thank you for arranging this." His concern touched her. "I haven't had an opportunity to tell you before now. When I see you at church . . . well, I know Jane needs her space." As did Ethan, but she dared not say as much.

"Time will help."

Miranda nodded. "I won't rush her. I will be here when you"—Miranda squeezed her eyes shut momentarily—"when she is ready." She twisted her skirts in her hands.

Ethan studied her for a moment. She could smell his musky amber scent. "I should call for the carriage," he said. His eyes grew soft like melted chocolate. How she longed to have him look at her this way again. Or did she just imagine desire there? Would she ever mean something to him again?

"Yes, the carriage," Miranda whispered.

Ethan extended his hand until his fingertips brushed the back of hers against her skirt. She held her breath, but he dropped his hand, as if only extending his friendship to comfort her, before retreating.

She pulled the daydreams and wishes back and tucked them into a safe place in her heart. With a weary sigh, she made her way back to the others. She wanted to at least be an option in Ethan's mind, but it seemed Miss Withers was filling the vacancy rather nicely. The old Miranda would have snagged his arm and boldly inserted herself back into his life, but the new her could not. Ethan deserved a chance to follow where his heart led him.

CHAPTER 21

OVER THE NEXT FORTNIGHT, THE days began similarly, but their end was usually Miranda's favorite. Her time spent reading with Lady Callister varied with long talks about when Lady Callister was young and the experiences life had blessed her with.

"I had three proposals before I accepted my Edward's hand." Lady Callister wore her perched spectacles, though she rarely looked down as she knitted. She easily produced yet another beautiful blanket for her tenants without missing a beat in her story or dropping a single stitch. "I was tempted by one particular suitor, but my Edward had something special about him, and he won out in the end."

"Three? Good heavens. What made Edward stand out?"

"He was better-looking."

Miranda laughed and let herself slouch in her seat. Lady Callister allowed it, and Miranda loved her all the more for it. "When I first met you, I never would have taken you for such a romantic. Now I know you live and breathe it."

Lady Callister chuckled. "There is enough sorrow and unhappiness to cover the earth several times over. We cannot dwell on hardships for too long, or our spirits wither away, whereas love sustains us. So I choose to be a romantic. Falling in love is one of those things that keeps us going. Staying in love is even better."

Miranda was mesmerized by her words. "How did you stay in love? I presume you loved your husband."

"I never would have married him otherwise," Lady Callister said. "But your question is warranted. Falling in love is the easy part, but we often complicate the rest of it. It is a lot like serving my tenants. I show them I care and do my best to meet their needs. It's the same with husbands."

"Really?" Miranda looked away for a moment. "And what about not-quite husbands?" She had never coveted someone's advice so greatly in her life.

Lady Callister whipped her needles around as she thought. "I do not see why the answer to that cannot be the same. Take Mr. Roderick, for example. Miss Withers recognizes his desire to help others, and she has matched him with her generosity."

Miranda's eyebrows slung together. "She has him figured out exactly."

"Has she?" Lady Callister asked. "Because needs are ongoing. She must continue to assess and meet those needs, or Mr. Roderick will lose interest. Love must be constantly nurtured."

"Whether Miss Withers is capable of keeping his attention or not, Mr. Roderick is not so very fickle. I believe he will be loyal to the one he chooses. He is unfailingly so toward his family." She looked down at her hands. He would not change his mind about someone who was right for him.

"Indeed, he is a good man, but he is still a man. None of us are perfect." Lady Callister smoothed out a row of completed stitches.

"He is close," Miranda admitted. Miss Withers was exactly that in a woman's form. They were disgustingly perfect for each other. Captain Grant should be more her taste—flirtatious but sincere. Perhaps they should discuss something else. "Tell me about the suitors you turned down."

"Ah yes. One of them was the son of a duke."

Miranda listened, but her mind kept reviewing their previous conversation. What needs did Ethan have? How would things have been different between them had she asked herself this question sooner?

✳

Captain Grant led Miranda through the vestibule of his house with a sort of nervous excitement. "It's a small but stately house. There are eight bedrooms upstairs." He pointed up the narrow staircase. "However, I would like to redecorate the downstairs first. The dining room is over here"—he pointed to the right—"and a single sitting room just beyond." Then he pointed to the left. "Behind the staircase is a shared study and library."

The high ceilings and large entryway encouraged an open feeling Miranda rather liked. Captain Grant motioned them into the drawing room, and Miranda followed Lady Callister. He beckoned her toward a sampler of fabrics, and she picked it up and sorted through it.

"I am completely useless when it comes to decor," Captain Grant said, flashing his crooked smile. "Mauve or rose or red? They all look the same.

And do I pair it with gold or crème or celestial blue? I am depending upon your kindness to guide me."

Lady Callister eyed her surroundings critically and placed herself in a chair by the fireplace. A book sat on the side table next to it, and she picked it up and began to thumb through it. Once Miranda was assured Lady Callister was comfortable, she turned back to Captain Grant. "Well, what color do you like best?"

"Black."

Miranda's brow lifted, and they both laughed. She had never decorated a room before, but she knew a thing or two about the popular colors and styles. Black was nowhere on the list. "You might need my help more than I thought. Is there a color on this swatch that stands out to you?"

Captain Grant stepped closer to her to study the fabrics. "The indigo."

Miranda stepped back a few inches, not exactly repelled by his nearness but not wanting to encourage anything just yet. "Indigo is an excellent choice. Now we must choose two accent colors."

"Two?" Captain Grant asked, stepping close once more. "This might take some time for me to decide."

"You have an hour," Lady Callister said, not even looking their way. "Try to be efficient."

Captain Grant motioned for Miranda to sit on a settee just large enough for the two of them. The frame and arms were gilded and the upholstery done in a rich burgundy.

"This is a lovely piece of furniture," Miranda said, wondering if she had ever commented on such a thing before.

"Thank you. It was my mother's."

"Was?" Miranda asked, wondering if his mother had passed away.

"Yes, I bought it for her, but she insisted it is too fine a piece for her cottage."

"Oh," Miranda said. She had never thought about Captain Grant's connections. His circumstances must have been drastically reduced prior to his time in the navy, and his house was likely bought from his prize money. She doubted Jane knew. Not that it mattered anymore. She was beginning to resign herself that this might be her future.

"Well, the settee is lovely," she said. "You should decorate the room around this piece."

"I am pleased you like it." Captain Grant held up the indigo against the red. "Not too awful, I daresay. Perhaps I should save the indigo for my bedroom."

"An excellent idea."

"Wonderful. I will do exactly that." Captain Grant smiled and appraised her face.

She dipped her chin to avoid the intenseness of his gaze. "Does your family live close? I imagine your mother would like to assist you in decorating."

"She lives in the next county over with my youngest sister, who has not yet wed. But they are currently both in Dorset to help with the children during my other younger sister's lying-in."

"You are fortunate to have a mother and sisters, then." Miranda would never have a mother to help with such a task as childbirth, if ever there were the need. "What about a father or any other siblings?"

"My father died when I was fifteen. I left for sea shortly after. Besides my two sisters, I have a younger brother apprenticed for a shipping company."

He was alone here—a feeling she was well acquainted with. "It must be hard being the eldest. I can't imagine worrying about everyone's needs, especially when they are not near enough for you to help them."

"Hard times find us all." Captain Grant reached over and rested his hand upon hers.

Miranda wanted to enjoy his touch. Oh, how she ached sometimes to be touched. But try as she might, the contact made her anxious. Her heart was neatly wrapped and ready to give to the wrong person. She would give anything to peel the wrapping back and let herself be cared for by this good man. It simply did not feel right. Maybe with time . . .

Lady Callister slammed her book shut, causing Captain Grant to yank back his hand.

"Well, well. An hour passes more quickly than it used to." She stood and motioned for Miranda. "Send for my cloak, if you will."

"Yes, Lady Callister." With relief, Miranda escaped the room. She did not even question why Lady Callister did not seem to like when Captain Grant paid her attention.

CHAPTER 22

MIRANDA WONDERED IF PERHAPS THE sun was informed of Ethan and his sisters' visit to Lady Callister's for tea, because its rays stretched forth and warmed the afternoon just for the occasion.

"Let us take our tea on the lawn," Lady Callister announced. "All last winter I looked forward to such a privilege, and then we practically skipped over the summer. This infernal weather has almost denied me of any sunshine at all."

"I hardly think the idea a wise one, Lady Callister," Ethan said, raising his hands as if to hold off a charging bull. "According to the papers, Scotland had quite the nasty snowstorm, and I saw our neighbor's sheaves of wheat draped in a coat of frost this morning. This glimpse of sun cannot touch the chill in the air."

Miranda couldn't hold back the thrill of seeing Ethan again. It made her want to forget her place. "Wise or not, the fresh air might do us good. As Lady Callister's companion, it is my duty to sit beside her during frenzied storms or the fairest weather." Miranda added a theatrical flair to her words. "Let us bask in the rays of the sun, sparse as they may be, and let our souls be invigorated." She adopted her usual tone once more to add, "Besides, we can all wear our wraps."

Ethan's lips twitched. "You're impossible. You know that, don't you?"

Was it his smile, or was she feeling the effects from the sun already? She wasn't even sitting by the window. "Incorrigible maybe, but never impossible." She ignored Jane's grumblings and let herself grin.

In a matter of minutes, the servants spread a fresh tablecloth on the outside table and carried out an extra chair or two to accommodate them all. Ethan insisted on a lap blanket for all the ladies, and the sweet gesture did not go unnoticed by Miranda.

Lady Callister turned to Ethan, who sat next to her. "Tell me truly. What are the long-term effects from such unyielding weather?"

The bridge of Ethan's nose pinched with his obvious concern. "I fear we are in for a long winter. Our harvest was poor. The papers say crops from here to America have failed. Next summer is predicted to be just as wet and cold."

Miranda never liked to talk about current events. Bad news was bad conversation. However, something about this news pulled at her heartstrings. "Will many go hungry?"

Ethan lifted his brows in surprise. "Yes, I am afraid many will go hungry. Wheat was already in short supply."

Miranda met Lady Callister's worried eyes.

"Our tenants will not go hungry if there is anything I can do about it," Lady Callister said.

Miranda cradled her teacup, letting the heat from the porcelain warm her fingers. Lady Callister and Ethan were an anomaly, and their way of thinking was beginning to rub off on her. "What is there to be done?" Surely even the rich would have a hard time buying food if there wasn't anything for the farmers to sell.

Lady Callister hesitated. "We will share what we can and economize on what we can't. There is *always* something to be done."

"That's the spirit," Ethan said.

Jane let out an unladylike groan. "Must we always discuss such bleak subjects?"

Miranda recognized the words as something she might have said once. She wanted to say as much to Jane and have a good laugh, but Jane wouldn't share a joke with her. Not anymore.

Jane set down her cup of tea and took Miranda off guard by turning to face her. "Will you take a turn about the grounds with me, Miss Bartley?"

"Oh, ah, of course." Miranda ached to have their friendship back. Perhaps this was their chance to mend things. She pushed back her chair and smoothed her dress below her spencer jacket.

Jane did the same and motioned Miranda to the left, and they quietly walked a good twenty feet from the others before either said anything.

The silence grew awkward, and Miranda endeavored to extend the olive branch. "The pale green of your skirt is very fetching, Jane."

"Don't be ridiculous," Jane said, lifting the hem from the dampness of the grass. "I didn't ask you to walk with me so you could pretend all is normal between us again. It never will be, so you can stop before you get any ideas."

"Very well; I don't like your skirt at all," Miranda teased.

Jane stopped dead in her tracks and then turned and glared at Miranda. "I'm not going to warm to you with your little witty remarks. I'm glad you are ruined. There, I said it."

Ice-cold water could not have chilled Miranda more. "What? Why would you say such a thing?"

Jane pursed her lips. "Captain Grant. You noticed my interest in him; I know you did. Why did you do it? I haven't spoken to anyone here about the unfortunate scandal surrounding your family name. Mostly, I refrained because speaking of it would condemn my brother's actions of inviting you into our home." Jane shook her head. "But I won't keep quiet anymore. Captain Grant deserves to know."

"Deserves to know what, Jane? That I am poor? He has figured out that much already. He is well aware that I am a paid companion. That isn't some great secret. Will knowing of my father's shame change his opinion? I cannot say. But I guarantee if you prattle about it, it will look poorly on you, not me."

Jane's mouth dropped open. Miranda was reeling as well, but not for the same reasons. She realized she had done that very thing—she had informed Ethan of every negative quality everyone else possessed. Instead of winning his favor, she had repelled him.

"I'm sorry," Miranda said, pressing her eyes closed. "I never should have said that. I tried to push him toward you, but—"

"I don't want to hear your apologies. Never speak to me again, Miranda Bartley. Never!" Jane stalked away, her tight fists swinging angrily against her sides.

Miranda watched Jane leave. Tears flooded her vision, and she did her best to blink them back. She swiveled so she would not have to watch Jane return to the others. She had promised herself she would give Jane more time. Why did she ruin everything? Several minutes passed, but no solutions came to mind. She heard a noise behind her. Hannah had come to rescue her.

She turned and saw she was mistaken.

Ethan had come. "I can remember when the two of you were inseparable."

"She doesn't seem to be coming around like you said." Miranda gave a weary laugh, hastily wiping at her eyes. Ethan had seen every emotion on her now.

"Yes, well, you reminded me last time how unlikeable you are." Ethan grimaced.

Miranda bit back her smile. "I am wounded."

"I will make it up to you by completing this circle around the grounds at your side." Ethan waggled his eyebrows as if he was dangling a treat in front of her.

"I daresay I will be completely disagreeable, and you will suffer a sound rebuke from your sister once you return home," Miranda replied with a heavy sigh.

Ethan shrugged. "I am far more used to Jane stalking away from me than you are." He seemed determined.

"Very well."

Ethan extended his arm, and Miranda felt a rush of pleasure and comfort as she rested her hand on it. This was what she had wanted to feel with Captain Grant but had not.

"Jane does not think Captain Grant is aware of my situation," Miranda said. The words slipped from her mind to her mouth easily. Why she would speak of such things to Ethan was beyond her. No, she did know why. She and Ethan were not a couple, but she did think they still had a friendship—something Miranda was relieved to find still existed despite everything.

"Jane thinks Captain Grant is a good match for her," Ethan said, shaking his head.

"You disagree?"

"I do. I think Jane doesn't know her heart yet. She wants what she cannot have, and that isn't love. It's jealousy."

That was easy for him to say. He didn't know what unrequited love felt like. "What is love if not wanting someone?" There her mouth went again, spouting as if it had a mind of its own.

The way Ethan scratched at the back of his head told her he was as uncomfortable with the topic as she was. "I would not discount attraction, to be sure." Wasn't he doing just that? Hadn't she sensed his attraction to her at one time? It clearly was not a large portion of his definition of the word.

When he finally looked over at her, she gave him a doubtful look. His smile was hesitant, and she knew he was thinking about their past. He looked ahead again, but his pace slowed. "I think love is the makings of poetry with all its passion and fervor," he said. "But mostly, I think it is simple everyday devotion. I wonder if Jane even thinks about the day-to-day part. All she cares for is the passionate beginning and how pleased she'll be to be the treasure on a man's arm. She's still young, and it'll come, but I fear she will rush into something before that happens."

"I have never heard love described in such a way." Miranda wondered how many times she could say the word *love* around Ethan before her face started on fire from the heat of embarrassment. She wished she had seen such devotion between her parents, but his words made sense. It was a balance between the heart and the head. She was all heart, and she knew Ethan was far more practical. Clearly, the two did not work well together.

"I am beginning to think love is also pain and heartache," she added. She felt his eyes on her, but she refused to look at him. "But what do I know about the subject? You must know a great deal more, as you are courting Miss Withers. Are you soon to be engaged?"

Surely she must enjoy torturing herself. She was eager to talk of only the most awkward and distressing topics. Ethan was quiet, so she stole a glance. The tips of his ears were already red from the cold, but Miranda sensed his embarrassment. It was only fair he feel as anxious as she did.

He cleared his throat. "Yes, I believe we will be engaged soon."

She'd known his answer before she asked, and yet, hearing it was so final. She had to look away so he did not see her eyes shining with emotion. She was a fool.

"Unfortunately," Ethan started, "she doesn't seem to know the language of the fan. If she does, she is always saying the most irrational, hateful things."

Miranda did not laugh at his attempt at lightheartedness. She didn't want to talk about Miss Withers anymore. Not every debutante knew the language of the fan. It was complex and rarely useful, but it had been their special connection, and that made it personal.

After a moment of silence, Ethan chuckled.

She snuck another glance at him. "Why do you laugh?" How could he find anything humorous about a subject that wrenched at her insides?

"I just remembered seeing you in Folkestone for the first time, covered in mud." Ethan shook his head. "You actually imitated a peasant's accent. I can hardly believe my memory."

A slow smile spread across her face. "The accent was absolutely authentic. I must have been a sheep farmer in another life."

"I don't believe it," Ethan said, eyeing her. "You? An animal farmer? Instead of sending them to the butcher, you'd probably try to dress them up as pets in frilly dresses and yards of ribbon."

"You know," Miranda said, warming to the new topic, "I think I could even improve a pig's appearance." They both laughed. But pigs made her think of Sarah, and she sobered. "To be frank, I don't care to think about my time in Folkestone. I have enough nightmares to fill my mind on the subject."

Ethan covered her hand on his arm with his own. It was hardly proper for him to do so, but he did not seem to care. "You are a part of Society again. Back to the old Miranda. There is no reason to think on it again."

He couldn't see that she had changed at all, but she had. She could never forget her time at Gray House. It haunted her. It drained her joy and smothered out all the light and hope inside her, but it had changed her. It might not be enough to win his affection, but she could never be the old Miranda. She knew it the same way she knew she wanted to be like Lady Callister. The way Miranda spoke and thought were not the same as before. Her perspective on life itself had altered.

She dropped Ethan's arm. They were nearly back to the others anyway, and Jane would take it as a dagger to an already open wound. "You must be happy to have Miss Withers in your life. She will make a lovely lady of Stonebrook Hall." Miranda did not know why she said it, but she could not retract her words now.

Ethan's eyes darted everywhere but to meet hers. "I agree." He swallowed visibly, his voice far too soft.

Miranda's heart settled heavily in her chest, and the emotional distance between them grew as wide as a chasm. By not denying his intentions with Miss Withers, Ethan had severed the last thread of hope Miranda held for him. A special place in her heart would always belong to him, but it was time to move on.

CHAPTER 23

NOVEMBER APPROACHED LIKE A STALKING lion. Reports said few managed to harvest anything, and the heavy rains destroyed the rest. Even Miranda, untouched by hunger and poverty now that she resided with Lady Callister, could feel the uneasiness in the air. On the first of the month, she received a letter while taking tea with Lady Callister.

She gaped at the wax seal. A large *A*. She had seen it before. Her stomach clenched. It was from Lord Aldington.

"What is it?"

"It's from my uncle."

Miranda fumbled while she attempted to break the seal.

"Do you need my penknife?"

"No," Miranda said, breaking it free. She pulled open the paper, and a few banknotes fell onto her lap. She smoothed the paper but found no written correspondence. "He sent me money."

"I can see that. The question is why."

Miranda's throat itched, and she reached for her teacup. "I can hardly understand it. I did not ask him for it."

Lady Callister was quiet for a moment. "Some people aren't good at communicating their feelings. Take it as a sort of peace offering."

Sighing, Miranda folded the money back into the paper. "I confess I don't know what to think." A winter had settled inside Miranda since she had told herself not to hope for Ethan. She should be thrilled to have received a letter from Lord Aldington at all, but it was too confusing for her to decipher, and it did little to bring her joy.

All day and well into the evening, the letter was on her mind. After finishing a chapter in their book, she noticed Lady Callister observing her with a keen eye. "What is it?"

"You have not been yourself for several days. Not to worry. I have news that will cheer you. I want to host a ball," Lady Callister said.

"Do not put yourself out on my account. I will be myself again; I promise."

"I believe you, but a ball is still on the calendar. I should surely like to enjoy the company of my good neighbors before several of them head to London before Christmas."

"I did not realize you hosted such large parties here." Miranda slipped a ribbon between the pages and closed their book. Ethan and Miss Withers would be at the top of the guest list, but Miranda would not let such a detail diminish the occasion.

"I would guess your definition of a country ball and mine are vastly different," Lady Callister said, taking the book and slipping it into her sewing basket. "I am rather loose about my standard of invitation. It's an informal affair and far more entertaining than the stifling London balls."

"You never speak of London except with distaste. Do you never travel there?"

Lady Callister sighed. "I rarely travel at all anymore. I am old, or did my timeless beauty fool you?"

Miranda laughed. "You are an artifice of deception."

"Yes, well, I used to enjoy the Season, but it wears on a person. I'd rather drink cold tea for the rest of my life than suffer some people's idea of good company. No, this is my home, and I prefer to stay in it."

Miranda reached forward and clasped Lady Callister's hand. "And it is a lovely home at that. Would you like me to start the invitations first thing in the morning?"

"Yes, and then we ought to see how you are at dancing." Lady Callister's shrewd eyes used to make Miranda fidget, but now she found them endearing.

"I would dance a pretty circle around your chair, but it might make you dizzy. I fear you will have to trust me."

"Ha!" Lady Callister said. "I cannot believe you have any rhythm after listening to you practice the pianoforte every morning."

Miranda feigned shock. "Well, I shall not embarrass you if I am by your side all night. You won't have to worry for a minute."

"Nonsense. You will be dancing like every other young lady."

"Lady Callister—"

"I insist."

Miranda pursed her lips. "Very well. If anyone asks me, I shall accept, but just because I know you will enjoy censuring me for my every move."

"Exactly. Now, we must send out invitations straightaway. There is too much gloom and doom about the countryside with this confounded weather. The harvest has been very poor indeed."

Miranda appreciated the subtle reminder that her concerns were not as great as many others'. Her uncle had sent her money today, and Lady Callister had sacrificed her own comfort to cheer Miranda—both reasons to celebrate. She knew Lady Callister was worried about a great deal of people, and Miranda no longer wanted to focus on Ethan. She wanted to help.

Before she retired to bed, she pulled out a sheet of parchment.

Dear Uncle,

Today, to my great surprise, I received a letter from you. I must thank you, for I did not expect to be granted such a generous gift! After opening your house to me, you owed me nothing. I find myself touched by your offering and hope you are warming to the idea of us repairing ties.

I hope this missive finds you in good health.

Until we meet again,

Miranda Bartley

⁕

Miranda spread the newspaper across the table. She read the headlines, took notes, and folded it back up. Then she replaced it with another paper, this one a week older. She repeated the process several times before Lady Callister found her.

"Ah, you found Mr. Lympert's stash of old papers."

"Your butler has kept every issue of this entire year," Miranda said, amazed at how he had stacked them with such precision in his room.

"Oh?" Lady Callister said, impressed. "I am surprised he would share his collection with you."

"I simply asked," Miranda explained. "I find the word *please* can be most effective."

"Agreed," Lady Callister said, coming over to stare at her notes. "What do the locations you have listed have in common?"

"These are locations of riots in London since the beginning of the year. From what I can gather, they are the result of the post-Napoleonic war, the high price of grain, and the ill effects of the weather."

She added the towns Ely and Littleport to her list of West Suffolk, Norfolk, Cambridgeshire, Hockwold, Feltwell, and Norwich.

"You gathered all this information by reading a few newspapers?" Lady Callister asked.

"Actually," Miranda admitted, "the gentlemen in Town spoke of these events off and on last Season. While a genteel woman does not converse about such topics, we are not deaf. The newspapers are to help put together the whole picture. Sadly, I find there is not a good solution here."

"Not in the papers, where every writer has an agenda," Lady Callister said, sitting down beside Miranda. "There is a lot of talking around the issue, but the unrest continues. Still, I must caution your abundant curiosity. Poverty and hunger follow every footstep of the working class. It is not a new problem, nor will your excessive worry change it."

"But the riots?"

Lady Callister sighed and fingered the newspaper with her gloved hand. "I do not blame them for being upset, what with their fear for their families, but it is out of our control."

"Upset?" Miranda shook her head. "Why, their motto is 'Blood or bread!' That goes well beyond upset."

Lady Callister's expression changed to a satisfied one. "I knew you would come around."

"Whatever does that mean?"

Lady Callister chuckled. "I am a good influence on you."

Miranda's mouth dropped open. "Oh, really?"

Lady Callister nodded. "I always take credit where credit is due."

"I had no idea you were a saint." Miranda hid her smile.

"Well, now you know."

A laugh escaped, despite her attempt to smother it. "Yes, now I know. But what I do not know is what to do about this wretched situation."

"You will think of something," Lady Callister said.

"You have blind faith in me." Miranda tapped her fingers on the table. "I cannot understand why workers cannot afford to feed their families."

"I don't pretend to be overly informed," Lady Callister admitted. "We ought to ask our neighbor. If he tells us to not concern ourselves with such matters, we will respectfully withdraw. We cannot forget our position. A genteel woman must act within her sphere, and no more."

"Ask Mr. Roderick?"

"The very man." Lady Callister nodded.

Miranda shook her head. "I would hate to trouble him. Captain Grant might—"

"Nonsense. His home is not as close. Go get your cloak and gloves."

Miranda would eat her hat if Ethan did not think her absolutely ridiculous for asking after matters that were inappropriate for a woman to discuss. It simply wasn't done. Further, he would think her fishing for his attention. This idea mortified her. She had promised herself she would bury her feelings, and she was doing everything in her power to do so.

✳

Ethan was surprised to see Miranda and Lady Callister come to visit at the same time he and his sisters were entertaining Miss Withers. Flustered, he practically jumped to his feet.

"Please, join us," Ethan said, welcoming them into the drawing room. He hadn't talked to Miranda since their walk at Crowfield and their in-depth conversation about love.

It certainly wasn't the reason he had passed up an opportunity to speak with Mr. Withers about marrying his daughter. Ethan couldn't quite explain why, other than the timing did not feel right, nor could he explain his reason for avoiding Miss Withers since then. Today, he had been determined to redevote himself to his purpose. He took a seat and glanced at Miss Withers, then back to Miranda, letting the awkwardness of having them both there together settle around him.

Lady Callister took a seat near the fireplace, where a warm flame curled around the wood behind the grate. She immediately set her eyes on Jane. "Jane, dear, take your sister upstairs, will you? We have business to discuss, and I assure you, it will bore you both to tears."

Jane scowled as she got to her feet, but Hannah seemed pleased enough to be excused. As they left the room, Hannah gave Miranda an affectionate farewell but did not spare a single glance for Miss Withers. She was a traitor, that one.

Miranda took a seat on an opposite sofa from Miss Withers, creating a triangle with Ethan in his chair as the third angle. Her hair was pulled back into a simple style. Her dress was overtrimmed, but there were no other ribbons or adornments on her person. It took him a moment to determine what was missing. There was no ready, bold smile.

"Perhaps I have stayed too long," Miss Withers said, standing.

He wasn't sorry to see her go, under the circumstances. It was too much having her in the same room as Miranda. "I thank you for coming," Ethan said at the same time Lady Callister bade Miss Withers to sit.

"No need to leave on our account," Lady Callister explained. "Before we discuss business, let us discuss pleasure. We have an invitation to a ball for both of you."

This was the first Ethan had heard of a ball. His sisters would be ecstatic, but he wasn't sure how he felt about it.

"Thank you for including me on your guest list," Miss Withers said, settling herself back into her chair.

Lady Callister acknowledged her with a nod. "We also require Mr. Roderick's educational opinion on a few matters."

Ethan's curiosity piqued. "What is on your mind?"

"Might you explain to us the Corn Laws?" Lady Callister pointed to herself and Miranda.

"Gladly. It is nothing more than a steep import tax."

"Is it doing us any good?" Miranda asked, her posture bent forward in anticipation of his answer.

Amusement made his lips twitch. "It is meant to encourage us to favor domestic producers, but the rise in cost of living is the most urgent reason for recourse."

She wrinkled her nose. "Is that why wheat is so expensive?"

Ethan remembered Miranda's statement back in Folkestone about the price of bread. "It is a factor, yes."

"What is being done about it?" Miranda asked.

"I do not sit in Parliament yet, as you well know, so I cannot speak for the lawmakers." He leaned toward Miranda and rested his elbows on his knees. "However, there is the Berkshire Bread Act, where the parish provides an allowance to cover the price of bread according to family size."

"You must still be poring over all those fundamental law papers of your father's," Miranda said with a half smile. So she had been paying attention. Miranda looked to Lady Callister. "Is that happening in the parishes here?"

"Oh, in parts, yes, but the act is not a national law. The problem is there are some who have taken advantage of the system and do not work at all."

"But surely, after such a cold summer and all the rioting . . ." Miranda trailed off. Her eyes darted to Miss Withers, and her cheeks went pink.

Ethan knew she was embarrassed to be speaking of a topic usually reserved for the men, but he had never thought Miranda so attractive as he did at that moment. She had taken an interest in something he was passionate about. While he missed her confidence, he was glad she was looking beyond herself. With both confidence and selflessness, she would be a force to be reckoned with. He found himself grinning and had to cough to cover his smile. If she saw him grinning, Miranda would think he was mocking her ignorance and call him a tease. But then there was Miss Withers and her gift of perception—she'd guess the real reason for his smile.

"If all the landowners raised the salaries of their employees, this would not be a problem," Miss Withers said. Her voice took on an interesting tone—perhaps a competitive edge?

"I agree," Miranda said. "But that sort of change could take years. People are starving now. We must see that Reverend Giles is giving the adequate allowances per the Bread Act."

"Why not do both?" Ethan asked. "We can encourage our neighbors to increase wages and see if the parish can supplement as needed." He had had to do just that with his own tenants after assessing the numbers with Mr. Dalkins. Ethan hoped many of his neighbors would be willing to do the same.

Miranda clapped her hands, and her wide grin emerged. Her eyes caught his, and he swallowed a sudden desire to be near her. He forced his gaze to focus on Miss Withers, who folded her hands primly with a pleased but guarded smile. Here sat two beautiful but very different women. His heart and mind were divided. One made perfect sense on paper, and the other conjured up fantasies he struggled to suppress.

He didn't have to look at Miranda to admit her behavior *had* changed. All his arguments against her had faded away one by one. He ran his hands down the arms of his chair. He could not let this sway him from all reason. Stories continued to circulate about the Bartley family, even though Miranda's time in servitude was still a secret. His connections had confirmed the disconcerting rumors about her father, and his family would never condone a match under the circumstances.

Even as he thought it, his own willpower seemed to wane. She was a woman who had blossomed in adversity. He would do his best to avoid her because that was the choice he had made, but there would be no escaping seeing her at Lady Callister's ball.

※

Reverend Giles gave a moving sermon about charity. However, as Miranda watched Ethan escort Miss Withers out of the chapel, she promptly forgot everything the reverend had said about the virtue. She eyed Miss Withers in her pink gown and azure spencer. She was likeable enough, but Miranda could not stand to see her with Ethan. Why did Lady Callister have to live in the same parish as Ethan and his family? The ball was next week, and Miranda would be forced to watch the couple dance together.

Thank goodness there was something more important at hand than nursing her pride. Lady Callister and Miranda made their way purposefully over to the reverend as the parishioners dispersed.

"How do you do, Lady Callister?" he said. "I trust you are well."

"Better than the hands who support us," Lady Callister answered.

Reverend Giles's smile dropped. "I do not believe I take your meaning."

Lady Callister was in royal form. "There are several prominent members of this community who insist this parish provide a bread allowance for the poor."

Miranda did not think the purple coloring in the rector's cheeks a good sign.

He cleared his throat not twice but thrice. "I do believe that would require money from the parish, and we must be careful—"

"We must be careful not to upset those who pay your salary," Lady Callister interrupted. "Not that I think for a moment that such a *charitable* man such as yourself would even think about only himself profiting."

"Never, Lady Callister. Never."

Lady Callister gave him a sweet, endearing smile. "I knew you would see things our way. You do have such a good heart."

Reverend Giles's smile could be interpreted as a grimace. There was something to be said about having a rich, influential person in one's life. Not that Miranda claimed such. No, she simply appreciated seeing power used for a good purpose. If she ever had money again, which seemed extremely unlikely, she would want to be exactly like Lady Callister.

"I don't think he took that very well," Miranda said once they were alone in the carriage.

"No, he did not." Lady Callister fiddled with her shawl. "We shall have to see if he is in better spirits at the ball. There is a reason issues such as these divide the people. The question is which side does our good reverend stand on?"

CHAPTER 24

A COUNTRY DANCE USUALLY CONSISTED of flirtatious glances and scheming matchmaking, but Miranda viewed tonight's setting in an entirely different way. Her goals included avoiding Captain Grant, ignoring Ethan's presence, and giving Lady Callister her complete attention. The gathering numbered about fifty people, with plenty of room to navigate around the dancers but not enough to hide.

Captain Grant caught her eye across the room where he stood by a desperate matron and her rather awkward daughter. Miranda sent him a smile of sympathy and hurried to find someone to talk to before he moved her way. Out of the corner of her eye, she saw him make his excuses and retreat. Her gaze frantically darted from one person to another. Whom could she attach herself to?

Aha! Hannah. She sat conveniently alone. Miranda walked so quickly she could have been mistaken for skipping with the dancers.

"Hannah!" she said with whispered excitement. "Are you well enough to take a turn around the room with me? My request is rather immediate, if you take my meaning."

Hannah's features, tight with apprehension, relaxed. She stood and took Miranda's arm.

"I have not been here for more than half an hour, and already I am a wallflower. How can I ever compete with the belles in London?" Hannah gripped Miranda's arm fiercely as Miranda weaved her in and out of people toward an empty corner of the room.

"The secret is to remember everyone is worried, even the prettiest ones. You must believe in yourself, or no one else will take you seriously." Miranda enjoyed giving such advice since she attributed the same tidbit to her own success—despite the fact she had left London with fond but empty memories, zero friends, and no husband. At least she could say she rarely was in want of a partner. Well, until now. She ought to take her own advice since her confidence was not what it once had been.

"Please tell me there is a code word for such a thing," Hannah said desperately.

They paused next to a potted tree—the only sedentary object in the room besides the chair and sparse enough to hide part of a leg if necessary.

"We might need to forget the code words, Hannah. Try telling yourself the gentlemen can smell fear and you do not want to attract a predator. Relax, smile, and pretend confidence, even if you do not feel it."

"Smile? Openly?" Hannah frowned. "But what about being demure? I dare not smile at a man. I would invite the worst sort if I acted in such a way."

Miranda opened her mouth to argue, but Hannah had a point. She did not want her friend to attract the men Miranda often found trailing her around. Ethan, of course, had been refreshingly opposite, and his goodness made him stand out.

"A modest smile, then," Miranda answered. This seemed to appease Hannah.

Miranda glanced around for Captain Grant's position, and in doing so, she met Ethan's eyes. For a moment, their gazes met and held. Her heart thumped in her chest. She heard Hannah speaking, but the words flitted around her. While he stood next to Miss Withers, it was Miranda he was staring at. Warmth filled her, and she started to smile at him, but Miss Withers said something to Ethan, and the spell broke. He turned away from Miranda.

Putting her gloved hand on the potted tree, she tried to catch her bearings. Surely Miranda had imagined the fondness in his eyes. Ethan had probably been searching for Hannah and his gaze had unintentionally fallen on her since she and Hannah stood near each other. Miranda had masterfully put him from her mind all day, and now she had to build up her resistance to him once more.

"Miss Bartley," Captain Grant said upon arriving by her side. He maneuvered himself in front of her and Hannah and grinned with satisfaction.

"Oh, Captain," Miranda said in a falsely cheerful voice. She could not even encourage the one man interested in her because of her lingering feelings for Ethan and her concern for Jane, and now he had her trapped. She thought quickly. "You know my friend Miss Hannah Roderick."

Captain Grant bowed his head to acknowledge Hannah. And then a plan came to Miranda's mind.

"I assume you would like to dance with Miss Hannah, so I will just slip over and see to Lady Callister's well-being."

The captain's mouth fell open, but he recovered quickly. Like a true gentleman, he turned to ask Hannah to favor him in the next set. Miranda made a quick dash to Lady Callister's side, relieved for her own sake but sad to have to brush off someone as nice as Captain Grant.

"This is not a footrace," Lady Callister said. "It is a dance. When you are finished circling this room, I do hope you will give some young men the pleasure of partnering you."

Miranda laughed lightly. "I cannot ask a gentleman to dance, now can I? And not a one desires to ask me."

Lady Callister scowled. "They cannot catch you. I saw the whole thing, so do not deny it."

Miranda bit her lip to hide her smile. The music stopped, and the dancers lined up for the next reel. Hannah beamed across from Captain Grant, her smile as undemure as they came. Her happiness made Miranda's trickery worthwhile indeed.

"All right, I admit it," Lady Callister said, watching Hannah. "That was well done."

"Yes," Miranda said, "but what will Jane say? She will not speak to Hannah the rest of the night."

Lady Callister chortled. "If Lady Gibson were here, she would see to Jane's manners. A letter might be in order."

"I do not think that is necessary," Miranda said. How could she explain to Lady Callister that it was she who was behind Jane's ill behavior? "I hate to worry Jane's parents. I think she will be more herself when she is with her mother again. Did you not say she will return to London soon?"

"Next week. Though, I find it silly the family wants to spend the entire month of December and the holidays in such an overpopulated, gloomy place instead of at home, in peace."

"Next week?" She thought she would be able to torment herself by seeing Ethan a few more times before his inevitable departure. Disappointment gripped her heart.

No, no, no.

It was Hannah she would miss and the opportunity to win Jane over again.

Lady Callister looked at her oddly. "What is going on in that head of yours?"

A loud crash prevented Miranda from responding. There was a clamor amongst the dancers, who now were bunched together instead of in their lines, and the music stopped.

Lady Callister grabbed Miranda with her strong, bony hand and propelled her forward. "Go see what has happened."

Miranda hurried over to find Hannah and Miss Withers on the floor. Miss Withers's white gown was drenched in red sherry, her face contorted with shock and disgust.

Hannah's sweet face crumpled with tears, and she stood and fled before Miranda could reach her. Captain Grant moved to help Miss Withers stand.

"This is disgraceful. Look at me!" Miss Withers cried.

It was easy to feel sympathetic for Miss Withers. Her dress would never be the same, and clearly the woman was humiliated. Miranda found herself wondering what Lady Callister would do. Just like she had with her tenants, Lady Callister would assess the problem and then find a way to alleviate it.

Miss Withers's problem was her dress. She needed a new dress and quickly. Miranda swallowed back any thoughts that argued against helping her. Miss Withers wasn't the enemy, not really. Miranda had never given the woman an honest chance.

She hurried over, ignoring the whispers and stares. "Fetch some towels," Miranda said to a footman. "Send a maid to mop this up and then another one to my room, please." She touched Ethan's arm. "Find Hannah."

"Of course." He nodded, appearing grateful for direction.

Miranda turned to Miss Withers. "Come with me."

"I really should leave straightaway," Miss Withers said once in the passageway. Distressed, she wiped at the stain, but her efforts made it worse.

"And end your night prematurely? Nonsense," Miranda said. "There is much fun to be had, and you would be sorely missed." She believed what she said to be true, even if she herself would not miss her. Together, they went up the stairs and around the corner to Miranda's room. Once inside, Miranda guided Miss Withers to her closet and waved for her to choose from its contents.

Miss Withers reached for the dress closest to her. "These are stunning."

"Yes, I know," Miranda said. "I have expensive taste, and my father lived to indulge me. There will be a few subtle changes to styles this Season, but these are still the latest and greatest, in my opinion."

"I agree," Miss Withers said, fingering a pretty yellow ball gown—Miranda's favorite. "But I cannot borrow one. You saw what happened."

"I saw a complete accident," Miranda argued.

Miss Withers turned to face her head-on. "Why would you do this? I was convinced you did not care for me in the slightest. We are not even friends."

Miranda ducked her head for a moment. Ethan had been ever so right about her. Miss Withers could see the truth just as plainly as he had. "Please, do me the honor of wearing one of my dresses." Had her icy heart thawed a little? She actually wanted to see how beautiful Miss Withers would look in her favorite buttercup ball gown. "This one. You and I are similar in size. I imagine it will complement your coloring perfectly."

Miss Withers looked cautious but finally gave a nod of acceptance. Once she changed, they returned downstairs. Several oohed and awed over the dress. Miranda stepped back into the corridor, content to let Miss Withers shine without stealing any attention for herself.

"That was very kind of you," Ethan said, stepping into the passage with her.

"Did you find Hannah?" Miranda asked, sidestepping his compliment.

"She is in the carriage, absolutely mortified. That blasted Captain Grant whipped her around so fast that her light frame spun right into the server. I would not be surprised if she refused a Season altogether. You know her shyness."

Miranda nodded. "I am sorry to hear it."

"Jane is saying her goodbyes. We are to leave for London the day after tomorrow. I received a letter from Mother before we left for the ball, urging us to hurry. She is impatient to oversee last-minute preparations for Hannah's debut."

"Oh," Miranda said quietly. Only one more day. Lady Callister had said they wouldn't leave for another week. "I wish you luck, then."

Ethan's somber face matched hers. He stared at her for a moment, then reached down and ever so softly took her gloved hands in his own. A touch so light and gentle should not stir Miranda, but it did. Her heart pounded in her chest.

"I was wrong about you," Ethan said softly. "Unforgivably wrong."

"No, it is the other way around. You must forgive me. I'm ashamed of my behavior back in London. I never should have acted the way I did, especially at the card party with your friends." Miranda dipped her chin. "I should not have been so rude to Miss Withers either. I felt threatened by her presence. I guess you could say I was jealous. I was reckless with my words."

"Jealous?" Ethan's brow furrowed. He shook his head in disbelief.

Miranda waited for him to drop his hands and walk away, but he tightened his hold on her and stepped closer.

"You had no reason to be jealous. Not one. No one could hold a candle to you."

His thumbs caressed her hands, sending gooseflesh up her arms. Miranda's dreams and reality seemed to be fusing into one, but it made no sense. He did not love her. He loved Miss Withers.

But his eyes said otherwise. "You should despise me for walking away when you needed me most, yet your grace astounds me. I wish . . ." His voice trailed off, and his eyes fell to her lips. He swallowed, and she trembled under his heady gaze. "I wish . . ." His head lowered, and she closed her eyes.

"Ethan!"

Ethan dropped Miranda's hands like they were hot coals and whirled around to face Jane.

"Hannah is expecting us," Jane snapped, tugging at the tops of her gloves. She turned to Miranda, her eyes and whole expression softening. "Oh, I thought you were Miss Withers. She frightened Hannah, and I . . . never mind. I know Hannah will be sad she cannot say goodbye, so I will say it for the both of us." Her expression turned sheepish. "I hope you will find happiness with Lady Callister." Jane's words were stilted but not insincere.

"Thank you." Miranda would treasure her words, even though they were hardly a white flag of peace between them. The butler approached with their cloaks, and a panic doubled inside of her. They couldn't go. Not yet. Why could she not contrive a reason for Ethan to prolong his departure?

"I, ah . . ." Ethan's features seemed just as conflicted. She sensed there was more he wanted to say. He pressed his eyes closed momentarily and then accepted his cloak. "Until the spring, then."

Miranda's hands already ached to be held again. Ethan could not just leave. Not like this. There was too much to be said—too much unresolved—too much she needed to apologize for.

"Hannah is probably beside herself," Jane said, as if unaware of the tension between Miranda and Ethan. "We had better hurry." She slipped out the door and left them alone.

Ethan's dark eyes met Miranda's, the intensity of his gaze like a sweet caress, filling her with longing. "I . . . had better go," Ethan finally said. "Goodbye, Miss Bartley."

His uncertainty compounded her own. "Goodbye," she whispered. It was all she could think to say. No other words came to mind until it was too late and the door had shut behind him.

⁂

Jane hurried toward the carriage, but Ethan couldn't pull himself away from Crowfield. His breath came in quick bursts. All night he'd not been able to keep his gaze from straying to Miranda—her beauty was unparalleled, her actions utterly selfless. Not once tonight had she tried to steal any attention for herself, even knowing that a husband would be the surest way to further her position. Ethan wanted to tell her how he felt. How he had spent months trying to deceive himself that he did not need her. He knew now that Miss Withers was not for him—and not just because she had frightened Hannah. No, it was because he could never love her like he did Miranda.

He put his hand up to knock on the door to end his torment but stopped. He might finally know his true feelings, but he still had an obligation toward Miss Withers. It would not be right to act on anything until he freed himself from the expectation Miss Withers had every right to have. He had made that mistake once before, and he knew now the damage of such a deed. If only he had given Miranda more of a chance those many months ago. He had judged her much too harshly. How could he have been so foolish? In agony, he ripped himself away and shuffled toward the carriage. It was simply too late.

⁂

The pace of Ethan's life sped and slowed at all the wrong intervals. Invitations to social events and demands from his mother filled his nights, but his mornings slumped with uselessness. London's poverty overwhelmed him, his friends bored him, and his blasted cravat refused to lie straight. Worst of all, he could not make a plan to save his life. After taking his horse out for some light exercise, Ethan received a note from his mother demanding he visit her. He rode over straightway, having little else to pass his time.

"You seem preoccupied as of late," his mother noted.

He sat across from her in his family's town house. His eyes strayed to a golden statue of the Roman god Mercury. This room was overdone, in his opinion. It had never bothered him before, but it certainly did now.

"Is that why you summoned me? To lecture me?" Ethan asked in a laconic tone. He finally focused on his mother. Her ebony hair still looked youthful, with a few strands of gray, but there were wrinkles in her face that Ethan could not remember from last spring, especially around the mouth—worry lines. His gaze sharpened. Was Father the source? His sisters? Or him?

"I never worry about you, dearest," his mother answered.

His concern relieved, he smiled. "I hope to keep it that way. Tell me what is on your mind."

"You."

"Me?" Ethan furrowed his brow. "Well, if you are not worried, then you must be pleased with me."

His mother took on her famous look of superiority, one Jane had clearly inherited. "I am neither worried nor pleased. Indeed, I find myself perplexed. I received a letter this morning from Lady Callister."

"Lady Callister?" Ethan gulped. He had hoped to avoid this moment a little longer, but Lady Callister was nothing but forthright.

His mother's pointed eyebrows arched ever higher. "There is truth to this, then? Miss Bartley is Lady Callister's new companion? How did this come to be? And why did you not tell me?"

Ethan shrugged. "You know I never gossip, Mama."

"And did this affect your courtship with Miss Withers? Jane refuses to tell me anything."

Nothing could have surprised him more. Jane had had the chance to slander Miranda's name to their mother and had resisted?

"Miss Withers and I get along well enough, and Miss Bartley is aware of my intentions toward our neighbor. There are not any complications to speak of." Just the small matter that he had almost kissed Miranda, and instead of feeling ashamed, he was disappointed. Acutely so.

How could he explain that he had made a fool of himself months ago by shamefully rebuking Miranda? Then, once she had proven herself opposite of what he had accused her to be, he had been too cowardly to fix the problem. If he did anything about it, he would be embarrassing Miss Withers by prematurely ending a courtship with her. Nothing rankled him more than being less of a man than he expected of himself. He had acted rashly and must be forced to pay the consequence for the rest of his life.

"I see. And Miss Withers travels to London after Christmas?"

Ethan crossed one leg over the other, relaxing now that he had successfully evaded his mother on the point of Miranda. "Yes, or so their family planned to do last I spoke with them."

"Excellent." His mother poured him some tea, and he accepted. "Now, what tasks are you furrowing away with these days? I expect you have been searching for another young lad to sponsor at your charity school."

"The school? Oh, ah, actually, I *have* been thinking a little about the food shortage with the terrible harvest and all."

"Your father speaks of little else these days." His mother handed him a plate of almond tea cake. She could never resist feeding him. "There is another matter I hoped to bring to your attention," she said in a lower tone.

"Hmm?"

"Your sisters."

Ethan sighed. "I did my best this summer, like I promised."

"Yes, and I had hoped that, without my presence, Hannah would no longer be able to hide behind me and Jane would be less temperamental. I am afraid Hannah is worse than before, and Jane is sullen and contemptible, brooding over every disappointment she meets."

Ethan rubbed his hand across his jaw and earnestly pondered the situation. He cared deeply for his sisters, but heaven knew he was enjoying a break from living with them. If Miranda were here, she could coax Hannah from her room and force a truce with Jane. But that woman had far too many hands in the pot as it was. He had missed his chance, and now he needed to extricate himself from her. His mind was too consumed as it was.

"I am out of ideas," Ethan finally said. That included for himself.

"Well, I am not. I want to invite Miss Withers and her family to join us for the holiday. I think we could all use the distraction, and Mrs. Withers and I are eager to press your relationship along."

Ethan's eyes widened. Yes, the plan was to marry Miss Withers. And he rarely deviated from his plans, despite what he had once told Jane, but he needed time to cleanse his heart.

"I'm not keen on the idea."

"Why ever not?" his mother asked.

Ethan cleared his throat. "Because the roads are terrible, and they should wait for drier weather."

"It could be a decade before the weather improves."

He struggled to muster another excuse. "Well, what does Jane think of this?"

"I do not intend to reward her behavior by letting her have a choice in the matter," his mother said almost petulantly.

"I think you should ask both Hannah and Jane," Ethan said desperately. "It is their holiday too." Hopefully they would say no.

"I cannot put my finger on it, but there is definitely something on your mind. I thought you would be anxious to hurry this along too." She folded her arms over her crème muslin gown. "Very well, I will ask them."

Ethan prided himself in being decisive, but his head was in a muddle. Whether he admitted it or not, he was straddling a line that he needed to cross and be done.

CHAPTER 25

CHURCH SEEMED LIKE A GOOD place to purge one's wicked thoughts. Miranda bore guilt for coveting and plotting a theft, but she was not ready to fully repent. On the pew opposite her, Miss Withers's profile was perfectly composed. Miranda, on the other hand, fidgeted with her prayer book and considered her sins. She dearly wanted to steal Miss Withers's beau. The ideas that flitted through her mind were anything but holy. Shame on her. Miranda knew she would not ever act on the silly ideas her mind concocted, not with the resolutions she had made for herself after her time with Sarah, but it was hard not to *think* wickedly.

Reverend Giles crossed to the wooden pulpit, his face severe. "All who frequent the gambling den of sin, I call thee to repentance! Proverbs 13:11 tells us dishonest money withers away. One in our congregation today represents the consequence of such vile behaviors. Having been cast from her father's side, she is reduced to living off the charity of others." Reverend Giles directed his gaze to Miranda and let it rest there.

Heat flooded her cheeks.

The reverend did not look away when he said, "Her reputation is indeed beyond repair, and we must shun her."

Shun? Miranda's heart pounded. Her bonnet shielded her embarrassment from the onlookers, but she felt their incriminating stares. She moved minutely so she might see Lady Callister. Her employer's mouth was tight, her stiff posture radiating tension. She seemed to dare the reverend to go on.

He did—preaching on and on about the perils of supporting sin.

Lady Callister's brow rose higher, and Miranda thought she might be contemplating murder. There was a great deal of sinning going on in the minds of this congregation.

"We cannot afford to be complacent," Reverend Giles continued. "We must protect our community from all affiliation of sin. Shake off these associations, and encourage your neighbors to do the same."

His words stung. How many people must Miranda be rejected by? Her ears tuned out the rest of the fiery sermon. When the hymn reached completion, Lady Callister catapulted to her feet. She gestured to Miranda and marched to the door. Shaking, Miranda hurried to stay by her side.

It was not until they were in the carriage that Lady Callister finally spoke. "I have never been so outraged in my life." She pulled the curtain closed on the carriage window as it lurched forward. The sound of wheels grinding against wet rock and damp earth did little to drown out Miranda's spinning thoughts.

"I am quite sure he did not mean to insult you, only me." Miranda sighed and tipped her head back against the seat. "I do not have to be in a church to worship. That much I know." God had already accepted her in her darkest hour and given her Sarah. He was perfect in his merciful nature, whereas Reverend Giles and all of High Society were incapable of such divine understanding. Even so, his condemning words reopened a wound that was still healing. She could barely hold back her tears. "You have no obligation to me. I will inquire for another position first thing tomorrow."

"Do not be ridiculous. If every man interpreted the Bible to support his own ideas, mankind would be lost. I specifically told Reverend Giles to leave it alone, and he deliberately ignored me. He must have sent out some inquiries about your name all the way to London. It is retribution from my insisting he provide food for the poor. No, my objection is with him, not you. I thought his refusal to attend my ball would be the end of it. I am sorry to be wrong."

Miranda had not even noticed Reverend Giles's absence that night. "I am most sorry."

Lady Callister dismissed her words with a wave of her hand. "Think nothing of it. It will stir up the gossips, but I will not dismiss you. I have more influence in this neighborhood than a tattling old man."

"A man of the cloth," Miranda corrected, pulling the lap blanket over Lady Callister. "Though you are a far superior person, you used to respect him greatly. I suspect the others do too."

"Humph," Lady Callister said with her mouth pursed tight with anger. "I do not want to speak of him."

"Yes, but you must be completely sure if you are to keep me. I will not come between you and your friends."

Lady Callister's shrewd eyes narrowed further. "Heaven forbid you have come to like me. Perhaps I need to increase your time on the pianoforte."

Miranda's gloomy thoughts began to dispel with Lady Callister's sudden candor. "I suspect more animated readings in the evenings might increase my aversion for you."

"Yes, Psalms and more Psalms."

Miranda pinched her lips to keep from laughing. "Very well, I admit it. I do enjoy being your companion. I never planned to like you, but then again, I never planned to be a companion. I thought I would be traveling the world with my father this summer past, but meeting you, I think, is far better. My friends are in such short supply, and I count you as a favorite."

Lady Callister finally softened her expression. "You are a good girl. Do not let anyone tell you otherwise."

"Thank you."

"You remind me of myself in some ways."

"Do I? In what way?"

"I never speak of this, as it is rather dear to my heart, but I think it is a story you would appreciate." Lady Callister looked away for a moment, her eyes pensive. Miranda was honored that she would want to confide in her, but she could tell the story would cost Lady Callister to tell.

"A long time ago," she began, "I lost a baby. Stillborn."

Miranda's body tensed with the unexpected words.

"It was a long time ago," Lady Callister said. "You need not worry for me. The first few years were the hardest. During this most difficult period of grieving, a tenant gifted me with a blanket."

"A tenant?" Miranda asked, surprised.

"Yes. We moved in different circles, but it did not matter to her. She sympathized with my hurt and simply reached out. The blanket was so lovely in all its simplicity and such a sweet token to remember my baby by. She was the first tenant I connected with, but from that moment on, I began to see them all as real people—equal in their needs and potential in life."

"I am so sorry for your loss," Miranda said, wishing she could say more.

"From my experience, sorrow can only be lessened with time and with love. And that meant me putting my energy into loving someone else. I decided to pass on the kindness and found I enjoyed helping others. Your loss, Miss Bartley, is of a different nature, but nevertheless, it has caused you sorrow. Regardless of your hardships, you have embraced your position as a companion. Your mannerisms are proof of your genteel breeding, as they ever were, but you are not the same Miranda who first came to Sussex."

"I've changed, then?" Miranda asked, hope rising in her chest. She believed she had felt it gradually over the past months, but she dearly wanted someone to confirm it. Despite Miranda's shortcomings, Lady Callister's honest appraisal of her character meant everything to her.

"You still speak rather candidly." Lady Callister's thin mouth pulled into a kind smile. "However, I find I am partial to a riveting conversation."

Miranda's throat lodged with emotion. She had found another person who believed in her as Sarah did. Miranda would do everything she could to be the woman Lady Callister thought her to be. Embracing her role with Lady Callister would be easy to continue, as long as Reverend Giles did not run her from town.

She need only forget Ethan, and she could truly be content.

CHAPTER 26

MIRANDA WOKE AND DID NOT want to leave her bed, still reeling from
Reverend Giles's sermon. Was this how she would wake up every morning
for the rest of her life—alone? She buried her face in her quilt. She wasn't
ill—not truly—but her mind did not know it. She ached to see Ethan—to
fix what she could not. She wanted to be sensible like Lady Callister, but a
penetrating ache of loneliness began to consume her. She thought quickly,
searching for a reason to keep going.

She needed help. Indeed, someone should know how to handle this.

Her father.

What would her father say? He would tell her to walk to the shops and
buy herself something. It had worked marvelously before, but something
told her it would not this time. She burrowed farther under her blanket
and thought about her maid and friend. Sarah would chastise her soundly
and tell her to stop thinking solely of herself. Miranda smiled a bit at that,
but her self-loathing ran deep enough already.

Restlessly, she rolled from her side onto her back. What would her
uncle advise? She had written to him again recently, a silly letter about her
day-to-day activities, but besides the money, she had yet to hear anything.
In this case, the cantankerous man would surely pour her a drink and tell
her to wash down her sorrows.

Ethan?

No, no, she was not to think of him again. Ever.

Lady Callister? Hmm, what would she say? She would pull Miranda
to the window and tell her to open her eyes and see a world of people
full of sorrow and empty dreams. Lady Callister would say, *"Find those
individuals, and mourn with them. Care for them. Serve and love them."*

Miranda did not care to serve anyone just now. It required a heart to serve, and hers was broken.

A soft knock at the door interrupted her melancholy thoughts.

"Come in," Miranda said, not bothering to rise.

A maid entered, holding a missive for her.

Who would write to her? Miranda pulled herself up long enough to take it from her hands.

"Are you well, miss?" the servant asked.

Miranda sighed. "Well enough. Please tell Lady Callister I overslept, but I will be with her shortly." Apparently, Miranda would get up after all. Yes, she would get up and plod through another day. But not yet.

She unfolded the letter, wondering again who would care enough to write to her. She dared hope it was from her father. She ached for his comforting presence.

No. The handwriting was feminine. Miranda's eyes followed the words down to the bottom. Miss Georgina Withers desired a private visit with Miranda.

Miranda groaned. "Can't she let me be miserable without boasting about her engagement and causing me further sorrow?"

Serve her.

What a silly thought. Lady Callister's imagined advice was as practical as it was sensible. But why not? Sure, Miranda wanted to despise the woman, but Miss Withers was too sweet to hate. It would not kill Miranda to be more amiable. Perhaps another effort would purge the immense jealousy she felt. After all, desperation to shed this cloak of heartache called for some sort of action. Then she could finally move forward knowing that Mr. Roderick's future marriage to Miss Withers was meant to be.

With a deep breath, Miranda went to her writing desk and penned a reply. An idea formed in her mind. Nothing big, since that would require more heart than she possessed, but one she would act on.

The next day, Miss Withers arrived at the precise moment she'd agreed to, and the two of them sat down across from each other in the sitting room.

"Tea?" Miranda asked after they finished their initial pleasantries.

"Yes, with sugar and cream, please."

Miranda fixed the drink as Miss Withers helped herself to dessert from the tray.

"I gave your ball gown to the maid when I arrived. I thank you for lending it to me."

"You're welcome," Miranda said, setting the teacup in front of her guest. She doubted the dress was the reason for Miss Withers's visit.

"This lemon shortcake is delicious," Miss Withers said, devouring a slice with a few quick bites. "I hope Lady Callister does not mind if we do not save her any."

Miranda smiled tentatively. "She doesn't know it is being served. I requested it after asking around and learning your preference for lemon."

Miss Withers stared at Miranda with puzzled amazement. "And here I thought my visit might be unwelcome. My many thanks."

Miranda ducked her head to hide her smile but felt the warm pleasure inside that she'd hoped would come. Sarah would be proud—and then she would pinch Miranda's arm and say, *Don't let it go to your head.*

"Will Lady Callister be upset you are missing your Thursday rounds? I hear she is very dedicated to her tenants."

"Her dedication is quite admirable," Miranda said. "While she was curious about why you wanted to meet with me, she did not begrudge me the time. Perhaps she thinks you are a good influence on me."

"Me?" Miss Withers laughed. "Everyone in the neighborhood seems to think me quite an angel."

"Aren't you?" Miranda asked, her tongue a mite loose for good taste.

"That's the point, isn't it? It doesn't matter who I really am, as long as they think I am perfect."

"I see." Miranda eyed her warily.

Miss Withers looked at her teacup. "I refuse to let you be so kind when you and I both know that I have hated you from the moment you arrived."

Miranda's stomach tightened, and she shifted in her seat. This was not the admission she'd expected. The entire neighborhood seemed to be shunning her since Reverend Giles's resounding rejection, so Miranda should hardly be surprised.

"I want you to know," Miss Withers said, "that Mr. Roderick—"

"You are engaged," Miranda finished, trying to hurry along the torture. "I am happy for you."

"We are not engaged," Miss Withers corrected. "Not yet, anyway. But I would like to speak to you about him."

Miranda groaned inwardly. "If you think I am in the way, you are wrong. I want nothing but your happiness together." This was a hard admission but part of embracing her resolute attempt to move forward, accept her role as a companion, and let go of what was not meant to be.

Miss Withers looked up and blinked several times. "I admire your fortitude, but I do wonder at your honesty. Such a passionate declaration cannot be sincere."

Miranda's eyes widened, and she took a long sip of tea.

"I want to marry a man who loves me," Miss Withers said, smoothing her russet curls. "I am still young and fortunate to have my parents' support of my wishes. I only need to know who Mr. Roderick loves."

It was Miranda's turn to stare. She knew what Miss Withers implied. "How could you doubt his affection for you? Everyone can see how well you complement each other."

"Oh, I am aware how well-matched we are," Miss Withers said. "No two personalities and temperaments could be more similar. However, we both like a challenge, which is why I have cause to wonder about you."

"Me?" Miranda set down her empty cup. "I challenge him in the same manner one would ruffle someone's feathers."

"Exactly. I don't ruffle Mr. Roderick at all. Do you not see why this is a concern?"

Miranda didn't understand how frustrating a man could be a good thing. Miss Withers was imagining a nonexistent problem. While Miranda would like to be a contestant to win Ethan over, it was far too late for her. For starters, he was in London, and she was in Sussex. "Mr. Roderick had his chance with me," Miranda said, "and he did not take it. Besides, I am no longer his equal."

Miss Withers set down her teacup too and folded her arms across her chest. "Jane told me about your past. I was predisposed to dislike you after Mrs. Grantham's card party, and maybe that was wrong of me. But I am not wrong to feel threatened by you. I sense you have a hold on Mr. Roderick. And do not tell me it is in my mind."

Miranda shook her head. "Even if he dedicated a small sliver of his heart to me, my circumstances are yet the same." Saying such a personal thought out loud threatened to disrupt Miranda's calm facade.

"It is that sliver I must eradicate," Miss Withers said, smiling sardonically. "I merely want to know what I am up against."

Miranda was disgusted by this conversation. It was hard to remember Miss Withers was a good person and acting only because she felt threatened—a feeling Miranda understood. "I assure you, Mr. Roderick has given me no reason to believe he feels anything for me beyond friendship."

Miss Withers frowned. "Come now, Miss Bartley, you and I are adult enough to know not everything has to be said to be communicated."

Another lemon shortcake was in order. Two slices down at rapid pace, and still Miranda could not choke down this topic of conversation.

"I hoped you would be more forthright, but I sense you are trying to protect yourself with your false assurances." When Miranda didn't answer, Miss Withers set down her teacup. "I should take my leave. You have eaten all the cake."

Miranda grimaced. "Forgive me. I have overindulged."

Miss Withers smirked as if she thought Miranda more odd than funny. "A problem that must run in the family, and one more reason to remember Mr. Roderick deserves better. Trust me when I say it would be wise for you to never think about him again." Neither of them said goodbye. Miranda stood while Miss Withers exited, leaving an unsettled feeling behind her.

Miranda took her seat once more, in utter shock. Miss Withers was not who she had been pretending to be. She was jealous and conniving. Besides that, she gave Miranda reason to hope for Ethan when she should not. She shook her hands, hoping it would relieve her anxiousness. When would Lady Callister return? Miranda walked to the sewing basket and dug out their novel. She thumbed through it, hoping the words would ease the sting from Miss Withers. But instead of seeing the words, she saw Ethan—a glance, a touch of his hand, his rescuing her from Gray House. She tipped her head back against her seat and stared at the ceiling. Did Ethan care, even a little?

How long would it take for Miss Withers to smother every shred of affection Mr. Roderick had for Miranda? *Be content*, she told herself. She adored Lady Callister. This was her place now. Ethan was in London, for heaven's sake. His future did not include her.

Lady Callister finally returned from her visits, looking rather worn out. Her presence snapped Miranda out of her head. She went straight to Lady Callister's side. "It was far too wet to go out today. I should have encouraged you to stay here for morning calls." Miranda rang for some hot tea and helped Lady Callister sit down.

"Before I took you on, Mr. Roderick warned me that you were a spirited girl and not to mind your strong opinions, so it would not have mattered. I would not have listened."

"How do you like that?" Miranda teased. "Mr. Roderick will hear it from me next time I see him." When would that be? April? May? It seemed forever away.

Lady Callister eyed her. "I hope such a meeting will be sooner rather than later." She closed her eyes and leaned her head back against her chair. "I should like to rest a moment before I dress for dinner. Pour me some tea, and then tell me a story from . . . what was that place called . . . Gray House?"

"You do not want to hear about that awful place, I assure you." Miranda's hands, especially her knuckles, ached at the very mention of Gray House. Dreary memories began to spill over into her tremulous presence of mind.

"I want to know more about your past. Please, humor me."

Miranda took her seat beside Lady Callister. Thinking of Gray House might distract her from her current concerns. She thought for a moment about what she could say. "Gray House schooled me in a new way of thinking. So much so that when I saw my reflection, I saw nothing but the loathsome virtues I possessed. I will never go back. I would meet my uncle again, but not there." She smiled as if the gesture lessened the severity of her words. "My maid, Sarah, was my only comfort. She stayed with me until she fell ill and the housekeeper dismissed her."

"I am sorry to hear it," Lady Callister said.

"Thank you. Sarah liked me even though I was quite bossy. I miss her."

"You have a strange talent for endearing people to you," Lady Callister said while pointing a sharp, bony finger her way. "I saw the way you had Captain Grant at your beck and call."

Miranda chuckled and handed Lady Callister her tea, fixed just the way she liked it.

Lady Callister took a sip. "I forgot to ask about your visit with Miss Withers."

Miranda looked down at her lap.

"Not well, then. No matter. I shall be the one to lift your spirits. I have an idea. I think we ought to go to London."

"London?" Miranda almost spilled the hot tea all over her lap. London meant a possibility of seeing Ethan again. "But . . . but you do not enjoy traveling. And you do not care for London. I hardly think—"

"You do hardly think, which is why I must do so for the both of us. We shall leave as soon as I can make arrangements."

Miranda sputtered. "What about the holidays?"

"We will celebrate there. I ought to be with my niece for the Season, and what is a holiday without family?" Lady Callister's lips turned up in a mischievous way. "Might you like to have a dress or two made for the occasion? I do pay you, after all."

"No," Miranda said, hardly processing the sudden change in plans. "I have other hopes for my money, if that pleases you."

Lady Callister looked at her with soft, satisfied eyes. "I am a touch curious about your monetary plans, but I will respect your privacy."

"Thank you." It would be hard to explain the need to save in case her position at Lady Callister's was threatened further. She would do anything to prevent returning to Gray House, even if it meant sacrificing the finery she often longed for. Whether her funds were used for practicality or charity, she was determined to put them to good use. Miranda took a deep breath. "I will accompany you to London, if you do not change your mind before we leave."

"I will not," Lady Callister said with some finality. "And I forbid any ridiculous excuses like those you employ when you do not care to practice the pianoforte."

Miranda bit back a smile. "Yes, Lady Callister."

Lady Callister hurried from the room and left Miranda with waves of emotion—a low tide of hope at seeing Ethan sooner than she'd imagined and a high tide of discouragement that Miss Withers's straight teeth and perfection of character would already have convinced Ethan of his future marital bliss with the woman.

❋

The morning before they were to depart for London, Miranda followed the easy routine established while at Crowfield. She sat down at the pianoforte, and by now, several songs flowed from her fingers without a single wrong note. It was a wonder. All those painful hours of practicing had improved her abilities.

"Pardon me," the butler said from the door, "but Captain Grant is here. He insists on speaking with you."

"At this hour?" Miranda asked. Whatever would he want? She hoped it was not the one thing she feared. "Tell him I will see him in here, and please leave the door open. Then inform Lady Callister of his arrival."

Miranda hadn't seen Captain Grant since the ball. After Ethan had left, the captain had remained by her side, but she had done her best to talk about Jane the entire time. It was, perhaps, too much to hope that he wanted Miranda's advice on how to court Jane.

Captain Grant entered the room and performed a deep bow. His head came up with a smile the size of England.

"Good morning, Miss Bartley. I have never heard such excellent music. You play very well indeed."

Miranda laughed softly, pulling herself to her feet. "I do not play well, but I am improving. Please come in and tell me what is on your mind. You seem much too good-humored for it to be an emergency."

"I am merely congratulating myself because I heard simply by chance that you were leaving town. I was afraid I would miss you. It seems fate has smiled upon me."

Miranda bit her lip. She was easy enough in Captain Grant's company, but whenever he attempted to breach the careful friendship they had established and make it into something more, she found herself searching for an out.

"You came to say goodbye," Miranda said, straightening a pile of music. "That was very kind of you. Please extend our farewells to anyone who asks after us." She knew they would be asking after Lady Callister and not her.

Captain Grant wasted no time in crossing over to her. He stood far too close and pulled her hands away from the music. "Miss Bartley—Miranda, if I may—I cannot let you leave without knowing how I feel. You are lovely beyond comparison. You . . . your heart is good and kind. In fact, to confess it all, I adore everything about you. I would be honored to have you as my wife."

Miranda had waited her whole life to be proposed to. She stared down at his hands grasping hers. She took a shaky breath. She had every reason to accept this man. Any sane woman in her position would do so. But this gesture, as sweet as it was, could not replace the recent memory of Ethan standing just as near to her. Miranda pulled her hands away as gently as possible. "Captain, I am not blind to the attention you have paid me. However . . ."

Captain Grant studied her. "What is it? My situation? My family?"

"No." Miranda could answer honestly there. "You are above reproach. It isn't that. I have loyalties to a friend who cares deeply for you. If you think on our past conversations, surely you will discover whom I speak of."

His frown melted into his crooked smile. "I am flattered"—he studied her for a moment—"but also selfish. I would rather her heart be broken than mine."

"There is more." Miranda fiddled with the music again, hardly believing she was laying her cards on the table like this. She was giving up a proposal to a perfectly good man, which would give her all the security she needed—and she had no guarantees for something better. "My feelings are otherwise engaged."

Captain Grant took a step backward. His mouth worked around as if he could argue with that too. Finally, he sighed. "There were times I wondered why you kept holding back, but then you would do something to encourage me."

Miranda dipped her head. "I am sorry I confused you. I wanted to care for you, but in the end, I cannot be disloyal to my heart. I hope we can still preserve our friendship."

Captain Grant cleared his throat and nodded with reluctance. "I will see myself out. Please make my excuses to Lady Callister."

"I will tell her that you came to say goodbye but were pressed for time." Miranda reached out and touched his arm. "My opinion has little value in this neighborhood, but from me you will hear only praise for you. Thank you for being my friend."

Captain Grant bowed and turned to leave.

Miranda squeezed her eyes shut. Could she not do anything right in her life? The list of people she had hurt seemed only to grow.

CHAPTER 27

LONDON WASN'T THE HOME MIRANDA remembered. No one from her past life wanted to call on her, nor she them. If only she had splurged her careful savings on a few new gowns to boost her confidence. She gazed at the streets of Mayfair through the window of Lady Callister's town house, remembering what had happened that morning. While walking with Lady Callister, one of Miranda's former friends and the lady's mother had given her the cut direct. They had averted their gazes and crossed to the other side of the street with nary a word. This had not come as a great surprise, but it was surely just the beginning of what judgment Miranda would receive from Society. Fortunately, securely tucked inside Lady Callister's London town house, Miranda could pretend all was right in her little world.

"Now that you are here, what do you plan to do about it?" Lady Callister asked.

Miranda dropped the lace curtain and put on a practiced smile. "I plan to be an excellent companion, same as I was in Crowfield. Despite the overwhelming amount of people who live in London, you shall not feel lonely with me by your side."

"How very comforting," Lady Callister said dryly. "What I meant is what do you plan to do about your father?"

"My father?" Miranda asked, her brow furrowing. "I can go by a false name and always keep my face down, if you feel his reputation would bother you."

Lady Callister pinched her lips with annoyance. "I am asking if you mean to visit him."

"In Spain? What an idea." Miranda laughed off the notion.

"Dear girl, you are beginning to worry me. Did you or did you not know your father never left London?"

The blood drained from Miranda's face. She gripped the back of a chair, her legs shaking. She took several deep breaths. "No, that is not possible. That would mean—"

"He is in debtors' prison."

Shock consumed Miranda, and for a moment, she could not even breathe. She raised her eyes to Lady Callister; her words came out in a croak. "Which one?"

"The Marshalsea." Lady Callister whispered the name, and Miranda recoiled.

"Do . . . do you know if he is still alive?" Stories of starvation, beatings, and other horrors followed every prison.

Lady Callister came to her and took her hands. "He yet lives."

"He never wrote to me. If he was here all along, why did he not write?" Miranda tasted her tears before she registered she was crying.

Lady Callister coaxed Miranda into an embrace. "Most men in his position could not write if they wanted to. It takes money to post a letter. You know that."

Miranda had not hugged anyone since Hannah and Sarah. She needed this. Craved it. She breathed in Lady Callister's sweet floral scent, wondering how she could have ever thought it was anything but comforting and perfect. Miranda's tears flowed more freely, and she mourned what this meant for her father . . . what it meant for her.

After a few minutes, Lady Callister pulled back. "There, there. Dry your eyes, and let us make a plan. No good will come of keeping focused on his bleak circumstances."

Miranda pulled out a handkerchief and dabbed at her eyes. She followed Lady Callister to a settee and sat down beside her.

Lady Callister put her hands in her lap. "For a while, he was in the common side, but now he has a private room and is more comfortable."

"How is that possible?" Miranda said, searching Lady Callister's eyes. "He must have a benefactor. He was sure no one would help him."

Lady Callister nodded. "Yes, there is someone helping your father, though I cannot say who. Your concern now is to look to the future."

"I . . . I can try to work off his debts," Miranda said hopefully.

"An admirable desire," Lady Callister said. "I thought you meant to do so when you refused new gowns. Perhaps it would be easier to marry someone with money. You are a beautiful girl, and there are plenty of rich merchants who would not mind your family's history."

Miranda again recoiled, and Lady Callister seemed to make note of her reaction. How could she admit her foolishness? She had just turned down Captain Grant.

"Never mind that just now." Lady Callister put out her hand to calm Miranda. "Would you like to visit him? I know my grand-nephew would take you."

Miranda pushed away her frustration and thought for a moment. "I know it will be hard, but I should like to visit. Who is your grand-nephew? Would he truly step foot in the Marshalsea?"

"Why, Mr. Roderick. Who else do you think I would ask to accompany you?"

Miranda blinked rapidly. Then she jumped to her feet. "Good heavens! You are related to . . . ?" Miranda put her hand over her eyes. "This whole time you have intentionally kept this from me?"

"Initially," Lady Callister said, not looking the least bit guilty. "We did not tell you because Ethan worried you would not accept the position. He said it was difficult to convince you to come to Stonebrook, and you might balk at the idea of further charity." Lady Callister's voice was soft and her words careful. "His sisters agreed to play along and give you time to settle in to your new position. I assumed you had pieced the relationship together naturally, but at times I wondered. You might be angry, and you have every right to be, but I assure you, the intentions were honorable. My grand-nephew worries about me so, and he created a solution that took care of us both."

Miranda folded her arms around herself. "You must both think I am a complete idiot. Does Mr. Roderick also know about my father?"

Lady Callister gave a firm nod. "He has been the means of all of my information."

"And"—Miranda felt hot tears once more on her cheeks—"you let my reputation affect your family. I am so ashamed and . . . and at a complete loss as to what to do."

"We took a risk, plain and simple. However, our decision does not change your situation overmuch," Lady Callister said.

"It does. Can't you see?" Having a father living overseas because of his debts truly could not be as horrible as one locked away as a prisoner. "How could you do this for a complete stranger? I want to thank you and call you a fool at the same time."

Lady Callister firmly grabbed Miranda's hand. "Sit down, and get ahold of yourself. We were responsible for our own choices and made them willingly. It is your turn to make some choices. In order to move on with your life, you must face your past."

"Is this why we came?"

Lady Callister sighed and looked at her lap. "I am an old woman. I have seen lives come into this world and leave it. I have ignored more people and problems than I ought to have. My husband, bless his soul, was not a generous man. After he died, I got to thinking that if I have been blessed more than most, then my money should have an obligation tied to it.

"Ethan helped me invest some of my funds here and there, but I haven't reached out past my own tenants—until I met you. I was given a second chance. You were like clay, and I could mold you into a musical performer, a scriptorian, or anything else I could imagine. And then you surprised me and started to worm your way into my affections. I noticed it first when Captain Grant came to visit, and I was not ready to part with you."

Miranda could not believe her ears. Her tears ceased, and she listened fervently.

"I got into my mind that I could bring you back to London, and with my influence, perhaps we could smooth your reputation. But we must deal with your past first."

This was the opportunity Miranda had hoped and prayed for. A comforting peace settled over her heart. She was no longer facing her future alone. She had Lady Callister—an angel with a halo of soft white hair, a wealth of experience, and a well of strength. With her help, Miranda could face her past.

CHAPTER 28

SEEING ETHAN AGAIN SHOULD NOT have excited her under such abysmal conditions. She was angry at him for the secrets he'd kept from her. And yet, there he stood in front of Lady Callister's open door, in his crisp black overcoat with his adorable, imperfect cravat poking out, and her heart could not be still. She stepped down off the last step of the staircase and waited for him to come in so the footman could shut the door behind him. He didn't move.

"How are you enjoying London?" Ethan asked, his mannerisms anything but easy.

Miranda's nerves were already frayed, but the awkwardness between them only increased her anxiousness. The last time she had seen him, the night of Lady Callister's ball, their parting had left her heartsick. She had thought she would not see him again until the following spring, with his new wife on his arm. She pulled her cloak closer around her, attempting to protect herself from his unnerving presence.

"I could not say I am enjoying London at all," she finally said. "I find I have lost my taste for the place." A drastic understatement, considering her light tone, but Ethan was aware of their destination, so there was no point in expounding.

"I am sorry you had to find out like this." He shifted his feet, further revealing his discomfort.

"Which part? That Lady Callister is your great-aunt or that you knew my father was incarcerated?"

Ethan winced.

Just then, Lady Callister came down behind her. "Why is the door open, Ethan? Never mind. I am ready now, so we can leave." Lady Callister and her maid were to accompany them to the Marshalsea but would wait in the carriage while Ethan and Miranda went inside.

Ethan held his arm out to his great-aunt, and Miranda did her best to dismiss her annoyance as she followed them. She had to prepare herself to meet her father in a place she never imagined she would ever go. Once inside the carriage, she turned her body so she might keep her gaze out the window. Silence permeated the enclosed space.

There must have been a reason to keep the criminals in the front eye of the public. Why else would the hub of England, even Buckingham Palace, be surrounded by prisons like Newgate, Fleet, King's Bench, and the Marshalsea? Miranda had frequented Thames Street often enough for the theater and musical halls. But across the London Bridge lay a community of prisoners bound by their debts. No one glanced their way unless they knew someone there, and even then, they stole only glimpses when no one was looking.

Lady Callister broke the silence. "Do not bring any money inside. The destitute can sniff out even a farthing."

Miranda nodded. She stole a glance at Ethan, but their bouncing view captured his full attention. She dreaded his company at such a humiliating time, but she craved his comforting presence too. He must have sensed her gaze. He looked over at her for a moment and gave her a grim nod.

She turned away just as the carriage pulled to a stop. Ethan alighted first, then put out his hand for her. She took it, and immediately her attention was drawn to the brick wall of their destination and the locked gate that separated her from her father. What condition he was in she knew not.

"I will be right here when you are finished," Lady Callister said encouragingly through the carriage window.

Ethan held out his arm, and Miranda took it, allowing him to lead the way to the gate. "I have arranged with the warden for us to see your father in his room." He lifted his hand and rapped the knocker against the wood.

A man's face appeared behind the grate in the door and asked their names and business. Ethan explained who they were, and the man swung the door open for them. Miranda wanted to shrink back, but one look at Ethan gave her the courage to step into the dark forecourt.

The turnkey led them a few paces into the courtyard, and the light gave Miranda a better look at him. His body was stooped like that of an older man, but his face was as young as Ethan's. His attire was equally contradicting, with his tailored clothes and grimy ungloved hands. The turnkey flicked his gaze to her, and she drew back. His beady eyes roved over the whole of her. He licked his lips and sneered. When her eyes widened with disgust, the turnkey laughed.

Ethan put himself between her and the warden and glared at him. "We don't want any trouble."

"Don't go makin' Mr. Blackett angry, then," the man said, pointing to himself.

"Arrogant lout," Ethan grumbled as soon as Mr. Blackett turned to lead them down a narrow, elongated courtyard. Ethan looked at Miranda, and his expression turned sheepish. "My apologies. This place is not fit for a lady."

It wasn't fit for her father, either. They followed the turnkey across the colorless strip of dead grass, which was contrasted by a lonely blue pail that lay on its side next to a water pump. A line of snow along the wall was the only sign that winter had touched the already-barren place. Miranda heard a child crying and several laughing and could make no sense of either since the voices came from inside the three-story brick barracks. A few men circled up alongside the first barrack were quietly talking amongst themselves. They looked over at Miranda and Ethan, and silence fell between them. She was sure their curiosity could not match her unease.

The warden brought them to the second of what seemed to be eight barracks clumped together. An entire neighborhood of people was locked away from the world, and Miranda had never thought twice about it. Each barrack had several rooms and outer doors.

The turnkey stopped in front of the last wooden door on the first floor and rapped twice before swinging it open. "Looks like yer both lucky to be on the king's side today. But warn yer friend to pay his fees, or he'll be rotting in the common side without any bread for his mouth."

Miranda squeezed Ethan's arm. She might be angry and confused by her escort, but the turnkey's words and odious presence allowed her to temporarily forgive Ethan. He put his hand over hers, which only made the warden laugh again. He stalked away from them, his cackle echoing through the courtyard like that of a crazed animal. Ethan looked down at her and gave her a vacillating smile before helping her down two steps into a small room with a single window.

Miranda's father was standing by a table with a plate of exactly three scones and a pitcher of water. He looked well enough—a mite thinner, with all gray hair instead of the mostly black she was used to. He wore no overcoat, though his room was as cold as the weather outside, and no fire burned behind the grate.

"Father," Miranda whispered, letting go of Ethan's arm. She hurried to her father and threw her arms around him. This was the man who had comforted her all her life and made her feel like a queen.

He squeezed her tightly against him. "My girl. My beautiful, darling girl."

Miranda pulled back and wiped at her streaming tears. "I would have come sooner, but I thought you were in Spain."

"Spain," he said with a laugh. "My driver turned me in for a reward no doubt greater than my debt. If I ever see the scoundrel again, I will—"

Ethan cleared his throat.

Her father looked up and sighed. "Ah, Mr. Roderick. Thank you for bringing my daughter to see me. Or perhaps I should not thank you. You should have had the sense to keep her far away from here."

Miranda put her hand on her father's arm. "Mr. Roderick brought me as a kindness to my employer."

"Employer?" Mr. Bartley swore. "You were supposed to be at my brother's."

"Your brother's house is a prison under a different name," Miranda said, wishing Ethan would step out so she could speak frankly. "I am a companion to Lady Callister, and I assure you, it is an extremely respectable position."

Her father shook his head. "I have brought ruin to the both of us. And I am sorry for my brother and his behavior. He is blinded with hate, but I never thought his feelings would extend to you."

"Why does he despise us so?" Miranda longed to know the reason behind it.

"A story best left for another time, my sweet."

Miranda recognized the patronizing tone as one that meant she was too young to be privy to such information. She was not the naive daughter she once had been. "Very well. What can I do to bring you greater comfort? Bring blankets? Food?"

"I have friends who have sponsored my rooms, though they wish to remain anonymous. Do you know who they are?"

Miranda shook her head. She had wondered if it was Lady Callister. "No, but I will repay them when I can. I do not earn much, but—"

"No, no, no," Mr. Bartley said. "I can handle myself well enough here. This never would have happened if I had regulated my spending over the years, though I still blame that infernal volcano." Her father shrugged. "Just take care of yourself."

"I will."

"Good. Now, understand this. You must not visit again. Tell your friends I am dead, and live your life."

Friends? Besides Lady Callister, she really had no one. Even as she thought it, she wondered if she could count Ethan. He had done so much for her, and yet, he was a man who intended to marry someone else.

"Father," Miranda argued, "I will do no such thing. I can't abandon you. We should be together." She didn't want to live in such a place, with the vile warden and the way the tight walls seemed to close in on them, but it made sense it should be that way. She had learned that when all else was lost, family was the only thing that remained. "I will come live with you here."

"Never." Her father balked.

"No," Ethan added at the same time.

She turned to see Ethan's features tight.

Her father grabbed her hand. "You must not even visit."

Miranda wanted to argue, but perhaps with time, he would feel otherwise.

"I know it is hard to understand," her father said, "but it must be so."

"Then, I will write as often as I can." Miranda clasped her hands in front of her.

Her father pulled her into a tight embrace. "I . . . I love you."

Miranda had never heard those words spoken to her before, and tears flowed freely down her face. "I know, Father." She would never doubt his love again.

She said goodbye and promised again to write often. She couldn't bring herself to say anything to Ethan as they walked back to the carriage. The ride to Lady Callister's town house was quiet. Both Ethan and Lady Callister seemed to sense her need for a period of reflection. Thoughts of her father and his situation mulled about in her head, and she ached for him.

Lady Callister invited Ethan in for tea once they arrived home again. Miranda's trance broke, and she once again became extremely aware of his presence.

"I will not intrude any longer. Miss Bartley must be exhausted." Ethan glanced at her with quiet affection in his eyes and turned back to his great-aunt. "My mother expressed her eagerness to visit me, and I should be home when she arrives."

Lady Callister nodded. "Tell your mother and the family to call on us tomorrow for tea."

"I will tell them," Ethan said, clasping his hands in front of him.

Miranda resisted the urge to beg him to stay. She wanted him to coax her to talk about everything. Tomorrow there would be absolutely no privacy. And worst of all, Lady Gibson would be seeing her for the first time in reduced circumstances. Amongst all the troubles that weighed on Miranda, she worried Miss Withers was scheming something.

Lady Callister smiled. "If I am going to be in London, I hope to see my family regularly. Unless your father comes and is in one of his self-aggrandizing moods, which he often is. Thank goodness Parliament will be in session soon."

Ethan chuckled and inclined his head to say goodbye. He gathered his cloak and hat while Lady Callister tottered off to the drawing room. Miranda stood frozen. She wanted him to stay but had no reason to keep him here.

The butler opened the door for Ethan, and Miranda's reason fled. "Wait."

Ethan turned, surprised.

She should apologize for her hurtful words and her anger, but she couldn't bring herself to discuss another failure of her character, so she quietly said, "Thank you."

Ethan's lips pulled upward, but there was a crease in his brow. "First time visiting debtors' prison, though I'm sorry you had to experience it." He sighed. "Sort of thrilling once you got past the ridiculous turnkey."

Miranda appreciated his effort to add levity and pursed her lips to keep from smiling. "You were very brave. You should reward yourself with chocolate when you get home."

Ethan gave a flourishing bow—one she knew he would never perform in public. A small smile tugged at her lips as she watched him take his leave. She traced her steps to the drawing room, where Lady Callister patiently sat, no doubt eager to hear every detail. A small sigh slipped past Miranda's lips. Unrequited love was an altogether different sort of prison—one she was sure to be locked in for the duration of her life.

CHAPTER 29

AN HOUR BEFORE CALLING HOURS began, Miranda sat in her room, staring at the banknotes on her lap. Again, her uncle had sent money, and without a single word of explanation. Pleased he was thinking of her, she tucked the notes away in her reticule and went back to the drawing room to work on her embroidery. Once she was settled, there was a knock at Lady Callister's front door. Miranda instantly concluded it was Ethan and tossed aside her needlework. She realized how foolish it would be to hurry to greet him, but the butler pulled the door open before she could retreat.

It was not Ethan. The face on the other side made Miranda gasp.

"Sarah!" Miranda flew past the butler and nearly knocked Sarah down the steps with her embrace.

"Oof! Miss, I can hardly breathe!"

Miranda pulled back to see Sarah's dancing eyes. "Come inside, where it is warm, and we can talk."

"I know it isn't proper-like to visit you at the front door, but I went to the servants' entrance, and they thought me ridiculous for requesting to see you."

Miranda pulled her inside the entry hall, and the butler excused himself so they could talk freely. "I am sorry you were not well-received by the servants. There are already rumors about me that have no doubt reached their ears. Is that how you found me?"

Sarah nodded. "As soon as I heard a Miss Bartley was in Town, I could not believe it. I knew it had to be you."

"It was all Mr. Roderick," Miranda explained. She was excited to finally tell someone she trusted and knew could understand. "He insisted I let him help me find a position. With his assistance, Lady Callister graciously took me in as her companion."

"That's wonderful, miss."

"Yes, and my uncle has sent me money twice now, though he communicates nothing. I have taken to writing him letters. I tell him random bits of things about myself that I am sure he does not care to read. I even had the audacity to tell him to find a hobby to improve his spirits. I said if I could play the pianoforte, then he could do just about anything. I hope he considers redecorating, but I will save that suggestion for a future communication so I do not overwhelm him with the idea."

Sarah giggled and then sobered. "Anything is better than the drink."

"Agreed," Miranda said. "Enough about me. Please, tell me how you have gotten along."

"I work for a newly married Mrs. Keene, and she never says please either." Sarah winked at her, and they both laughed. "Your recommendation was better than gold with everyone I applied to. Apparently, I'm a sight better at fashion than you gave me credit for."

"I do not doubt it," Miranda said, knowing in the past that she had credited her own expertise more often than was likely true. "I was wrong about a great deal of things, of which you are already well aware." She had once yearned to return to her old self, but not anymore. She loathed the idea. As uncertain as her future was, she was happier with herself. Miranda glanced back at the door behind her. "Will you come in and meet Lady Callister?"

"It isn't my place, miss. I've used up all my bravery today, I'm afraid."

"She is like the mother I never knew. Please, indulge me." Miranda pulled Sarah inside, despite her many arguments, and toward the drawing room. Lady Callister was napping in her chair, but her eyes fluttered open with the commotion. "Lady Callister, you must meet my dearest friend, Sarah. She was the maid who followed me to Gray House and cared for me."

Sarah kept her eyes down like a well-trained servant and dipped into a curtsy. "How do you do, Your Ladyship?"

Lady Callister's nearly absent brows shot upward. "And why do we have the honor of receiving you this morning and in my drawing room?"

"I insisted," Miranda said without an ounce of regret.

"You would," Lady Callister answered. She eyed Sarah. "Where do you work now?"

"I am the lady's maid to Mrs. Keene."

"What sort of employer is she?"

"She treats me well enough," Sarah said.

Lady Callister narrowed her eyes. "Does she pay you well enough?"

"Yes, Your Ladyship."

Miranda reached over and squeezed Sarah's hand. "Can I see you again? Perhaps I can meet you for a walk in the park."

"I should like that very much. There is something I dearly need to speak to you about. Can you meet me the day after tomorrow, say after luncheon?"

Miranda turned to Lady Callister with a request for permission on the edge of her lips.

"Most companions have afternoons or Sundays off," she said before Miranda could speak. "You have never asked for either. I should think a walk and the use of my carriage a perfectly acceptable arrangement."

Renewed appreciation for her employer filled Miranda. She saw Sarah out and returned to the drawing room. Ethan's family arrived a few moments later—without Ethan.

Miranda refused to be disappointed after seeing Sarah again, but it was hard to lie to herself. She curtsied deeply to Lord and Lady Gibson, Jane, and Hannah.

Lady Gibson started to smile at her but quickly cast her gaze down. Miranda did not blame her. She knew Lady Gibson had high expectations for her son's marriage, and even if she cared for Miranda, the situation necessitated that her loyalty remain with her son.

Hannah immediately crossed to Miranda and took her hands. "I am so glad you have come to London."

"Hannah," Lord Gibson censured. "Please sit down and compose yourself."

Hannah gave Miranda a look of apology. She found a seat next to Jane, who seemed rather quiet and avoided her gaze. Miranda hated the tension her own presence brought to the room. She wanted to greet Lady Gibson as warmly as Hannah had her, but it was not to be. She took a seat near Lady Callister and averted her eyes from the company.

"Are you well, Aunt?" Lord Gibson asked Lady Callister.

"I am well enough. Thank you, Charles."

"And Miss Bartley?" Lord Gibson asked. She looked up to see his dark, discerning eyes pinning her to her seat.

Miranda always felt like Ethan had received the best qualities of both of his parents. However, both Lord and Lady Gibson could be quite intimidating. Their lack of smiles and Lord Gibson's expression of annoyance made Miranda squirm.

"My health is excellent, thank you. And your family?"

"Tolerable," Lord Gibson answered. "My gout is much improved since Bath."

"Hannah is preparing to take her bows," Lady Gibson said rather proudly. She spoke to Lady Callister, though, as if Miranda were not even there. "We are all happy for such an occasion. And Jane's prospects are most excellent. She has already entertained several gentleman callers since our arrival." Jane beamed, and poor Hannah's gaze remained in her lap.

"Very good," Lady Callister answered. "And what of my nephew?"

"Ethan?" Lady Gibson asked, hardly surprised. "Why, we all know he is to marry Miss Withers."

"Have they announced their engagement?" Lady Callister sounded almost skeptical.

"Not exactly, but these things take time."

Lady Callister frowned. "My nephew is not one to take his time. He is punctual in every aspect of his life. Is something amiss?"

What was Lady Callister hinting at? Miranda would dearly like to know.

Lady Gibson gave her husband a pointed look. "He is preoccupied, to be sure. In fact, more than a week ago, I heard tell he rescued another stray boy. I do not know the details, but his cause is always worthy."

"Worthy?" Lord Gibson said with raised brows. "The boy has too much heart and not enough backbone. He'll learn the hard way like the rest of us."

Lady Gibson gave him a patronizing nod. "Mark my words, he has a good head on his shoulders and will not disappoint us where Miss Withers is concerned."

Miranda wanted to defend Ethan's nature, but her desire to excuse herself was stronger. There was only one door, and it was located behind Lord Gibson. There was no way to leave the room without drawing unnecessary attention her way. However, if she stayed in her seat, any more discussion about Miss Withers and Ethan would make her ill.

"It is Ethan we are discussing," Jane interjected. "He considers himself a moral giant among men. He will do exactly as he pleases and will rationalize it in a way that makes us feel apologetic for being contrary."

"We will simply have to remove any distractions he has." Lord Gibson briefly glanced at Miranda. "I do not have time to lecture him."

They must not have been informed of her visit to Stonebrook until recently. They seemed quite put out toward her. She wanted to laugh off Lord Gibson's comment and explain that there was no way she would ever induce Ethan to marry her now. Their worry was needless.

"Lady Callister," Lady Gibson began. "We know you care for Ethan's happiness. You will help us?" Everyone, including Miranda, took her meaning.

Lady Callister frowned. "Your son has extended every kindness to me. I shall do what is in his best interest."

"Good, and we all agree what that is." Lady Gibson cleared her throat. There was a glimmer of remorse in her pronouncement, but it did not change Miranda's awkward position. Lady Gibson motioned for her daughters to stand. "Come, girls, we have several important visits to make this morning, and your father has business he must attend to. Thank you, Lady Callister, for the tea."

The tea service had arrived only a few moments before, and not a single drop had been served. Jane stood but was the last to leave. She turned toward Miranda, her expression full of regret. She seemed to want to say something, but her mother said her name, and Jane turned away and departed. Was Jane sorry for the way her family had treated Miranda? No, that could not be. Still, the sad look in Jane's eyes nagged Miranda. The family left, but the heaviness of the situation did not. Miranda poured Lady Callister a cup.

"Is it time for me to seek different employment? It seems I make all of your acquaintances, including your own family, uncomfortable."

Lady Callister stared at her tea, deep in thought. "It was only a matter of time before they learned about your stay at Stonebrook. I am going to request Jane's company tomorrow, and all will be put to right soon enough."

Miranda's eyes widened. "Jane?"

Lady Callister nodded slowly. "When you return from visiting Sarah tomorrow, Jane shall be here. Bring me my lap tray and writing things. Lady Gibson will not refuse me."

The solution was unclear to Miranda. Jane despised her. The entire family was agitated with Miranda's presence. She could not keep relying on Lady Callister's generosity and burdening her relations. The time had come to make a plan of her own.

✳

Arm in arm, Miranda and Sarah walked around Hyde Park. The morning riding hours were over, and the fashionable time for carriage rides was not for a few hours more. That meant Miranda could actually relax and enjoy herself away from the prying eyes of the *haut ton*.

"You said you wanted to tell me something," she coaxed.

"Yes," Sarah said, pulling Miranda to a stop. "I am afraid it is bad news."

Miranda put her hand to her throat. "My father?"

Sarah shook her head. "No, but I did hear he was at the Marshalsea."

"I just discovered it myself." Miranda sighed and let her head fall forward.

Sarah gently squeezed Miranda's arm. "There is no good time to tell you, but there are some who find exploiting others a sport."

"You mean someone is exploiting *me*?"

"Your family," Sarah said. "I was growing suspicious of Mrs. Keene, but now I have no question in my mind. You see, I have a letter in my possession to be printed in the Society papers. When I attempted to refuse, I was told to deliver it at the risk of termination."

"What sort of letter is this?" Miranda's eyebrows drew together.

Sarah seemed to weigh her words. "Mrs. Keene asked me several questions about you during my initial interview. I thought nothing of it at the time. She continued to press me here and there for more details, and I started to worry. I wanted to talk to you before, but it's worse now. Last night, a Miss Withers came to see Mrs. Keene. The name seemed familiar, so I started asking questions amongst the servants. It was then that I learned Mrs. Keene's maiden name is Karlson. They are the two women from the card party you spoke of. None of the servants overheard their conversation, but the result was a slanderous letter."

"But why?" Miranda wrung her hands. "Miss Withers does not care for me, but why would she resort to such ruthless tactics?"

"Whether Miss Withers wanted to do it or not, the former Miss Karlson has a mind of her own. She is loyal to her friend and fiercely determined. She is not as well-connected as you once were, but her new husband is a wealthy man, and he has influence enough. It seems you have made an enemy of her." Sarah blew out her breath. "What am I to do?"

Miranda had to think before she could answer. Her reputation was already fragile, but this letter would throw poor Lady Callister into further gossip. How on earth would Miranda find another position after this was printed? "We need to discuss this with Lady Callister. She deserves to have a say since she insists on keeping me as her companion."

Sarah chewed on her lip.

"Do not fret," Miranda said. "Your friendship means more to me than this letter."

Sarah shook her head. "Wait until you read it."

"Then, we must go to Lady Callister directly," Miranda said, taking a deep breath to steady herself. "This needs to be resolved before you return home."

Sarah agreed, and they took the carriage back to Lady Callister's town house, where they saw a second carriage waiting. When they stepped out, they could see the Gibson family crest emblazed on the door. Jane had arrived. Miranda's heart tugged inside her as she remembered the last time she had seen Jane and the softer side she had glimpsed.

Sarah pulled out her coin purse and loosened the ties. "I suppose I should show you this before Lady Callister sees it." She removed the folded letter and handed it to Miranda.

Miranda unfolded the paper. She skimmed the beginning, then stopped. "'At the Marshalsea, rotting in his debts'—what a horrible thing to say!"

"There is more," Sarah said.

Miranda read on, and her eyebrows rose higher with every line. "She says here that I have leeched myself on to Lady Callister and have my eyes on Mr. Roderick and every other wealthy man in Town." Miranda gasped. "I care not for my father's well-being but only for my own. The entire time he has been incarcerated, I have not written or visited once." Miranda lifted her gaze to meet Sarah's. "But I just learned he was there, and I visited him the first opportunity I had."

Sarah's eyes filled with tears. "I don't know where she gets her information. I swear I said very little about you. I am ashamed for my part in all this."

"Miss Withers could have supplied most of the ammunition, especially if Jane confided in her about my father. Do not blame yourself!" Miranda pulled Sarah in for a tight hug. As she did, a sharp wind snatched the letter from her hand. Miranda gasped. "Quick! No one else must see this." The letter danced across first cobblestone, then grass. The wind picked up again, and the letter flew high into the air and right into a pocket between two branches, high up in a tree.

"Dash it all!" Miranda cried.

"Well, one of us must climb this tree. We cannot risk that letter getting into anyone else's hands," Sarah said.

The door of Lady Callister's town house opened, and the two women turned to see Ethan's amused expression, his arms folded across his chest. "Bird-watching?"

Sarah looked to Miranda for help.

"Oh, good day to you." Miranda quickly curtsied, taken off guard. "I did not know you were with Jane."

"I was with my parents and offered to drop Jane by on my way to purchase a few things. What is it you keep staring at?"

"'Tis nothing, Mr. Roderick," Sarah said, her eyes gleaming with fear.

Ethan looked up at the tree. "Is that paper?"

"Yes, and it is very important we retrieve it." Miranda rubbed her forehead.

Ethan stripped off his greatcoat, and Miranda caught it when he tossed it to her. "Very well."

"No," she said. "Absolutely not. I perfectly remember the last time you climbed a tree."

Ethan scowled. "It seems we have had a role reversal. You suddenly care, and I do not." He unpinned his shirt sleeves and rolled them up above his elbows, exposing his muscular forearms. "Stand back, ladies." Miranda had a hard time not staring. "I will have that paper back to you before you can sneeze."

"Only because neither of us feels like sneezing," Sarah whispered to Miranda. They watched Ethan jump and grab the lowest branch. She continued in hushed tones. "Have you considered what you are going to do if he reads the letter? The part about your scheming to win him?"

Miranda shivered. "It is not too far from the truth."

Ethan managed to pull himself up on the branch without the awkwardness of the last time he climbed a tree. Once up, he maneuvered his way close enough to snatch the letter. Then he lowered himself down and dropped to the ground. He bowed and ceremoniously handed the letter to Miranda. The sight nearly made her swoon.

Sarah snatched the paper for Miranda, and Ethan looked at her in surprise.

"You must have been practicing your tree-climbing skills." Miranda pushed her bonnet back and smiled. "I thank you kindly for your help."

"It was nothing." Ethan unrolled his shirtsleeves. "Physical exertion has become part of my daily routine."

Miranda bit her lip to keep from grinning like a ninny. "Well, we have benefitted from your efforts today."

Ethan motioned to the letter. "Important, is it?" When Miranda nodded, Ethan's eyes narrowed, his curiosity obvious.

The door opened again, and this time Jane came outside. "I wondered where everyone had gone. Lady Callister saw you out the window talking and insisted you all come in for tea."

Ethan offered Miranda his arm, his brows raised in question.

Miranda gave a slight shake of her head. "Please, go inside without me. I will be in shortly." Ethan did as she said and retreated inside. Miranda turned back to Sarah. "Take heart. I won't let you lose your position over this."

Sarah played with the strings on her worn purse. "I can find another position. My concern is for you, miss. This letter will sever what is left of your good name. We must take it seriously."

"I understand all too well. When Lady Gibson called here the other day, I never thought she could be so cold toward me. Now I wonder if Miss Withers revealed everything to her too. If Lady Gibson could turn me away, I haven't a chance anywhere." Miranda wrung her hands. "Lady Callister will know how best to handle this. Wait in the vestibule while I speak to her, and then I will return to you."

Once in the town house, Miranda went and stood at the threshold of the drawing room. "Lady Callister? Might I speak to you privately for just a moment?"

With a curious expression, Lady Callister came without delay, leaving Jane and Ethan in the drawing room. Once she stepped out, Miranda shut the doors. "Forgive me. It is very important, or I would not have taken you away from your guests." Miranda handed Lady Callister the letter.

Lady Callister held it away from her eyes so she might see it better since she did not have her reading spectacles nearby. She read quietly for a moment, her mouth pinched together. "Utterly disgraceful." She returned the letter. "We must burn it." She crossed the corridor to a smallish library, and Miranda watched through the open door as Lady Callister tossed the letter into the fire. The flames made short work of the paper as Lady Callister returned to Miranda's side. "Sarah will gather her things, and I will employ her. I shall ask Jane to speak to Miss Withers about this so we do not see a repeat offense from her or this Mrs. Keene."

"I would love to have Sarah here—thank you! But Jane? Surely we can think of a different solution." Miranda blinked her eyes rapidly. "She would not like to be asked to do a favor on my behalf."

Lady Callister nodded. "We came to an understanding this afternoon. Have you never wondered why Jane would not say a thing against you to anyone else? Not even to her own mother? Think on that, and do not concern yourself over this letter for another moment."

Miranda shook off her thoughts of Jane. She was more concerned than ever about Lady Callister employing her. "Surely you must see why I need to leave here."

Lady Callister shook her head. "Promise me you will not do anything hasty. Everything will right itself soon enough."

Miranda's confusion heightened. "You are up to something. You had that guarded look every time you tried to keep Captain Grant away."

Lady Callister beamed. "You are catching on. Well done."

"Those gothic novels are a bad influence on you. I have not the faintest idea what you are thinking, but I know you are capable of imagining something terrific."

"Not just imagine," she whispered. "I follow through." Lady Callister opened the door to the drawing room again.

Miranda hurried back to Sarah in the vestibule. "All is in order." Those four words were all she managed to get out before Ethan walked out of the drawing room toward them. Her stomach flipped. Curse her weakness where this man was concerned.

"Is everything all right?"

Miranda nodded.

"I'm relieved to hear it. Lady Callister wanted to speak with Jane privately," Ethan said, putting his hands behind his back. "She should be but a moment; then we must take our leave. Might I offer our carriage to take your maid home?"

"Thank you, no." Miranda smiled at him, her heartbeat picking up pace. He was always so thoughtful. "Lady Callister is arranging for a carriage to be prepared for Sarah." She turned to Sarah. "You are to gather your things and come and live here with us."

Sarah clasped her hand. "Gladly." She eyed first Miranda, then Ethan. "I shall wait in the garden." She stepped outside, leaving them alone. Miranda called for a footman to ready the carriage for Sarah and then turned to face Ethan.

❋

Ethan had been anxious to be near Miranda, especially after the hard night he had endured. He had gone to meet with Miss Withers, and it had not ended well. She had asked him directly if he still had feelings for Miranda. Ethan had not been able to deny it. He'd apologized for his weakness and offered for her with a promise to stay faithful.

Disgusted that he had toyed with her affections while being devoted to another, she'd stomped her foot and behaved in a very surprising manner. She'd agreed to marry him on the condition that Miranda would leave Lady Callister's employ. But when something slipped about a plan to see Miranda leave London as well, Ethan refused to indulge her. They were at an impasse and had finally agreed to mutually end their courtship. Ultimately, by being honest about his true feelings, he'd ruined a chance at a decent match all for a woman he might never have. But he did not regret it.

Then Jane had given him an earful on their way to Lady Callister's town house, burdening him with her story. Apparently, Miss Withers had made the rounds after he had left her, letting Jane know exactly how she felt about him. The two had developed quite a friendship since Miss Withers's arrival as their neighbor, and Jane had been deeply offended by the row. Unlike when things had ended between him and Miss Bartley, Jane had chosen *his* side, not her friend's.

He was a free man, so why didn't he feel free? He wanted to rush to Miranda and beg her to consider him again, but the letter in the tree confused him. Had it been from Captain Grant? What if he had proposed? Could Ethan endure the torture of watching them begin a life together?

Light spilled into the corridor through a window over the front door, enshrouding Miranda in a sort of halo. If it was so wrong for him to be with Miranda, why did it *feel* right? A sort of thrill stole through him. The memories of Miranda had been working in his heart, trying to speak to him, to explain what his mind couldn't understand. Even if he could not see a way to make things work between them, it did not mean it was impossible. If it was right, they would find a way.

They could start over.

But first, he had to know if she would even give him a chance. He needed to know if she was still angry with him for his secrets and if she loved Captain Grant. A memory came to his mind, giving him an idea of a way to test her. He set his jaw, determined to breach her defenses.

"Do you remember the second time we met?" Just thinking about it gave him courage to step closer to her.

She didn't look at him, but a glimmer of recognition touched her face. Her head bent his way, and she adopted a bland expression. "Not very well, no."

Why wasn't she smiling? She must still hate him. "It was a memorable moment. *I* have not forgotten it."

Her eyes took on a challenging glint when she met his gaze head-on. "I haven't the slightest notion what you could be talking about."

Now she was practically goading him. She was too serious to be the Miranda he knew. He stepped closer to her until he was an arm's length away. "I had hoped to see you again after our time together at the modiste's shop, but this meeting was unexpected. I can still vividly recall the rather high-pitched opera singer at the musicale." He could see her demeanor cracking. "I fled the room only to find you dancing around the corridor."

"I wasn't dancing!" She folded her arms across her chest. "Why would I be dancing in the corridor, where anyone could happen upon me?"

He saw a little twinkle in her eye and called her bluff. "Such a dance I had never seen before. I recall some jumping and spinning too."

"Oh, please." Her mouth twitched.

He could smell her vanilla and lavender scent, and his heart raced. "What was I supposed to think with such a scene before me? Your hand was up fanning your face and your eye winking."

"I was never so saucy."

"Ridiculously so." His own grin spread across his face. He rested an arm over her shoulder against the door and leaned closer to see if she would crack. Another push would get her there—or so he hoped.

"You know I was not dancing but was in desperate need of assistance. Are you saying you helped me that day because I enticed you? You could not help yourself. You—the epitome of a gentleman."

"I had no idea you thought so well of me." Ethan relished her nearness, now that he had no inhibitions about it. He needed to know how she felt. "But as I recall, I was going to pass by, but you threw yourself at me."

Finally, a laugh burst from her mouth. "Your memory is faulty, sir. I might play coy at times, but I am completely without guile in this. I had an eyelash caught in my eye—*not* a scheming plan to catch a suitor. Besides, I did not know you from Adam."

"Are you sure you did not recognize me? I knew you instantly."

"My vision was quite affected."

Ethan chuckled. "You must have sensed my trustworthy nature. You clearly needed my help that day, and yet you wouldn't even let me look at your eye."

"The eye is a sensitive organ."

Sensitive but profound. Hers seemed to be drawing him ever closer. He was mere inches from her. Was he testing her or his own willpower? "I was this close and you couldn't handle yourself in my presence. Your heart was palpitating."

"Blinking rapidly is not a sign of palpitations." Her lips spread into a beautiful smile.

He lowered his voice. "You had gooseflesh up and down your arms. Isn't that sign enough?"

Suppressing a laugh, she lifted her hand and put it around the back of his neck just above his cravat, bringing a shiver to his skin. "You had your hand at the nape of my neck, and I was ticklish there. You deliberately left it there to torture me."

And now she surely meant to torture him. "You started wiggling about"—he leaned another inch closer, her scent nearly undoing him—"and at the same time, you were begging for assistance." Assistance he had willingly given and wanted to vow to continue.

"Mr. Roderick," she breathed, relaxing her back against the door. "I have never known you to twist a falsehood."

Ethan grinned and studied her. Did she want him as he did her? Her eyes gleamed with a hint of laughter, making the blue even brighter than normal. Lands, she was beautiful.

Full lips too.

He glanced back up, and her eyes were half-lidded. She met his gaze with a question in her eyes. One he finally knew the answer to. But what of *her* answer? If he kissed her, would she accept it? He had put her through so much, and his own soul was in turmoil.

The drawing room door opened. Ethan was not a cursing man, but his frustration was on the tip of his tongue. For a moment, he did not move. If eyes could speak, surely hers would tell him everything, and he could be satisfied. When he doubted what he saw, he reluctantly stepped away, coughing into his hand. Finally, he looked over to see Jane step out, her gaze on the floor.

"I hope you don't hold my slight exaggeration about your behavior against me," Ethan whispered to Miranda, his smile widening—whether from the memory or the excitement of the moment, he could not say.

"I am glad we can laugh together again." Her smile appeared. She did not hate him. But would she if he dared to press his suit again? Would she accept a proposal from Captain Grant before Ethan could come up with a plan?

Ethan pushed back his tailcoat and put his hand on his hip. "Good. Well, I really was on my way out." He cleared his throat and reached for the door, a lifeline for his racing heart.

Miranda dipped into a curtsy. Her easy smile slipped away and was replaced by the careful, guarded one she had worn before his teasing.

He left before he could get ahead of himself. It was one thing to want a woman. It was another to convince one's parents to accept her.

❅

Miranda could not regret the moment between her and Ethan. She should hate herself for being so weak. Instead, if he married Miss Withers tomorrow, she would now have this feeling stirring within her to treasure. She met Jane's sad eyes, but Miranda's thoughts were still on Ethan. Why had such a good man crossed paths with her in the first place, if not to stay? She blinked and focused in on Jane. And why did she have to be at odds with her dearest friend?

Jane stopped short when she reached Miranda. "I am sorry I said those hurtful things at Crowfield about you and Captain Grant."

Miranda blinked, surprised by the unexpected apology. "I tried many times to turn his attention toward you, but I made a mess of it. I am sorry too."

Jane played with her reticule. "I saw the way you avoided him at the ball and arranged the dance with Hannah. I should've thanked you that night."

"Do not think of it again. I wish there were more I could do to make amends," Miranda said.

Jane nodded. She gave Miranda a half smile and said goodbye. The soft shut of the door seemed to awaken Miranda from a sort of haze. She put her hand over her chest. What a day! She slipped back into the drawing room to find Lady Callister looking a picture of calm.

"What on earth did you say to Jane? She apologized to me."

Lady Callister picked up her teacup. "She saw the light all on her own. Do you remember at Crowfield when you and Jane took a walk and had a little row?"

"Yes."

"Through her tears, Jane told me she despised you and she despised herself. She has been trying to bury her affection for you to protect herself. Many times, I caught her watching you. There was sadness in her eyes that did not match her words or behavior. She has been mourning the loss of your friendship, but I believe coming back to London has helped her understand that her emotions were misplaced. She is a young lady with a great deal of expectations placed on her shoulders. She is still learning how to cope with the pressures that exist in Society and the difficult task of managing her feelings."

Miranda's wide eyes pricked with moisture. "I understand." A part of Jane was returning to her—she could feel it. The day's events compounded, and suddenly she wanted to lie down to digest them all. "How can I ever thank you, Lady Callister?"

"By promising you will not run away."

The request caused her to choke on her words. She did not deserve such loyalty. "I promise to not be hasty." Miranda would stay as long as her presence did not harm anyone. As it was, hers seemed a precarious situation ticking toward an inevitable end.

CHAPTER 30

ETHAN HANDED HIS HORSE TO the groomsman and stalked into the house. He had no plan, no speech prepared, but he must speak with his parents immediately. He was not one to put off a task, but this was more important than anything he'd ever done before, and he was anxious to see it through.

He found his father in his study. "Might I have a moment?" he said from the doorway.

"Certainly," his father said. "I am tired of reviewing these proposed bills. Everyone wants something for themselves, and sometimes the right decision is unclear."

Would his father think the same about what Ethan planned to say? He entered the room and shut the door behind him. The last thing he needed was his sisters eavesdropping and Jane spouting her opinion.

"I am no longer courting Miss Withers. I want it made clear to my mother and sisters so they leave it alone. I am to marry Miss Bartley."

"Miss Bartley? Do not tell me you proposed to the daughter of a man in the Marshalsea! The *ton* will jump on such a foolhardy, cockeyed agreement."

He had never done anything to disappoint his parents before. This was new territory, but he was determined. "I have not proposed yet. But I plan to, and I hope she will have me."

"You do realize your actions reflect on this family? You will not marry Miss Bartley, and that is final!"

Ethan would not be intimidated. "I understand your reservations since I have reviewed them in my mind continually these many months. But it is of no use. I cannot live without her."

His father stood and put his hands on his desk to emphasize his authority. "When you are young, you think your body is ruled by the heart. When you are old, you learn to balance your passions with reason. I will not let you waste your life on a silly inclination you will later regret."

"You know I am a practical person, Father." Ethan shook his head. "Miss Bartley and I were meant to be together all along. It is my fault we were not married long before this. I let my rationale ruin something real and living. A beautiful girl has suffered because of it."

"Your blasted conscience is what has altered your mind, not your heart." His father huffed. "This is what we will do. I will tell your mother and sisters you are leaving London for a short time to pacify the rebellious farmers."

"Rebellious farmers?" Ethan had left their tenants in peace, thanks to a small raise and the charity from the parish.

"Not ours, but there are plenty enough to go around. You do what you can to assist your neighbors, and get this woman out of your system."

Ethan pulled at his choking cravat. "And when I return unchanged?"

His father sighed and collapsed back into his chair. "If you feel the same, then we will reexamine the situation. I am not promising anything."

Ethan shook his head. "You are buying time. My goal will not change."

"You will listen. A father always knows what is best for his child."

"I will go, but you must prepare yourself for when I return." He and his father rarely disagreed, but when they did, it was not pleasant. His father was always firm in his opinion. Well, Ethan could be just as bullheaded.

✳

Jane surprised Miranda by calling early in the morning while Lady Callister was still asleep and Miranda was in the breakfast room.

"I need to speak with Lady Callister. The house is in an uproar," Jane said, waltzing into the room and grabbing a sweet roll as if they had been on friendly speaking terms for some time. "Ethan is leaving London again!"

Miranda's chest ached with disappointment. Disappointment she had no right to feel. "What sort of business is taking him out of Town?"

"There have been uprisings from the farmers." Jane's expression grew serious. "There is not enough food to go around. My father says the real problem is not the food but the beginning of a revolution! Surely you heard about the second Spa Field riot. Who knows what will happen next?"

Miranda had heard, but she was surprised Jane would acknowledge it. "Go on."

"It is all my father and Ethan have talked about since we arrived in London. Ethan came over last night and argued with him about something— surely pleading the farmers' case." Jane's lip suddenly quivered. "I'm worried. When he bid my mother and me goodnight, I saw fire in Ethan's eyes. I've never seen him so determined. He never loses his temper. Then my father drank himself into a stupor and was ranting like I have never seen. Ethan cannot involve himself in such a tumultuous situation. He could be seriously injured or worse. Someone must speak sense to him."

"Lady Callister?" Miranda asked.

Jane sighed. "I had hoped, but now I wonder if she would dare interfere. Will you do it?"

Miranda blinked rapidly. "Me? Why not ask Miss Withers?"

Jane gave an impatient snort. "I have reason to doubt her ability to sway Ethan. Besides, she would never risk upsetting my parents."

"And your father already dislikes me, so there is no risk there." Miranda wanted to know what had come between Ethan and Miss Withers, but she was more concerned about Ethan. She moved to finish her breakfast. "You have missed one thing. I will agree with your brother, so I will not be able to persuade him to stay."

Jane huffed. "Of course you would agree with him. You always loved him more than you did me."

Miranda's spoon stilled over her egg. "Jane, is this why you have been angry with me all this time?"

Jane shrugged. "I knew our friendship would dissolve as soon as he jilted you."

"It wasn't like that. You know I love you both."

"At least you admit that."

"What?"

"You love Ethan."

Miranda's cheeks colored, and she risked the confession. "I have always loved Ethan."

Jane nudged the edge of the rug under the table with her foot. "I wasn't sure because of Captain Grant's interest in you. If you do love Ethan, go to him. Beg him to be careful and return to his family to make peace."

"And then marry Miss Withers," Miranda finished for her.

Jane's bluster seemed to fizzle out, and she lowered her gaze to her half boots. "No, I do not wish that."

"You don't?"

"I know I have been horrid," Jane admitted. "It makes no sense, but your family's tragedy was mine as well. I know it's not the same thing, but you were always there for me. We relied on each other. Whatever party I was to attend, I made sure you were invited too before I accepted. Then this happened, and I felt like you betrayed me. You left me alone, and I hated you for it."

"I couldn't help what happened!" Miranda said much louder than she'd intended.

"You should have known!" Jane cried. "Your father always did as you asked. You could have stopped him. We could have been sisters!"

Miranda put her hand over her mouth to hold back a sob. Jane's condemning words reopened an old wound. Miranda would do anything to go back and remedy all her failings. She forced a fortifying breath before she spoke. "I'm sorry, Jane. I should've been a better daughter for my father and a better friend for you. I didn't know how to handle all that transpired, and when I turned to you for help . . . you sent me away that night like I was nothing to you."

"I know." Jane clutched her hands together. "I didn't know what to do either. It frightened me to involve myself in a scandal. Lady Callister said I have been grieving our friendship through my anger. I don't want to keep living like this. I hate myself, and you remind me of the person I am not."

"Oh, Jane." She knew better than anyone what Jane was feeling.

"I love my brother, and I dearly want him to be happy. His choice is what matters. If he chooses you over Miss Withers, I promise I will be happy."

Miranda pushed her food away and stood. She moved quickly to Jane's side and threw her arms around her. "I'm so sorry," she whispered. "And not because of Ethan. Because I have missed our friendship." Jane hugged her back, and they both cried.

When they pulled apart, Jane bit her lip. "Is it even possible for us to be friends once more?"

"Friends," Miranda repeated. "I should like that."

"Me too." Jane sighed. "I have been awful to Ethan and simply everyone. Will you help me? Will you speak to him?"

It wouldn't do any good. It wouldn't *look* good. But Miranda could not resist the appeal to see him again. "I will come with you, but you mustn't leave my side."

Jane smiled then and nodded. It was the first real smile she'd directed Miranda's way in many months' time.

The Gibson family carriage awaited them, and Miranda joined Jane and her maid on the short ride to Ethan's town house.

"Couldn't you just go to the door?" Jane begged.

"You promised."

"I didn't exactly promise." Jane put her hands together in front of her chest. "Please? I will keep watch. All you have to do is beg him to stay safe and reconcile with my father. Then my conscience will be easy."

"Why did *you* not ask, then?" Miranda didn't understand.

"I have harassed Ethan all summer and driven him half mad with my rancor. He won't let me in because he's tired of me always inserting my opinion into his decisions." She put her head down. "I came here before I came to see you. It isn't his fault. I don't even like being around me anymore. Why would anyone else?"

Miranda blew out her breath. "You can change, Jane. You don't have to be the same person forever." She looked out the carriage window to the town house. She had never worried about whispers with her name attached to them before her fall from Society, but now she had Lady Callister's reputation to protect. An urge to see Ethan again brought her hand to the carriage door.

"All right. Keep watch," Miranda warned. She did not want any onlooker to assume something untoward was happening since she was paying a call on a man, and at this early hour too.

In a few quick steps Miranda made it to the door and knocked. The butler let her in and brought her to Ethan's small sitting room. She had never been there before, but it resembled him. Everything was neat and orderly. The books on the mantel were even color coordinated. As she took a seat on a settee, she fingered the fringe on a sage-green pillow and imagined Ethan doing the same thing.

"Miranda," Ethan said from the doorway. He had never called her Miranda before, but the slip did not register on his face like it did to her insides.

She stood, feeling color flood her cheeks. "How do you do?"

He smiled. That was a good sign.

"Jane came to see me," Miranda began.

"Oh."

"Don't worry," Miranda said, smoothing the front of her dress with her hands. She was glad now that she had worn her green morning dress, as it at least made her feel pretty. "She came in friendship. Things are not what they were between us, but I believe we have made a fresh start."

Ethan's smile grew, but he did not leave his place at the door. "Excellent. I thank you for telling me that. I know how much you once meant to each other."

Miranda took a deep breath. "I came to see you because Jane said you were leaving."

Ethan's smile wavered. "My father and I have conflicting opinions on a matter. Nothing a little time apart won't fix."

"I heard," Miranda answered.

"You heard?" Ethan's cheeks reddened.

"Yes, Jane told me. That is why I came." Miranda had no idea it would embarrass him.

"Were you surprised?" he hedged.

"No, not at all." A knowing smile came to her lips. "I fully support you."

"You do? I mean, I am so glad to hear it. I thought you would be angry. And . . . and I would not blame you for a moment."

"Why would I be angry?" Miranda furrowed her brow.

Ethan took several steps toward her. "Because of the awful things I once said to you, only to have a change of heart."

Miranda processed his words not once but twice. Her mouth dropped open in shock. Suddenly, her breath was in short supply. "Change of heart?" The question came out significantly louder than she'd intended it to.

Ethan gaped back at her. "Ah, er, I thought that was what we were talking about."

Miranda shook her head violently. "I was speaking of you helping the starving farmers, which I ardently approve of."

Ethan pulled at his cravat, turning the knot to face his shoulder. "Starving farmers? Yes, I am hoping to, ah, help them."

Miranda clasped her now-trembling hands in front of her. "And . . . and then you will . . ."

"Marry," Ethan said abruptly. "That is, I hope to marry."

"Oh?" Miranda asked, feeling her courage mount. "Miss Withers?" She said the name breathlessly.

"No, not Miss Withers," Ethan said, stepping closer until he was but a foot away. His gaze fell to the exposed wood arm of the settee she had been sitting on, and he reached out and ran his finger along it. "We spoke the day before yesterday and mutually agreed not to pursue an alliance."

She could hardly believe such miraculous news. She attempted to process what it meant for her, but Ethan was too near for her to think straight. "Truly?"

"We were not quite matched."

She agreed. In fact, she was surprised she hadn't seen it all along. There was only one woman for Ethan Roderick. "You must have a plan to marry someone else, then. You always have a plan."

Ethan finally looked up and met her gaze. "I want to make plans." He paused. "I want to make them with you."

She could barely breathe. His smell intoxicated her. She nervously reached forward and straightened his cravat. She had wanted to do that for the longest time. "I might have a fit of jealousy and be unkind. Would you change your mind about me again?"

Ethan grinned. "I'll have you know I have been insanely jealous of Captain Grant. I think I can stand a jealous wife now and then." His hands found their way to her waist. "My love for you is stronger than it was before. There is no changing my mind."

She could see no indecision in his eyes or posture. His words were sure, like his character. "I saved the muddy gown I wore in Folkestone. I promise to wear it often so you will not worry about my vanity."

Ethan slid his hands up along her arms and rested them on her cheeks, cradling her face. "You could wear rags, and I would still find you enchantingly beautiful. Or you could dress like a queen, and I would worship you as your faithful, passionate servant."

Miranda melted against his touch, and her whole world shifted. Surely this could not be possible. "I had no idea you cared so much."

"Do you care for me?" Ethan's brown eyes were pools of vulnerability.

She nodded. "Can you not see how your touch affects me? You have had my heart since the moment I met you."

Her words were an invitation, and Ethan pulled her close. One of his arms wrapped around her back, and the other slipped down to her neck. He dipped his head, and their lips met—his soft and tender against hers. He loved her. He finally loved her. How she had longed for this. She had kissed him a thousand times in her mind, but this was real. His mouth moved around hers, deepening their kiss. She stood on her tiptoes, letting him hold her up. All the worries of the world faded away. He was warm and wonderful, and new hope seemed to spring up between them.

Ethan broke free for a moment and smiled like a boy on Twelfth Night. "That . . . was worth waiting for." Miranda grinned. He captured her mouth once more, stirring her with his heartfelt embrace. When he pulled back the second time, his smile faded and his expression turned serious. "If I had simply discussed my concerns in a more open manner, perhaps together, we could have worked through our problems."

Miranda put her finger to his lips. Their differences had shaped them into people who fit together as nicely as two pieces of a puzzle. She could not wish away their year of challenges, because it had made this moment possible. "Only look back to see how far we have come."

Ethan studied her, his fingers playing with the curls by her face. "I'll have only to look at you to know it was worth enduring it all. My future will be bright with you in it." He bent down as if to kiss her once more. "Our future," he added, grazing his lips against hers.

"I rather like the sound of that."

Ethan grinned. "I will have to make a list of people I want to tell. I think everyone in the entire world should know how happy I am this very moment."

Miranda giggled. "Your parents are not going to like this at all. We should caution ourselves until we speak with them."

Ethan took a step back, and a rebellious glint entered his eyes. "My parents already know exactly how I feel. They have their reservations, but they will come around." He abruptly released her and turned away. He crossed to the window, bent over, and pulled it wide open, sticking his head outside. What was he doing?

Then he yelled, "I am getting married to Miss Miranda Bartley, the most beautiful woman in the world!"

Chasing behind him, Miranda did her best to pull him from the window. "What in heaven's name are you doing?"

"You taught me not to make decisions based on others' judgments and to say how I really feel. And you're right. It feels excellent." He put his head back out the window. "I love Miranda Bartley!"

Miranda pulled his arm with all her might, which was hard to do while laughing. "Stop! They will all think you are mad."

"Or drunk," Jane said from the doorway to the sitting room.

Ethan froze in surprise and then opened his arms. "Come congratulate your brother and future sister."

Jane's stern expression faded into a smile. "I have never seen you so ridiculous." She hurried over and stepped into Ethan's arms. "Congratulations. I hope you are still this deliriously happy when you realize you have a mountain of challenges to climb before this wedding." Jane turned and gave Miranda a hug. "And I will be truly happy to call you sister."

"Oh, Jane, thank you!" Miranda felt her eyes water. "You knew the perfect way to trick me into coming."

"Trick you?" Jane asked, confused.

Ethan cleared his throat. "She thought my quarrel with Father was about the farmers, when in truth it stemmed from my insistence on marrying you," he said to Miranda.

Jane's mouth fell open. "Father said . . . well, I guess we will have to tell him it was all his fault you ended up together. He will love that!"

Ethan grabbed Miranda's hand and squeezed it to reassure her. "He had better. Only a fool would think otherwise. I will still need to go back to Sussex and see if there is anything I can do to help, but not until after we settle our engagement."

CHAPTER 31

"ABSOLUTELY NOT!" LADY GIBSON SAID, her eyes wide and her skin pale. "I will see to it that your father revokes your monthly allowance."

"Mother," Ethan begged, "how can you change your opinion so easily? Just last Season you insisted I hurry along my courtship with Miranda."

"It's not that she isn't a delightful girl; it is her circumstance. If you can change your opinion, so can I."

Ethan rubbed his temples. His head was splitting. They had been at this for far too long. "I am going now to see Mr. Bartley to secure his blessing."

"To that dark hole?" Lady Gibson pulled out her fan and started flapping it back and forth in front of her face. "Think very carefully about this."

"I have been thinking about nothing else for months!" Ethan stood to leave. They were getting nowhere. "I will see if Lady Callister will sponsor me until I find employment."

"You cannot be serious. A man of leisure such as yourself would not know the first thing about working. What about the title you are to inherit? It is your duty."

"You are wrong there," Ethan said. He was not an emotionally driven man, but he was a determined one. "Richard can take the title in my place. I won't back down, even if I must shovel sewage."

"Ugh!" Hannah said from the door.

Lady Gibson's eyebrows shot upward. "I told you girls not to spy at the door. Remove yourselves this instant!"

"But I like Miranda, Mother," Hannah said.

"I do too," Jane said, catching everyone but Ethan off guard.

"Wonderful," Ethan announced. "By the time I return, I hope my sisters will have convinced my parents of Miranda's virtues."

"Ethan." His mother's grim tone stopped him in his tracks. "Something must be done about her father, or your future will be ruined."

There was more truth in her statement than Ethan wished to acknowledge. He clenched his fists in frustration and walked out the door. Before speaking to Miranda's father, he needed a better plan. He thought of the old Miranda back in London and her unchecked, almost thoughtless behavior. *She* would not need to write out a speech or map out every step, but he did. Spontaneity should be reserved for his future wife. He was not very good at it, but love was a great motivator.

⚹

Sarah opened the curtains in Miranda's bedroom, filling the room with streaks of sunlight. Miranda smiled from her bed, and not because she had her very own lady's maid—a rare luxury for a companion such as herself—but because it was Sarah.

"Good morning, miss," Sarah said. She poured water into the washbasin and began tidying up around the room.

"It is a good morning, is it not?" Miranda curled up on her pillow and sighed dreamily. "Today I shall tell Lady Callister about Ethan's proposal. Then, in six weeks, you and I shall be moving once again."

"Will Lady Callister be happy for you?" Sarah asked, returning her smile.

Miranda pulled herself up and shrugged. "Of all the people in this world, she wants what is best for me."

Sarah pulled out a dress for Miranda and soon had her ready to go down for breakfast.

"Just ease her into the news," Sarah suggested. "It is one thing to like you as a companion and entirely different to have you marry into the family."

"I never thought of it in such a way," Miranda said, frowning.

"Chin up." Sara moved to pull the covers straight on the bed. "She might finally have a good reason to be rid of you."

"Enough of your cheekiness," Miranda said, sticking out her tongue. "It is so hard to find good help these days."

Sarah grinned. "Oh, get on now. You know I will be praying mightily that everything works out."

Miranda sighed contentedly once more and skipped down for breakfast feeling thankful for Sarah and even more thankful for having secured Ethan's love.

Lady Callister sat at the table with her eggs untouched and a letter in her hand. She glanced up at Miranda's beaming face and frowned. "You had better sit down."

Sensing bad news, Miranda did not even feel the chair beneath her as she sat. "What is it?"

"A letter from Lady Gibson. My grand-nephew Mr. Roderick has engaged himself. Can you guess to whom?"

Miranda's tongue felt twice its normal size. She finally managed, "Me."

Lady Callister nodded once. "And Lady Gibson says here that such a marriage can never happen whilst your father is in the Marshalsea. She even goes as far as to offer you money to reconsider." Lady Callister held up the banknotes.

Gasping, Miranda shook her head fervently. "Never."

Lady Callister gave a small sigh. "Money could help your father."

"But surely not enough to free him. I would be indebted to the family but never accepted by them. No, Ethan and I must make our own way."

"And how does my nephew feel about losing all his financial support?"

The blood drained from her face. "Has it come to that?" She never thought the family would go to such extremes to avoid a connection with her. But this was not a game of pretend where every person received their happy ending.

Lady Callister folded the letter up and set it aside. "I admit I employed you because I suspected Mr. Roderick's feelings for you."

Miranda gaped.

"I knew your name from letters I received from the family the Season before while you and my nephew courted. I am an old, foolish romantic. I did my best to keep Captain Grant at bay and deliberately brought you to London to encourage this union." She tapped the letter with her finger. "I am responsible for this. My nephew will be a baron someday, and I thought with my influence, I could smooth your reputation. Unfortunately, I have been removed from High Society for too long and have forgotten how strong tradition can be."

"No, you are without fault here." Miranda hugged herself. She swallowed back a lump in her throat. "This must end. I will write to Mr. Roderick and explain my refusal."

"I don't like giving up on such a good cause. Still, should you choose it, you will still have a place with me at Crowfield."

Miranda could not speak without crying. She nodded and excused herself. She hurried back to her room to find Sarah still there.

"Did you forget something, miss?"

"Pack our things," Miranda said, her voice cracking. "I am leaving."

Sarah's eyes widened, and she dropped the scarf she was folding.

"I cannot marry Ethan. And Lady Callister cannot continue to shoulder my disgrace."

Sensing Miranda's feelings, Sarah excused herself and let Miranda have some privacy. Miranda fell onto the bed and wept. It was worse than the day at Gray House when she had convinced herself that no one loved her. Now she had someone who wanted her, and she was walking away from him. Why was this happening? Why did every glimpse of happiness seem to be ripped away from her?

✳

Ethan crumpled up the missive from his father. No marriage or no money. It was absolutely ridiculous. His father's reputation would suffer from their connections, but it would blow over. Some other scandal would replace this one. At least, that was how Society had reacted when he had called things off with Miranda before. He massaged his forehead. No, he knew this was different. This time, if Mr. Bartley could not be helped, there would be no recovering from such a blow. Society already had its teeth into the Bartley family, and it would rip them to shreds. If only her blasted uncle would exert some of his influence.

Ethan gathered his hat and overcoat, determined to find a way. They had not endured this much just to give up. Nothing else could possibly be more important for him than starting a family with Miranda. There had to be a way out of this mess. He would start with a visit with Mr. Bartley.

Entering the Marshalsea was like walking into the slums of London. There were those who suffered but could be trusted and those who deserved to be locked away for life. Ethan's eyes darted in every direction as he wondered if someone would jump him from behind to try to rob him.

It was with some relief that he entered the prison room. He faced Mr. Bartley and shut the door behind him. The prisoner's shirt was wrinkled and yellowing, and he did not have the same sparkle in his eyes as when Miranda had been with him.

"How do you do, Mr. Bartley?"

Mr. Bartley, pale and thin, stood and bowed like a gentleman. "To what do I owe the honor of your visit?"

Ethan faltered. How would he broach this delicate topic? "Mr. Bartley, might I speak plainly?"

"Of course," Mr. Bartley said. He waved Ethan toward the only chairs in the room, near the small wooden table.

"I would like to ascertain the amount of your debts. Will you tell me?"

Mr. Bartley rubbed the stubble on his chin, his eyes suspicious. "And who will buy this information from you to further shame our family? What benefit will you receive?"

Ethan glanced at the door, wishing he were already removed from such a place. The odor alone seemed to penetrate his clothes. "I would like to apply some of my own funds to your debts."

"Whatever for?" Mr. Bartley leveled him with a hard stare.

"It can hardly surprise you, sir, that I have been paying for your rooms on this side of the prison for some time. Your comfort is important to me. I left your family subject to gossip when I removed myself from London at the end of last Season. My conscience urged me to make amends in some way. Now I will try all that I can to see you are released from this place."

"Why?" Mr. Bartley asked, his eyes wide and curious.

"I know this might prove difficult for you to reconcile with, but I have once more attached myself to your daughter."

Mr. Bartley waved the idea away with his hand. "You cannot buy Miranda's love, Mr. Roderick. I am obliged to you for your generosity, truly I am. But you hurt her badly. I might not be able to prevent anything from the confines of this jail, but my girl will marry a man she loves and respects."

The acid in Ethan's stomach burned in his throat. He had not worked things out with Miranda at last only to have both their fathers thwart their happiness.

"I assure you, Mr. Bartley, I regret walking away from your daughter. I give you my word when I say we love each other. If you will not let me pay your creditors, then I do not see any further reason to remain here. Good day, Mr. Bartley." Ethan rose and, with regretful steps, made his way to the door.

"Mr. Roderick," Mr. Bartley said.

Ethan turned to face him.

"If Miranda truly loves you . . . then you have my blessing. But you must forget about me. My debts are significant indeed."

Ethan swallowed hard. He could not break the news to Mr. Bartley that without freeing him from prison, it would be hard to support Miranda as his wife. "Thank you, sir. I promise to love her always."

"See that you do."

Nothing in his situation was truly resolved after his visit to the Marshalsea, but Ethan considered Mr. Bartley's blessing a godsend. At least one parent supported them. Ethan was not finished though. He had one last idea. A sort of fever burned inside of him. This had to work.

CHAPTER 32

MIRANDA AND SARAH WERE PACKING Miranda's things when Lady Callister entered the room.

"What are you doing? You promised you would not be hasty."

"I need a fresh start," Miranda said, her voice cracking with emotion.

Lady Callister sighed, her age showing with her deep frown. "Do you know where you will go?"

Miranda glanced at Sarah and then nodded. "A boardinghouse. I will stay there while I advertise for work. You will keep Sarah on, won't you?"

"Most certainly," Lady Callister said. She walked into the room and sat on Miranda's bed. "I will send out inquiries to my friends to find you a position."

"I cannot keep taking your charity."

"Nonsense." Lady Callister's grave eyes spoke volumes. "It will ease my conscience; I must insist. Take Sarah with you until you are settled. I shall pay her wages and send word once I have received an opportunity for you."

Gratitude for Lady Callister nearly overwhelmed Miranda. "Thank you," she breathed.

"For what it is worth, there will always be a place for you here should you find you need it." Miranda had never seen Lady Callister cry, but the woman's face crumpled, and she held a handkerchief to her nose.

Within the hour, Miranda used her savings to pay the coach fare for her and Sarah. With all their things loaded inside, she turned to say goodbye to Lady Callister.

"Have you told my nephew that you are leaving?" Lady Callister asked.

"No," Miranda said, her throat swelling with emotion. "But I have a letter here explaining everything." She pressed the note into Lady Callister's hands. "Delay as long as you can to give it to him so there will be no chance of him following me."

Lady Callister took the letter. She appeared older than ever. "I will give it to him, though I will not enjoy the task."

Miranda wiped away an errant tear before pulling out a second letter. "This is for Lady Gibson. She once was fond of me, you know. I was tempted to go to her and throw the money in her face, but for everyone's sake, I constrained myself."

Lady Callister's lips twitched. "How decent of you."

Miranda nodded. "Instead, I am begging her to forgive my poor conduct in this matter." She dipped her chin and sniffed. "They do not know it, but I loved each of them too."

"I understand," Lady Callister said. "I shall send word when I hear of a position."

Miranda embraced the woman she had grown to love. "*Thank you* seems so trifling. I owe you so very much."

"You owe me nothing. But just the same, I shall miss you."

How many people would Miranda have to walk away from? What more did she have to learn?

CHAPTER 33

THE LONG RIDE TO FOLKESTONE exhausted Ethan. Each mile was filled with tormenting thoughts. He should have told Miranda he had left London. Would she think he'd given up on them again—that he'd given up on her? He could not bring himself to offer her empty platitudes as comfort. No, he would face her when he had a viable solution.

Instead of resting up at Stephen's estate, Ethan rode directly to Gray House. It was time to introduce himself to Lord Aldington. He looked up at the grayish-white stone and grimaced. It did not bode well to think his last hope resided here. He knocked on the door and waited. When it opened, he introduced himself and was invited to sit in a shabby drawing room. He took in the crack in the mantel and the half-drawn drapes. What sort of ill will had Miranda experienced here? He was already imagining all sorts of unnerving things.

After several minutes, the butler returned to the room. "Lord Aldington requests to see you in his bedchamber."

"Bedchamber?"

"His Lordship is feeling under the weather. If you will follow me."

Ethan followed the butler, taking in the house as they walked. There were not enough windows or candles, and the passageway was full of shadows. Once they arrived, the butler let himself in and announced Ethan.

The butler moved to the side, giving him a view of Lord Aldington lying in his bed. His salt-and-pepper hair was pasted across his forehead, and his skin was damp and sallow. Ethan noticed one bandaged arm was lying atop the bedsheet. Beside Lord Aldington was a middle-aged man, likely the doctor. At seeing Ethan, the doctor took a bowl from Lord Aldington's bedside table and approached him. Ethan momentarily drew back when he saw the bowl sloshing with blood.

"I am Dr. Ferris."

"Mr. Roderick, recently from London." Ethan kept his voice low. "What is wrong with Lord Aldington?"

The doctor's short blond mustache drooped in unison with the man's eyes. "His liver, amongst other things. Not to worry. He has been gravely ill before and always pulls through. Today has been especially hard, though, as he is convinced he is going to die. I do not think he is up for conversation, but you may sit with him for a time. I will return in a few minutes, and then I must insist he rest."

Ethan stepped past the doctor and moved slowly toward the bed. Lord Aldington's eyes were open, and his gaze followed Ethan as he drew closer. This man was ill indeed—his eyes held a hollow emptiness.

Ethan cleared his throat. "Lord Aldington, I am Mr. Roderick, son of Lord Gibson of Stonebrook. I have come from London to speak to you."

"Why?" Lord Aldington turned his head and stared at the ceiling.

"I have recently engaged myself to your niece, Miss Bartley."

Lord Aldington's smile came out as more of a grimace. "Miranda?"

Ethan had not expected to hear the longing in this man's voice. Lord Aldington had neglected Miranda, but it seemed the memory of her brought him comfort. "Yes, Miranda."

"She mentioned your family name." Lord Aldington squeezed his eyes shut.

"I knew her before she came here, and she stayed with our family until she found employment as a companion."

Lord Aldington chuckled. "She is a hard one to forget, isn't she? What do you want from me? My permission?"

"I have come for one purpose: to seek assistance in paying Mr. Bartley's debts."

Lord Aldington gave a sharp laugh, followed by a groan of pain. "Never."

"I will not be able to marry Miss Bartley until her father is released. It is no secret you and your brother are not on good terms, so I have done my best to see to his care while he is in prison."

"Foolish man." Lord Aldington shook his head. "Why would you waste your money on my brother?"

Ethan clenched his fists. "I do it not for him but for his daughter. Unfortunately, it is the most I can do. Until I inherit, I lack ready funds to pay off his debts." He paused, knowing his explanation was getting him nowhere.

It would not help to scream at the man, but he was beyond frustrated with the whole thing. "Your niece suffered greatly while in this home. Do you truly have so little care for her happiness?"

Lord Aldington said nothing. Ethan put his hands on his hips and glanced around. Next to the bed was a small bedside table. On top were several open letters stacked in a careless pile. With little shame, Ethan bent his head to read the one on top.

It was from Miranda.

He snatched up the letters. They were all from Miranda.

"That's not your business," Lord Aldington snapped. He was too weak to move or do anything about it, so Ethan held firm to the papers.

"Despite everything you subjected her to, she still cared enough to send these." Ethan glared at the sickly man. "Have a heart. You're likely to die at any moment. Let one person in this world remember you fondly."

Lord Aldington lay there as if in a trance—as if Ethan were not in the room at all.

Exasperation overruled his sympathy, but Ethan knew he needed to stay calm. "Miss Bartley deserves her family."

The words took effect, but not in the way Ethan expected. Lord Aldington's face screwed up, and he moaned. He clutched his stomach and rocked back and forth.

Ethan leaned over the bed. "Shall I call the doctor back?" He was tempted to tell Lord Aldington that his sickness was brought on by his hatred, but the pain looked too intense to jest about.

Lord Aldington turned his head an inch or two until his eyes were once again upon Ethan. "You are right. About everything. How I treated her. How she deserves more. But I shall die soon . . . alone . . . and there is nothing to be done about it." His weak voice was close to a whisper and his breathing labored.

Despite what the doctor said, Ethan believed Lord Aldington did not have much time left. He felt as if the man were slipping away in front of his eyes. "You can still fix things, man. You don't have to be alone."

Lord Aldington stared at him for a while, as if deciding whether or not he believed him. Then he lifted his bandaged arm and gestured behind Ethan. Ethan turned his head back to the bedside table. Several medicinal vials littered the surface, along with a glass of water, but he didn't know which one the sick man wanted.

"The drawer," Lord Aldington said.

There was no drawer. Ethan almost told him as much, but then he stooped down to analyze the wood. He placed his hands on the front panel around the top of the small table and gently pulled. It was a drawer.

Inside was a single handkerchief folded in a neat square. It covered something. Ethan gently lifted the silk to reveal a small painting of a woman.

"My love." Lord Aldington sneered. "And my brother's wife."

It was enough to draw a picture in his mind of what might have happened between the brothers. Ethan could see a slight resemblance to Miranda.

"I cannot carry my sins any longer," Lord Aldington said, his words slurring. "There is a time to bury what needs burying—both the man and the deeds."

Their eyes connected once more, and Ethan understood only that Lord Aldington meant to put behind him his past.

"You will help me, then?" Ethan asked.

Lord Aldington groaned, and perspiration broke out again on his forehead. "Not for you . . . but for her."

"That is enough for me," Ethan said.

"Stay with me," Lord Aldington said, his breath short. "Please."

Ethan was planning on staying until the solicitor was called for, but seeing a grown man so desperately afraid to die alone humbled him. Didn't Lord Aldington have anyone else he could call on? It seemed he did not. Ethan pulled a chair by the bed and sat down, pushing aside his own anxiety. "Don't worry. I'm not going anywhere. You won't have to suffer alone."

※

By the time Ethan returned to London three days later, his eyes were bleary, and he was saddle sore. His trip had not gone anything like he had expected. As worn through as he was, Ethan had to see Miranda right away. He stopped at his home long enough to eat, shave, and change his clothes. Would she be angry that he had disappeared? He rubbed his freshly shaved jaw. He had promised himself he'd find a way for them to be together, but his natural optimism in the future seemed to fade with his weariness.

Refusing to get on his horse again, Ethan sent for his carriage to be readied. He stretched his back before climbing inside. The conveyance jerked into motion. The clopping of horse hooves and the clank of wheels nearly lulled him to sleep. His eyes snapped open when the driver stopped in front of Lady Callister's town house.

Sighing, Ethan made his way inside. He paced in the drawing room, eager for Lady Callister and Miranda to come down.

Lady Callister finally entered the room, her expression downcast. "I waited for days for you to come." She shook her head. "You're too late. She is gone."

"Gone?" The words were like a punch to his gut. "Where is she?"

"I thought she would send me the address of her boardinghouse, but she did not." Lady Callister eyed him. "Where have *you* been?"

"To Miss Bartley's uncle's house in Folkestone." Ethan waved his hand to dismiss the subject. He didn't want to talk about his melancholy visit. "Why wouldn't she send her forwarding address? You must tell me everything."

"Please"—Lady Callister took a seat and waved to the chair next to Ethan—"sit down before you wear a pattern into my carpet."

Ethan didn't want to sit. He wanted to run to wherever Miranda was so he could plead his case and explain. Reluctantly, he sat on the edge of a chair, if only to appease his great-aunt.

"Miss Bartley received a letter from your mother asking her to withdraw from the engagement."

"My mother?" Ethan clenched his fists.

Lady Callister gave a brisk nod. "Miss Bartley was too much of a lady to throw the money back in her face, so I did it for her. Sometimes a well-meaning set-down is just the thing to soften hard hearts."

Ethan would have liked to witness that. "Miranda must have been hurt. My mother always doted on her in the past."

"Your mother's intentions were not wholly bad. She might still be fond of Miss Bartley, but she was more frightened for the well-being and future of her son. Miss Bartley recognized a connection to her was damaging to your family and your position. She left here to ensure your happiness."

"What ridiculous nonsense," Ethan muttered under his breath. How could he be happy without her?

"It was very sensible—something I thought you would understand." Lady Callister quirked her brow. Was she implying that his practicality had put him in this position in the first place? "One more thing. She left you a farewell note, which I took the liberty of reading."

"You did what?"

Lady Callister shrugged. "I needed to know if she had left hints as to her whereabouts. You are not the only one concerned."

"Well? What did it say?" He was almost embarrassed to ask.

"A lot of sentimental sweetness. I quite enjoyed it. But it hardly matters what it says. It makes no difference. She is gone. You need to consider the facts. I could offer enough money to release her father from prison, but it would do no good. Miranda will never earn any respect. From the moment you are married, she will be treated with disdain. Don't you understand?"

Ethan leapt to his feet. "I would never let anyone treat her that way! She has already suffered enough."

Lady Callister nodded. "I agree. What are you going to do about it?"

"Is she still in London?" Ethan would not be dissuaded. He would chase Miranda to New South Wales if he had to. He would find her.

"I told you I know not where she is."

Ethan's jaw tightened. All his efforts would mean nothing if he couldn't be with Miranda. He could hear her telling him to look forward, but his regrets were suffocating him. He dropped his head in defeat. His whole life he'd craved certainty, wanted to earn the respect of his colleagues and maybe make a difference in the world. None of those things mattered without Miranda. He'd give it all up if he could just find her and convince her to marry him.

"Excuse me," he said. "I must take my leave."

"What are you planning now?" Lady Callister asked.

He lifted his head to meet her steady gaze. "I'm going to find her."

Lady Callister smiled. "Godspeed."

❈

After a week at the boardinghouse, Miranda was ready to move on. She opened her reticule to make sure she had everything she needed. "Remind me to leave you with Lady Callister's spectacles and book. She has surely missed them. You'll explain I took them by mistake?"

Sarah nodded. "She knows you often carried them for her. But are you sure you are ready to leave London?" Sarah took a seat on the edge of the lumpy mattress in their rented room.

Miranda nodded, fastening her cloak. "I am sure. I won't have a fresh start here, and we both know it."

She could tell Sarah agreed but was hesitant to say goodbye. "It is true your name is circulating, but that will not last if we are patient. Please, you mustn't act in desperation. If you leave here and find a job washing laundry or some other lesser means, you will never be able to return to your previous status. Think, miss."

"I am thinking." Miranda sighed. "I will live off what I have while I advertise for work. I simply cannot be so near Mr. Roderick and stay sane. It is the best I can do."

"What if Lady Callister finds you a position? Would you take it?"

Miranda collapsed onto the mattress next to Sarah. "I must break ties with the family. Don't you see?" She had caused enough trouble for them as it was.

"Oh, luv." Sarah put her head on Miranda's shoulder. "I hear heartache is the same whether in love lost or in death. I'm ever so sorry, miss."

Miranda wiped at tears stinging her eyes. "It pains me to imagine being parted from him for always, and yet, I will accept such pain if it means he is given the life he deserves."

Shortly later, Miranda and Sarah climbed inside a hackney to return Sarah back to Lady Callister's town house.

"I don't want to say goodbye again." Miranda grabbed Sarah's hand.

Sarah squeezed Miranda's fingers and smiled. "Who is to say this is forever? We thought that much last time."

"You will forget all about me soon enough," Miranda said. She had never been completely alone before, and fear twisted at her insides.

"How could I forget you?" Sarah asked. "I still see you facedown in the mud when I'm dreaming. That is, when I am having a good dream."

Miranda choked on her laugh. She turned and pinched Sarah in the side, which brought out a ticklish giggle. The carriage pulled to a stop in front of Lady Callister's home. The drive had been far too short. She feared this goodbye and hoped she had the courage for what lay ahead.

Now Sarah grabbed Miranda's hand. "It's time."

Miranda turned in her seat and threw her arms around Sarah. "Thank you. For everything."

The sound of wheels coming to a stop behind them caught their attention.

"Who could that be?" Miranda frowned at Sarah. "Lady Callister?"

Sarah lifted the curtain and poked her head out. "You are not going to like this, miss."

"Ethan?!"

Sarah nodded.

Miranda pinned her back to the seat. "No. I can't face him. I just can't." She thought quickly. Her eyes fell on their travel bags at their feet, and an idea launched in her mind. "Listen carefully, Sarah. You must get out and tell him that you left me somewhere."

"Miss?"

"Please! Tell the coachman to ride on. And I will need to borrow your thick wool shawl." She unpinned her cloak. "Here, take this instead."

Sarah's face contorted, showing several fleeting emotions. "Oh, very well." They traded outerwear, and Sarah let herself out. The coach door closed before Miranda could see anything.

Not wasting a moment, Miranda opened her valise, scanning the contents. She put on Lady Callister's perched spectacles and put the gothic novel on her lap. It wasn't enough. She pulled open Sarah's travel bag, and a sly grin stole across her face. *Perfect!* Miranda put the spare mobcap over her head, combing her fingers through her loose curls around her face and ratting her hair up toward her scalp. It was all precautionary in case the coach didn't move fast enough. Why wasn't it leaving?

She heard Ethan's voice before she saw him. It was muffled but growing louder. He was coming! She knew she could not escape him now. Turning away from the door, she wrapped the shawl high around her neck and chin and held the book in front of her face. Her heart raced like that of a helpless newborn kitten.

The coach door swung open, and Ethan poked his head inside. "Oh, pardon me, miss. I thought—"

Miranda didn't turn to acknowledge him.

"Why, you little rascal!"

Miranda furrowed her brow behind her book, not expecting her last moment with Ethan to begin with him calling her names. "Rascal?" she said in her best peasant's accent. She turned her body slightly toward him and slowly lowered the book so her bespectacled eyes could be seen over the brim. "Sir?"

Ethan looked haggard and irritated, but upon meeting her gaze, his features softened. Had she fooled him? There was no way she could refuse him should he touch her or beg her to stay with him. This was for his own good!

"Forgive me. I thought a lady was in here. Never have I seen such fine gloves."

Miranda gulped. She'd forgotten to remove her gloves. "Thank ye, sir."

"Nor heard such a lovely voice."

Miranda nearly swallowed her tongue.

He climbed inside and took a seat very near her. "Nor seen such an exquisite pair of eyes."

She was finished. She had not fooled him half-starved and covered in mud. Why had she thought she could she deceive him like this?

Pushing her book down to her lap, Ethan captured her hands in one of his. Then with the other, he removed the spectacles from her face. "I know we are strangers, but I am overcome by your beauty."

Miranda's heart was in her throat, and she could not muster a false accent. "Once again, you have failed to compliment my hair."

"You're right," Ethan said. He reached up and tugged the mobcap off her hair, smoothing the wayward curls with his hands. "There. Now I can bring myself to compliment it."

Smiling regretfully, she said, "I am sorry I had to say goodbye in a note."

"Never mind that, my love." His expression was one of weary relief.

How she ached to hear him call her his love for the rest of her days. His words and his nearness tortured her. They couldn't be together. She cleared her throat, hoping to dislodge the emotion. "Before you leave, I want to give you some money. I've been saving for some time, and I want it to help a poor family in Sussex. When you return to help the farmers, please take it with you."

Ethan smiled. "It is admirable you are thinking of those in need at a time like this, but you can give them the money yourself. I'm not going anywhere—not without you. All is going to right itself now. I don't want you to worry or be afraid for our future. But before I get ahead of myself, there is someone outside I must introduce you to." Ethan released her and climbed out of the carriage.

Confused whether to hope or feel dismayed, Miranda smoothed her hair once more and accepted his extended hand. Once her foot hit solid ground, Ethan pulled her to him in one quick tug. Still hidden from view of the others behind the carriage door, his lips grazed hers, and her breath caught.

"Ethan, you mustn't!" she whispered fiercely, pushing him back. She wanted to yell and cry and sing with all the emotions his simple kiss caused.

"Oh, but I must," he said, ignoring that half-hearted complaint on her lips. He kissed her again, lingering this time. When he released her, she was breathless. "Come." He tucked her under his arm and drew her away from the protection of the carriage door toward a strange man standing outside Ethan's carriage. "This is Mr. York." Ethan motioned to the tall, willowy gentleman she did not recognize. "He arrived in Town just this morning."

Mr. York removed his hat and bowed to Miranda. She turned to Ethan, curious as to the need for an introduction.

"Mr. York is your uncle's solicitor. Darling, you might want to listen to what he has to say."

"Miss Bartley," Mr. York began, "I must first impart grievous news. I am sorry to inform you of the passing of your uncle, Lord Aldington, lately of Gray House."

Her hope of her family ever reconciling left in one breath. He was gone. Truly gone. The thought devastated her. Miranda's world tilted, and her legs buckled. Ethan wrapped his other arm around her to steady her. This could not be real. Her uncle had often had a sickly demeanor, but she'd fully believed he had much more life ahead of him—enough for her family to make amends.

"When did this happen?" Miranda asked.

Ethan squeezed her closer to him. "I was with him at his last."

"You?" She could not believe it. "You were at Gray House?"

Mr. Roderick nodded slowly. "He made me read your letters to him over and over again. He said if I was going to be his nephew someday, it was my duty to do it."

Astonished, Miranda shook her head.

"Your kind words brought him a great deal of comfort," Ethan continued. "Your uncle's dying wish was to tell his family he was sorry."

"There was a heart at Gray House after all," Miranda whispered almost to herself. Her eyes pressed closed, and a feeling of peace permeated through her. She had thought time had a way of stealing one's best self, but now she knew that time was a gift and an opportunity to change. Because of this dark year, her family could finally be reconciled. Death could not undo the gift God had given them—the gift He'd given her. She would forever be grateful her uncle's heart had softened.

Mr. York cleared his throat. "I know the news comes as quite a shock, but I have papers that must be signed. I always say there is never a good time to discuss business."

"Yes, of course," Miranda said softly, grateful for Ethan's firm grip around her.

Mr. York pulled a paper from his shoulder bag. "The short news is, without an heir, your uncle signed the estate and all his entailing to your father as the next of kin."

Miranda lifted her hand to her mouth. "My . . . my father?"

Mr. York nodded. "Mr. Roderick confirmed your father's location. I was specifically instructed to find you first so that the will could be read with you and your father together. I know money cannot ease the sorrow death brings, but your uncle lived a rather sheltered life and hardly touched the family fortune. I daresay there are enough funds to pay off your father's creditors."

"And then there is the title," Ethan added, his eyes dancing. He handed her a handkerchief. "Your father will inherit money and renewed respectability. Not that I make light of your loss, dearest, but it does take care of certain problems."

Miranda dried her tears with the white cloth and tried to smile. "Forgive me. I am baffled. It is not so unusual for a family to be estranged, but I had no idea I would be so affected by his death."

"We will throw Lord Aldington a grand funeral," Ethan said.

"Yes," Miranda agreed. "A wonderful idea."

Ethan released her. "You are to stay with Lady Callister until we sort this all out. And I defy you to talk yourself out of this. My great-aunt and I have it all arranged."

"As you command," Miranda said softly. She felt the emptiness in her soul begin to fill once more with hope. She did not dare ask the single question burning inside her. Would this be enough to win over Ethan's parents? She now believed Ethan would not let anything stop him from marrying her. His trip to Gray House testified of this. However, his future mattered too, as did his family relations. And once lost from Society's favor, one could never return to one's former glory. Miranda had learned that lesson the hard way.

CHAPTER 34

ETHAN'S HEART POUNDED. THE ANXIETY of Miranda's departure, coupled with sleepless nights, should have made this sensation impossible. But his racing heart was not from an overtired body leaping out of a carriage to keep from losing Miranda. While the timing had been miraculous, his racing heart stemmed from the anticipation of closing an ugly chapter for Miranda and, hopefully, making her forever his.

They made their way to the Marshalsea and to Mr. Bartley's small apartment. Mr. York recounted all the details of the will to Miranda's father. Ethan followed this by telling everyone about Lord Aldington's final hours. Mr. Bartley collapsed into his chair, covered his face with his hands, and wept. Ethan had never seen a grown man sob like a babe before.

"My brother," Mr. Bartley cried. "My poor, lost brother."

They all bowed their heads and let him lament his loss. When Mr. Bartley finally came around, he looked directly at Ethan.

"We were once the closest of friends—the dearest of playmates." Then he turned to Miranda. "He loved your mama. When she chose me, it devastated him. We were both smarting after our parents' deaths, and he never welcomed us into his home again. He nursed his loneliness with the drink. Heaven knows I have done the same from time to time, yet I live and am free to have all the joys he did not." He bowed his head and bawled.

Touched by the effect a man's life had on the world, Ethan swore he would never let anything come between him and his family. Somehow, he must make his family see that he and Miranda needed each other.

He put his hand on Miranda's shoulder. "Mr. York and I will give you both a moment and wait outside. When your father is released, he is welcome to stay at my town house until he is ready to travel to Folkestone."

Ethan led Mr. York out to the brown Marshalsea lawn filled with patches of snow. The sun was going down on a day that would never be forgotten. Ethan shifted his feet, observing the life inside the prison around him.

"When can Mr. Bartley leave?" Ethan asked.

"As soon as tomorrow, if he wishes," Mr. York answered. "I need only obtain his signature and permission, and I shall see to his creditors in the morning."

"Good," Ethan said.

Finally, Miranda stepped outside her father's apartment. Mr. York switched her places and went in to finalize his business with Mr. Bartley.

"How are you coping?" Ethan asked, a little unsure how he could help Miranda in her grief. He wished he could carry this burden for her.

Miranda stepped closer to him. "Confused, sad, happy, elated."

"Lord Aldington expressed his regret for the way he treated you. He kept your letters by his side until the end."

"Truly?" She put her hands over her heart. "I can't thank you enough for being there for him when no one else was."

When she dropped her hands, Ethan snatched one, covering it with his much larger one. "I know this isn't the best time, but will you come with me to see my parents?"

Miranda fervently shook her head. "I cannot bear to see or hear their rejection."

Ethan tugged her ever closer. He never wanted to be parted from her again. His desire for her had only multiplied when she had disappeared. There was no way he could simply return her to his great-aunt if she could be at his side.

"I will meet with my parents while you visit with my sisters, then. I promise you this news will take away their reservations."

"All of them?" Miranda asked. "Because I do not think you can promise that."

"I have a plan," Ethan said.

Miranda bit back her smile. "You do, do you? Now my reservations are gone."

"Excellent," Ethan said, his lips drawing to Miranda's, "because I cannot bear to think of you deserting me again. I must protect what is mine."

"What is to be yours, you mean."

Ethan captured her mouth with his. She responded eagerly, almost desperately. He drew back long enough to say, "Your lips disagree. They already know they are mine."

She giggled, and he kissed her again. The fire between them could not be defined by his situation or hers, but by their shared love. This was a fight worth enduring. The door to her father's apartment opened, and he quickly pulled back. He caught a longing glance from Miranda and knew she would brave his parents rather than give up on what could be.

⚶

It was not much longer before they made their way to Ethan's parents' home. For a moment, Miranda thought she might rather spend the evening with Mrs. Guttridge. Her long day was about to get even more eventful. She gripped Ethan's arm fiercely all the way up the walk. The butler looked mildly surprised to see Ethan pulling Miranda inside after him. Once they shed their cloaks and Ethan requested to see his family, she was tempted to keep her distance, though it seemed ridiculous to act as if they were polite strangers when she knew Ethan wanted to prove they were so much more.

He led her to a chair in the drawing room and stood beside it as if to threaten anyone from coming close.

After a few desperately drawn-out minutes, the family gathered around them. Dressed for dinner, they arrived with a myriad of expressions etched in their features. Lord and Lady Gibson's mutual frowns added a sour note to the room's tone, making Miranda wish Ethan could hold her hand once more.

Ethan finally took a seat in a chair placed near hers, but it still felt a world away. While Ethan's greeting exuded confidence, his knee bounced up and down in a nervous rhythm. Miranda's knees kept still, but her mind did not. She could not fathom his parents' acquiescence. Lady Gibson caught her eye, and Miranda squirmed beneath her regretful gaze.

"Have you had dinner?" Lady Gibson asked Ethan, peeling her eyes away from Miranda.

"I have not and would prefer to speak with you before I do. Perhaps Jane and Hannah could find some refreshment for Miranda while we step into the study."

Lord Gibson looked like he was the one used to doing the maneuvering and was not too pleased for the unwelcome interruption to his night. He begrudgingly put his arm out to his wife, and Miranda watched Ethan follow them from the room.

Jane shut the door behind them. "What was Ethan thinking bringing you here?" she asked. "He knows Father's stubbornness. He could have spared you all this."

Hannah slipped down beside her and put her hand on Miranda's arm. "I am glad you came. You are a storybook damsel in distress. My brother is going to rescue you from poverty and whisk you away where you will live in marital bliss without another care the rest of your days."

Miranda could not help but grin. "I don't know about that. But I will confess I had no idea how deep his affections could be. He is a romantic at heart."

"Ethan?" Jane asked, handing Miranda a cup of tea the maid had just brought in.

"Yes. I am afraid he will marry me whether or not your parents relent."

Jane sighed. "Do you think I will find someone who adores me like that?"

Jane used to share her insecurities freely with Miranda, but this was the first time in months she had done so.

"I did once promise you I would help you find a husband. Whether or not I am ever your sister will not keep me from fulfilling such a promise."

"And what about me?" Hannah asked.

"Oh, Hannah," Miranda said. "You and Jane should not worry for a moment, as long as you avoid the mistakes I made."

"That should be easy," Jane said. "Neither of us is obsessed with our brother."

Hannah giggled. "You are right that Jane does not have to worry. Did you know Captain Grant has come to London? He called on us only this morning. He was watching Jane with a great deal of interest."

Miranda clasped her hands together against her chest. "How wonderful!" Then he had figured out her hints about Jane's feelings, which also meant he wasn't as in love with Miranda as he had thought. "If he has come all this way, his intent must be serious."

"We shall see," Jane said with a pink blush. Her attempt to appear collected quickly dissipated, and an excited smile blossomed across her face.

They all giggled, only to be silenced when Ethan returned with his parents. They rose to their feet, none more anxious than Miranda.

Lord Gibson approached her, his face grim. He extended his hand, and she tentatively placed hers into his.

"Welcome to the family," he said.

Everyone erupted in cheers—Jane's being the loudest. Hannah hugged Miranda tightly but was shooed away by Ethan.

He took her hand and brought it quickly to his lips. "You look surprised. Surely you did not think I was going to waste my second chance with you?"

"Our second chance." Miranda's voice caught.

"Yes," Ethan said, "and now we can start making plans together. Starting with a funeral but ending with a wedding."

Lady Gibson came up beside them. "How about starting with an apology?" She turned to Miranda. "I once thought you fit perfectly into our family, and I am happy to see you were meant to be there all along. I hope you will forgive us for our previous reservations."

"I do, Your Ladyship," Miranda said, "as long as you forgive me for wanting to marry your son despite what Society might think of me."

Jane came over to her opposite side. "Ethan is determined, so do not feel guilty. You know how set he can be once he is decided. I would not be surprised if he would willingly walk to the guillotine for you. Those few days while you were gone were rather scarring for my brother."

Miranda looked to Ethan, who smiled at her with his boyish grin and nearly straight cravat.

"Oh, be off with you to dinner," Ethan said to his family. "Miranda and I shall be there shortly."

"Just this once," Lady Gibson said. "Behave yourself." She motioned everyone toward the door. Lord Gibson, having just sat down, groaned but obeyed his wife and stood once more.

Ethan followed everyone to the door. Once they were all out, he shut it behind them.

Miranda wanted to laugh at the triumphant gleam in his eyes and his silly grin.

"Finally," he said.

"Finally," she echoed back.

She rushed to Ethan. He put out his arms and caught her to him.

He hugged her tightly, lifting her off the ground. When he set her down, he did not release her.

"Remember that day we ate ices at Gunter's?"

"I hated that day," Miranda said, wrapping her arms around his neck. "You called me vain and conceited."

"I meant it too." He grinned, tucking his head near her ear. "But now I am going to be the one to spoil you." He pulled back, and she could see the eagerness in his eyes. "I have something for you. It's not with me, mind you. I did not foresee finding you today."

"What is it?"

"A present. A bonnet, actually." He laughed at himself. "Jane picked it out and assured me it was the finest in Town."

Miranda laughed. He had remembered how much she had wanted him to like her bonnet that day. "How very kind. Thank you!"

"I promise to be the kind of husband who will make you *feel* beautiful. I will tell you every day for the rest of forever."

Miranda grinned. "Will you sketch my dress patterns too?"

"I will not. You have a gift for such things, and I should have appreciated it. I was too quick to criticize. I missed seeing the radiant girl right in front of me. I promise to love you always. As a demonstration of my love"—he pulled one of her arms away from his neck—"I want to make several more promises, actually."

"Oh?" Miranda asked, eager to hear anything that involved their future together.

He brought her fingers to his mouth. "I will never again watch you walk through town, shivering from the cold. You need not fear the direst of winters, in whatever form they come, as I will always be by your side to keep you warm." He kissed each one of her fingers, lighting her skin on fire.

He set her hand against his chest, and she blushed at the familiarity. She could feel his heart pounding just for her. Lifting his free hand to her face, he caressed his thumb against her mouth. "I will feed you, even when the world is hungry. There is nothing I won't do to take care of our future family." Her eyes filled with moisture, and she knew the fears she had faced this past week would never prey on her again.

God did love her. This was proof. She could see now that He had never really forsaken her. He had refined her so she could be forever with this man. Ethan wrapped his arm back around her, and she melted against him.

He whispered into her ear, "I will hold you when you are worried. I will make up for all the nightmares you have suffered since I let you go the first time." She could no longer contain her tears, and she quietly wept into his waistcoat. They stood that way for a moment, relishing the miracle they'd been given. "I miss seeing your ready smile, and I will be perfectly ridiculous if it means I will see it more."

He leaned back and lifted her chin, gently wiping her tears with his fingers, his breath warm on her skin. "I promise to love you always. Never again will I walk away from you." He pressed his lips to hers, assuring her that all would be right in their world. She'd never dreamed a second chance could taste so sweet.

AUTHOR'S NOTE

HISTORICALLY, MORE THAN HALF THE population of prisoners in London were incarcerated because of their debt. The Marshalsea (14th century–1842) is famous for being the prison where Charles Dickens's own father resided in 1824, just eight years after our fictional story takes place. Dickens wrote about the Marshalsea in three of his works.

The year without a summer is also just as legendary and true. Mt. Tambora erupted in 1815, bringing a volcanic winter to the year of 1816. This catastrophic event affected the entire world. Famine was widespread. However, this dark year also had cultural and spiritual significance. *Frankenstein*, *The Vampyre*, and Byron's poems "Darkness" and "A Fragment" were all written during this time.

While reading many heavy and difficult accounts of both of these topics, I also studied the Bible's references to the poor and downtrodden, my favorite being Matthew 5:3. It reads, "Blessed are the poor in spirit: for theirs is the kingdom of heaven" and reminds me of the hope possible for all those who suffer. While some might think I chose an unlikely setting for a romance, it made me realize the crucial role love has in bringing light and comfort during dark times.

ABOUT THE AUTHOR

ANNEKA WALKER IS AN AWARD-WINNING author raised by a librarian and an English teacher turned judge. After being fed a steady diet of books, she decided to learn about writing. The result was a bachelor's degree in English and history. When she isn't dreaming up a happy ending for a story, she's busy living her own together with her husband and adorable children.

Subscribe to Anneka's newsletter at https://mailchi.mp/a278fdec4416 /authorannekawalker or follow her on social media.

Facebook: @AnnekaRWalker

Instagram: @authorannekawalker